Gloria

# THE POINT OF FRACTURE

*a novel by*

## FRANK TURNER HOLLON

OTHER BOOKS BY
FRANK TURNER HOLLON

*The Pains of April*

*The God File*

*A Thin Difference*

*Life Is a Strange Place*

*Glitter Girl and the Crazy Cheese*

# THE POINT OF FRACTURE

*a novel by*

## FRANK TURNER HOLLON

MacAdam/Cage

MacAdam/Cage Publishing
155 Sansome Street, Suite 550
San Francisco, CA 94104

ISBN 1-59692-126-9

Manufactured in the United States of America

Book design by Dorothy Carico Smith.

*For my wife, Allison, and the kids.*
*Without them I'd be lost.*

How life is strange and changeful, and the crystal is in the steel at the point of fracture, and the toad bears a jewel in its forehead, and the meaning of moments passes like the breeze that scarcely ruffles the leaf of the willow.

*All the Kings Men*
Robert Penn Warren

# PART I

*Before*

1

Michael Brace opened his eyes. It was 3:30 in the morning, and he awoke for no reason. There was no sharp sound, or flash of light, or bad dream. He just woke up in the middle of the night and stared into the darkness for a few minutes from the living room couch. His wife was asleep in the other room. It had been a long time since they shared a bed. The house was small and modest with a long hallway leading to a kitchen and two bedrooms. Michael preferred the couch over the guest-room. At thirty-seven, Michael Brace was mostly a stranger.

It was summertime in south Alabama. Michael's eyes adjusted, and he could see the ceiling fan above spinning. He sat upright and felt the familiar twinge of pain in his knee. Michael walked quietly to the glassed-in porch and sat down in a white wicker chair. He looked out across the slick bay waters to the city of Mobile on the other side with its sparkling lights. The moon was nearly full. A streak of moon-white light stretched across the waters in a single bright line, ending in the dark horizon underneath the white circle pressed against the black sky.

Fifteen years earlier, before Michael and Suzanne were married, life was different. Michael turned his head to look down the long hall. There was light in the kitchen. Next to Suzanne's bedroom door stood a black umbrella. She got headaches. Pounding, consuming headaches that some-times lasted for days. The umbrella was a signal that still had a purpose: a demand for silence. Suzanne Brace was inside the room curled up in total darkness, unable to think beyond the dull pulsing pain in her skull.

Michael turned his eyes back to the shallow bay waters. He spent his childhood in the small town of Fairhope swimming and fishing the waters of Mobile Bay. He kissed his first girl at the end of the Fairhope pier and watched his first jubilee as a small boy on the beach behind his huge family home. Staring at the bay brought only calm, a contrast to the view of a black umbrella just a head-turn away. For a moment, it seemed to Michael Brace the bright white beam of the moon's reflection on the water actually came in his direction, starting from the other side, cutting through his chest at the present moment, and then continuing behind him down the hallway toward the next morning.

Michael remembered the time when he and Suzanne drove around town naked. It was before they were married, around two o'clock in the morning on a summer night. They'd had a few drinks. Michael couldn't remember whose idea it was. They stripped off all their clothes and raced out to the car. They drove around in his blue Volkswagen Bug until the sun came up, completely naked, drinking beer and laughing out loud. Michael could still remember clearly. He smiled in the dark.

Behind him there was a noise. Michael turned his head to see Suzanne's bedroom door slowly open. She stepped out into the hallway, her bare feet light on the hardwood floor. Suzanne put her hand against the wall and guided herself down the hall toward the kitchen. Michael turned his body slightly in the chair to watch. The light in the kitchen allowed him to see the outline of his wife. She wore only a white T-shirt that hung just at the bottom edge of her ass. Michael tilted his head downward just a bit to see all he could see. She was a beautiful woman, slender, but with gentle curves and hazel skin.

Suzanne stepped into the kitchen. She stood in front of the stove and then moved to the right, outside of Michael's vision. He heard the water from the faucet, and then Suzanne stepped back into sight. She placed a silver pot on the stove. Suzanne's long black hair was in all directions. It seemed an extension of her headache.

Michael watched. Suzanne edged the silver pot off the heat. He could see her looking down at the red-hot eye and watched her put her hand just above the heat and then pull away. Suzanne had a fork in her other hand and placed the tines on the hot stove. She held it there, and then slowly and deliberately Suzanne took the fork from the heat and pressed it against the palm of her hand. Michael's face twitched with the anticipation of pain. He expected a scream, but there was none.

Michael watched as Suzanne clenched her hand back and forth as the blisters rose. For a moment she had forgotten her headache. For a moment there was something more important. Pain sets its own priorities.

The smell of burnt skin drifted all the way to the porch only a few minutes after Suzanne poured her hot tea and closed herself away in the bedroom. Michael remembered how Suzanne once described the pain in her head with such honest detail that he could almost feel it himself. He wanted to understand, but it was like imagining colors he'd never seen.

On their first date, Suzanne told Michael she wouldn't talk about her family. She never did. There were no phone calls, no Christmas cards, nobody knocking on the door for her birthday. Michael had met a man once in a bar in Florida who had gone to high school one year with Suzanne. He remembered her because she was pretty and because she was only in school for one year, and then no one heard from her again. Besides a few general memories, the man didn't know anything else about Suzanne except she had a little sister named Elizabeth. Michael had once loved the fact that Suzanne was a mystery in a town where mysteries were usually very far away. He didn't feel that way anymore.

Morning was near. The world outside the porch windows began to lighten. Michael saw something move on the sidewalk between his house and the bay. He leaned forward in his chair. There was movement, stillness, and then movement again. It was Jerry. He was around fifty years old, seemed retarded, with a pair of black hard-rimmed glasses held to his head by an elastic strap around the back of his neck. Jerry had been roaming around Fairhope picking up aluminum cans for as long as Michael could remember. He usually wore cutoff blue jeans and the same brown button-up shirt. There were more rumors and made-up stories about Jerry than anyone could count. As a teenager, Michael had heard them all.

"He's a millionaire from France."

"He graduated top of his class at Harvard."

"He did it with a dog."

"He killed Joey Brunson in the woods behind the school."

Joey Brunson showed up two days later. He had run away from his home and stayed at the fish camp. Not all the rumors were as easily disproved, especially the one about the dog.

Jerry never spoke to anyone. He never smiled. He just walked around the town collecting cans in a green garbage sack and smoking cigarettes. Michael watched him pick up a cigarette butt on the sidewalk, light it, and look upward as the smoke rolled from his nose. When Jerry would pass by the house, Michael found himself unable to take his eyes away from the strange man. There was an underlying touch of envy. The feeling died away with Michael's failure to form a word to describe the feeling.

He had been a writer. Three days after his twentieth birthday Michael's short story was published in a national magazine. He had known it was good while he wrote it, and he knew it was good when it was done. People would look up from the words on the page and wonder how they had come from his hand. Suzanne would tiptoe by his door when he wrote, quiet, careful not to disturb the process. But then the words stopped coming. Michael closed his eyes. He could remember the slow turn from the golden beginning to the now familiar gray failure. His daddy had gotten him a job at the local newspaper. A diversion. A chance to pretend he was a writer in between brutally boring newspaper articles. Start a short story. Stop. Rewrite. Start again. Lie to Suzanne. Check the spelling. Maybe another whiskey would help. And then he got fired.

The novel was different. All these many years later Michael wasn't sure he could write a sentence, much less a novel. But he started anyway. The idea for the book was nothing Suzanne had ever said out loud. It was just some feeling inside of Michael that came from Suzanne, something he could see when she didn't know he was watching. It was nothing she could have formed into a sentence, but somehow it had seeped into Michael like brown poison. He had to write it. It wasn't a choice. One way or another, emotions squeeze out from each of us, in different directions, in touchable forms, whether we wish them to or not.

Michael fell asleep in the white wicker chair. It was Saturday morning. He heard the little squeak of tennis shoes on the wooden floor. Jimmy Butler stood about fifteen feet behind Mr. Brace. On Saturday mornings he would come with his mother to clean the Braces' house. He was seven and liked to come to Fairhope. Fairhope was fancy and clean and colorful. There were flowers on the corners of the streets, and a breeze blew gently off the bay. The stores in the old downtown square were full of shiny and sweet things. Jimmy's home was thirty minutes away, but it seemed like a million miles.

His mother was in the kitchen. Jimmy had eased past the bedroom door. He was afraid of Miss Suzanne. She moved like a planet, disconnected. She made him worry about things he didn't understand.

Without turning around, Michael Brace said, "That you, Jimmy?"

Jimmy stopped in his tracks. His eyes got a little bigger. He whispered, "Yes, sur."

Jimmy Butler waited. He turned to look at the black umbrella against the wall.

Michael said, "You bring your glove?"

"Yes, sur." Jimmy smiled.

"Where's mine?" Michael asked.

"In the garage."

"I'll meet you in the backyard," Michael said.

Jimmy turned around, ran past the bedroom door, and knocked over the black umbrella. It hit the floor with a crack. Michael turned his head. Jimmy stopped in midstep. They looked at each other. The whites of Jimmy's eyes against his black skin were as bright as the moon had been across the water. Jimmy turned and ran through the screen door and into the backyard. Michael followed in his sleeping clothes, a T-shirt and boxer shorts.

They threw the ball in silence. The crack of the umbrella was still alive in Jimmy's mind. He liked Mr. Brace, but Jimmy's mother didn't. She said he was lazy. She said he didn't work, and she said, "A man who don't work ain't worth the food he eats." Sophie Butler could forgive a person for anything except not working. "Idle hands are the devil's playthings," she would say. "Besides, he drinks too much."

Jimmy didn't care. His Uncle Raymond drank beer every day, and he liked Uncle Raymond, too. Mr. Brace told Jimmy about curveballs, and home runs, and a black man named Jackie Robinson who played second base for the Brooklyn Dodgers. He stood in his underwear in the backyard at eight o'clock in the morning and pretended Jimmy Butler was the best shortstop that ever lived on God's green Earth.

The front door slammed. Michael walked to the gate in time to see Suzanne climb in the car. She looked up, saw him standing there, held his stare, and then backed out of the driveway. It was the same driveway where they pulled up naked in the blue Volkswagen and dared each other to run inside in the morning daylight. There was no way back then, so many years ago, Michael Brace could have known how broken his life and marriage would become. And there was no way, standing by the fence on that Saturday morning with a baseball in his hand, Michael Brace could possibly imagine what would happen to him at the hands of his wife.

## 2

Suzanne sat in the waiting room of Dr. Betty Riis. During the past year, beyond the doctor/patient relationship, the two women had bonded. Suzanne could hear voices on the other side of the door. She was curious to see the face of the person who would walk out of the psychiatrist's office. Even on Saturdays Dr. Riis was almost always running a few minutes behind schedule.

The receptionist didn't come in on Saturdays and Suzanne Brace sat alone. She picked up a magazine and put it back down. She remembered Michael would be leaving that afternoon to spend the weekend at the fish camp with his brother, Phillip, and his stupid friends. She thought about how she used to hate when he would leave, how jealous she was of the time he spent with Phillip and Mark Simpson and Hardy. Now she looked forward to the empty house. She used to be afraid to be alone. She would think about things she didn't want to think about. Michael's presence would push all those bad things away. Now the bad thoughts came anyway, even when Michael was there. It was worse since she'd found the first four chapters of the novel Michael was trying to write.

She had sat on the cool floor of the kitchen and turned the pages slowly, one by one, in the quiet of the night. She had never told him those things. How could he know? It was like she was there again. The place was different, and the names and the faces were all different. But the feelings, the smells, and the fear. God, the fear, the sleepless expectation of childhood evil. It was exact. Michael's words brought her back to the point of fracture. They surrounded the emotions and squeezed them into exact patterns of light that crept across the white walls of a child's room. How could he possibly describe pain he had never felt, anger he couldn't see? How could he know with such precision and disgust, unless he was there? Unless he had picked clean her secrets? How could she feel safe again?

Suzanne tried to think of nothing, but nothing was hard to imagine. She couldn't really remember how old she was the first night, but she knew it was the night after her birthday party. The candles were blown out, and she thought everyone had gone to bed. Her baby sister slept in the bed across the little room. There were red and yellow balloons above her on the ceiling. There was a loud noise and a scream. Her mother's scream. The bedroom door flew open and in the light from the living room Suzanne saw her mother come through the door. And then she saw her father behind. His hand swung down against the back of her mother's head and they crashed to the floor at the foot of Suzanne's bed. Her mother and father were hidden behind the end of her bed. She remembered the soft sound of her mother crying, and then she remembered her father rising up, his eyes like the eyes of a monster, and his hand again and again, rising up and coming down against her mother below.

It was impossible to understand. And when her father stood that night, and walked to Suzanne where she lay crying in her warm bed, there was no way she could understand the smell of the whiskey, or the mental illness, or the open hand she felt hard against her own small face.

In the waiting room, Suzanne closed her eyes. The pounding inside her head was down to a slow hum. The voices through the door were distant. Images melted around her mind. She remembered the way she felt when they told her that her father had died. She knew even before the high school teacher or the policeman said a word. She had prayed it would happen, and when it did, she felt more alone than ever before. The only time he had told her he loved her was after she would feel the fire of his hands. Sometimes she would wake up the next day with him by the side of her bed crying and talking to people who weren't in the room.

Suzanne believed no one could know the feelings, or find the words to describe such boundaries. But on a rainy night two months earlier, after Michael had fallen asleep on the porch, Suzanne had found the beginning of his unfinished novel. He had written the words she had never spoken, not even to Betty Riis. Suzanne stood above Michael as he slept that night. She stared into his face and saw the face of her father.

The door opened and Betty Riis walked out of her office ahead of a slender elderly woman. Suzanne opened her eyes and tried to adjust back to the reality of the place she found herself. The elderly woman nodded politely to Suzanne.

Suzanne stepped into the office and sat down in her usual chair.

"Well, good morning, Suzanne."

"Good morning, Betty."

Dr. Riis kept her reading glasses perched on top of her head all the time. She was in her midfifties and loved her job. She was unmarried and childless. Her work was her life. She was a small-town psychiatrist, and Suzanne had proven to be one of her greatest challenges. Intelligent, complicated, and always one step away.

"You look like you've got one of those headaches again," Betty Riis said.

"How can you tell?" Suzanne asked.

"The skin on your head gets real tight."

They both smiled. A few seconds passed before Suzanne changed her face and spoke again.

"There's some things I've been wanting to talk to you about."

Dr. Riis was patient. She believed in giving her people time to say what they wanted to say. Sometimes too much pushing and pulling took away their momentum. Suzanne seemed to be struggling with whatever she came to say.

"I want to talk about Michael."

The two women had spent many hours talking about Suzanne's life. The discussions about Michael were limited to Michael's part in the big picture. Suzanne had always talked about her husband the way she would talk about a place.

"I'm scared."

Dr. Riis leaned over and reached her hand out touching Suzanne on the arm.

"What scares you?"

"Michael. Michael scares me. Different things."

Suzanne stopped herself and looked down at her hands in the lap of her dress.

"Has he hurt you, Suzanne?"

The hands were pressed against each other. The nails were painted and unbitten. The skin around the nails was smooth.

"Has he hurt you, Suzanne?" Betty repeated.

"Yes."

Dr. Riis waited before asking another question. She still had her hand resting on Suzanne's arm. She had never seen Suzanne so upset and off balance.

"How did he hurt you? Did he hit you?"

Dr. Riis' eyes instinctively looked across the body of the woman in the chair next to hers. She looked for scrapes and scratches and places of black and blue, but couldn't see any.

Suzanne felt a tear roll down her face.

"Not this time. He burned my hand."

Suzanne turned her palm upward. Betty looked down to see the redness. As she moved to look more closely, Suzanne closed the hand and turned it away.

Dr. Riis looked up into Suzanne's eyes. "What happened?" she asked.

"We were arguing in the kitchen. Michael was drunk again. He gets so angry. I'm afraid he doesn't know what he's doing anymore."

Suzanne had never cried in front of Betty Riis before. Her eyes filled up.

"How did he burn you?"

"The stove was hot. I was boiling water. He just pushed up against me. I tried to get my balance, and my hand ended up on the stove. It was just an accident. I don't think he meant to hurt me on purpose."

"Jesus Christ, Suzanne, do you know how many times I've heard that from women who are abused by their boyfriends or husbands? They get the shit beat out of them and try to blame themselves. It's typical. It's part of the control. You need to get out of there, now. Do you understand me? If he's hitting you, if he's drinking too much, you need to get out now."

Suzanne lowered her head. Dr. Riis reached up and rubbed the back of

Suzanne's neck. "Why didn't you tell me about this before?"

Suzanne took a deep breath. She appeared to gather herself.

"I thought I could work it out, Betty. I still think we can work it out. Michael's just under a lot of pressure. He can't find a job he likes. The money from his grandfather's inheritance is almost gone. He's trying to write again. I think he needs me now."

"I'm sure he needs you, Suzanne, but you need to be thinking about yourself."

The women stopped talking. Dr. Riis walked across the room and took a cigarette from her top desk drawer. She was down to ten cigarettes a day and the clock on the wall said it was time for number two.

"I thought you quit smoking," Suzanne said.

"I did. We're talking about you, not me, Suzanne."

Suzanne turned her head back down to her hands. She fidgeted like a schoolgirl.

"How many times has he hit you?"

Betty Riis lit her cigarette and sat down. The first drag felt good. She knew there were only ten or fifteen good drags on each cigarette. She couldn't have cigarette number three for at least another hour. Betty looked up at the clock on the wall.

Suzanne said, "He's going fishing this weekend. He'll be out of the house."

"That's just for a few days, Suzanne. You need to have a plan to remove yourself from the situation."

Suzanne wasn't crying anymore.

"I can't leave him right now," she said. "I just can't."

"What's the alternative, Suzanne? Spend every day locked in your room, afraid? That's not an alternative."

Suzanne flashed back to the face of her father at the foot of her bed. The raised fist. The sound of bone against bone. The fear she felt every night after that, when her mother would tuck her in, and the door would close, and she would lie awake listening for the sound of her father's truck in the driveway, the slam of the truck door. Wrapped inside all the little-girl fear, she remembered the night she pulled Elizabeth's bed with all her strength to the far side of the room, away from the door, as far away as the walls would allow.

Suzanne looked at Betty Riis and knew the woman could never understand. "I've got to go," she said.

"Don't go, Suzanne."

"I can't talk about it anymore right now. We can talk about it next time. I'll call and make another appointment."

She stood to leave and stopped at the door.

"Thank you, Betty. I appreciate everything you do for me."

"Be careful, Suzanne," the doctor said, and Suzanne left the room.

Betty Riis finished her cigarette and smashed the butt into the red glass ashtray. She didn't have another appointment until after lunch. As usual, she was left with an uneasy feeling after Suzanne was gone. They were never able to get past certain barriers. Her childhood remained unexplained in their discussions. Suzanne Brace was a strikingly beautiful woman, obviously bright, but Betty Riis saw signs of problems she couldn't quite piece together. It was disturbing to think about Suzanne being abused by her husband. Through their conversations, Betty saw Michael Brace as a spoiled rich man, the son of a prominent lawyer, who had never really grown up. She imagined him living off family money, calling himself a writer, spending weekends at a fish camp drinking whiskey until he passed out. Suzanne would always defend him when Betty had something bad to say.

Betty Riis looked at the clock. She eased past the guilt and took another cigarette from the pack. She lit it up and promised herself not to have number four until after lunch. It was a promise she wouldn't keep.

## 3

It was nearly noon and Michael Brace sat in the same wicker chair. Jimmy Butler and his mother had long since gone to the next house on their list. Michael felt the need to get up and take a shower. His bladder was full of his third cup of coffee and his knee was stiff. The house seemed empty when his wife was gone, but even more empty when she was home.

Michael stood under the shower and slowly made the water colder and colder. His breath would catch with the shock of every turn of the knob. Michael thought about the feeling he used to get when he would give things to Suzanne. It was selfish. But then, later, she could always make him feel like it wasn't enough or wasn't right. If he got her exactly what she wanted, she expected it and would be disappointed that he hadn't gone out and gotten something wild and unpredictable. If he got her a surprise, it was never right, because nothing could be right, and she would be disappointed she hadn't gotten what she asked for. Suzanne hated her own birthday. There was something wrong about that, Michael thought, as he turned off the water.

The phone rang in the other room. Michael wrapped a towel around his waist. On the second ring he decided he wouldn't answer. On the third he changed his mind and walked into the living room.

"Hello."

"You outta bed, Asshole?"

Since the eighth grade Mark Simpson had been calling Michael "Asshole."

"Yeah, I'm outta bed. What time we leaving?"

Simpson was a few years older than Michael and worked as a boat mechanic down at one of the marinas. He was tall and skinny and had three ex-wives in town. Each one hated him more than the one before.

"I've got one or two things to do. I'll come by the house around one," Simpson said. "How's that?"

Michael asked, "Just the two of us in the big red bomb?"

"Hardy might ride. His car's in the shop. I gotta go, Asshole. See ya about one."

Michael could hear him laugh before hanging up the phone.

Simpson had an old red Chevrolet. There was no air-conditioner, no radio, and no back window. There was a hamburger and a bag of fries under the seat from a fishing trip ten years ago. Simpson thought it was funny. He thought most things were funny.

Michael stood naked in front of the mirror above the sink in the bathroom. The mirror was old and distorted the angles of his face when he shaved. There was a particular spot he had learned to stand in to see himself more clearly. Michael wondered if his wife would come home before one o'clock. She hated his friends. She had always hated them. Michael had allowed her to take away so many pieces of his life. He had wanted her so badly he was willing to let her ruin his friendships, put weight on his family relationships, and change the way he felt about himself.

At 12:45 his duffle bag was packed and propped up next to the front door. It was only a weekend trip. The bag held two pairs of underwear, three individual socks, tennis shoes, blue jeans, three T-shirts, and two bottles of Jack Daniels. There were aspirin loose in the bottom of the bag.

Michael stood at the window and watched Suzanne pull into the driveway. She was smiling until the car door opened and she started to walk up the path to the house. There were times in their relationship when they had walked on emotional tightropes. There were long complete swings from happy to sad, and wonderful to intolerable. Somewhere along the line it changed. Michael sunk back into himself.

Suzanne walked slowly. She wore an orange sundress and sandals. Her black hair fell down around her shoulders. From the window, Michael imagined that if he had never seen her before, he would fall in love with her all over again. There was no clue in the way she walked. The sun shined all around her.

Suzanne opened the door. Without the window between them, from just a few feet away, Michael could see the hatred in her face. It was an old and frozen hatred. A hatred, it seemed, for everything she had never had and everyone who had never given it to her. Michael had become the symbol of these things. She would blame him, and he would blame himself. He was never strong enough to understand it or stop it. Now he was long past the point of arguing. She would attack, and he would sit. The same arguments, the same dead ends. Nobody learned anything.

Michael said, "Good morning."

He knew what was coming back at him before she said it.

"It isn't morning. If you'd get out of the house, maybe you'd see that. Or do writers need seclusion?"

Suzanne sat down at the desk in the bedroom. Simpson's big red Chevrolet pulled up at the street. Michael threw the bag over his shoulder and stood in the bedroom doorway.

"I'll be back tomorrow night," Michael said loud enough for Suzanne to hear.

She smiled. Years ago, in this same situation, Suzanne had made him feel guilty for leaving her alone. She knew just the right buttons to push. Now it didn't matter. She smiled again, thinking about how he used to plead with her while the car horn blared in the yard and his buddies yelled outside.

Michael waited for a response from his wife. None came. He turned and walked out the front door. He knew when he got to the car, she would come to the door and wave good-bye so Simpson could see.

Nobody knew about their problems. At least none of Michael's friends or family. Suzanne would smile at the right times and sometimes even brag about her husband in front of other people. For some reason it seemed very important to her that everything look nice even if the walls were falling down all around. At first, Michael thought it was good to keep their private lives private. Now, it just seemed weird to see her in that orange dress at the door smiling and waving as Simpson pulled away.

"That's a hell of a woman you're married to, Brace. I think I'd eat a pile of my own shit if she asked me to."

Michael didn't always like Simpson, but sooner or later Simpson could almost always make him laugh. He was lanky and had a mischievous disrespect for authority. He never tucked in his shirt or wore socks. His arms were longer than they needed to be. He floated through the world like a kite.

"Let's get the fuck outta here," Michael said.

"I gotta pick up Hardy."

Hardy weighed 245 pounds and was five feet five inches tall. He worked at the post office and drank beer. Some people have one or two real good nicknames. Hardy had fifteen nicknames. He was famous for one punch he had thrown when he was a senior in high school. Hardy knocked out Perry Reynolds at a party. Perry Reynolds ended up a proud member of the Fairhope Police Department. He had to have his jaw wired, and Hardy became a legend. Now he thought of himself as semiretired at thirty-eight.

Hardy was waiting in his yard with all the traditional fishing gear, including the hat with the hooks. He hadn't actually caught a fish in years. His eyes were blue and the brows above were blonde. Hardy walked with a curious quickness in his step. He and Simpson didn't spend that much time together, but they were very good at it anyway. Hardy spoke with an English accent on their fishing trips, which made Mark Simpson laugh uncontrollably.

"Get in the car, Hardy. Asshole's in a big hurry."

"Jolly good."

Hardy pointed to his penis and said, "Shake hands with the future, my boys. Shake hands with the future."

Michael laughed. He hadn't seen them in months and it felt good to feel good. He wasn't sure exactly what Hardy meant, but it didn't matter.

"You gonna catch any fish this time, Hardy?" Michael asked.

Hardy answered with the English accent, "Don't expect to, no. Mostly I expect to get drunk and speak highly of women's genitalia. Which, I suppose, could be associated in some ways with fish, if we allow ourselves as gentlemen to bridge these two subjects, if you know what I mean?"

After a while Simpson was laughing so hard he was bent over the steering wheel. Hardy looked kingly sitting in the backseat of that old car between the beer cooler and the fishing poles. He lit up a fat cigar and imitated Winston Churchill.

Time went fast. Soon there were only trees. The road turned from hot cement to red dirt. There were no houses or fences. The skinny pine trees lined the road in timber rows that stretched into the woods. There was a deep green calm.

"What's the matter, Mikey? Your wife giving you problems or somethin'?"

Michael hadn't noticed he'd been staring out the window for the past ten minutes. He wondered why Hardy assumed it had to do with his wife.

"Have a beer. It won't make anything better, but drink it anyway," Hardy said as he handed a beer up to the front seat.

"Don't worry about it, Mike. Learning to like women is like learning to like Scotch. When you're a kid, you don't like either one. Then, when you get older, people keep telling you you're supposed to like both. First you learn to like girls, then you end up teaching yourself to like Scotch. Neither one of them comes naturally."

Hardy was just talking to hear himself talk. Michael stopped listening and stared out the window again. He thought about the fishing trips he used to take as a child. The ones he remembered best were those with his father and brother. The Brace family had been in Baldwin County a long time. Michael's grandfather had been a good lawyer in the county for fifty years. Old people still stopped him on the street to tell stories about his grandfather and the things he had done. Michael's father and brother followed in his grandfather's footsteps to become lawyers, too. Michael had learned at a very early age the shadows he walked in were older and longer. At least they seemed that way. That was one of the reasons Suzanne had seemed necessary. She was wild and unpredictable. Nobody knew her family or where she was from. She was the personification of his rebellion against the family walls.

"You still sleepin' on the couch?" Simpson asked.

Michael turned to him. "How'd you know that?"

"I've slept on more couches than I can count, boy. Hell, I remember the couches a lot better than the beds."

Michael turned back to look out the window at the trees. Baldwin

County was a beautiful place to live. There were sugar white beaches to the south in Gulf Shores, Mobile Bay on the eastern shore, and acres of cotton fields and pecan trees in the center of the county. Up north there were rivers that flowed south and dumped their dirty waters into the bay, with fishing camps and miles of woods full of oak trees and dogwoods.

"Oh, no," Hardy said in his English accent. "I believe maybe Mikey's got his mind back on Laura Simmons. Homegrown, good ole Laura Simmons."

Michael said, "Shut up, Hardy."

Laura Simmons was twenty-five years old. She worked as a cashier at the grocery store outside of town. She was young and naturally pretty, with shoulder-length brown hair, and had a thing for Michael Brace. Ever since the first time they saw each other, five years earlier, Michael could see something in her eyes. He was older and would come into her store sometimes. He would always go through her checkout line. For Michael, Laura Simmons had become something good for him to think about. A refuge. She smiled in the middle of the day. Thinking about her was free, but Michael had never taken the smallest step to make her real. He never called to hear her voice, and then hung up. He never drove past her house in the middle of the night to see her light on in her room. Something always stopped him. He didn't love her. He didn't even know her. And she didn't love him. She didn't even know him.

"I haven't thought of Laura Simmons in years," Michael said.

Hardy said, "Liar, liar, pantyhose on fire."

Michael tried not to smile.

"You know what I think?" Simpson said. "I think Michael is an alien. He was dropped off at random and ended up in the house of the amazing Brace family. At night I think he sneaks off in the woods and sucks the blood from donkeys' butts."

Michael couldn't hold back the laugh. It was the reason he still went on the fishing trips. He reached back for another beer even though the one between his legs was still half full.

A deer ran across the road in front of the car. All three men saw it, but nobody pointed or said a word.

"Why don't you just kill her?" Simpson asked.

"What are you talkin' about?"

"Your wife, if she's causing you this much grief, why don't you just kill her?"

"It's not my wife," Michael answered.

"Bullshit! The only thing that can make a man look like you look is a woman."

"I told you, it's not my wife. Nothing's wrong with my wife. I got some things on my mind."

Simpson smiled and caught eyes with Hardy in the rearview mirror.

"What are you talkin' about anyway, Simpson? You've got three ex-wives, I don't see you killin' any of them off." Michael's tone was sharp. He surprised himself. Simpson thought it was funny.

"Settle down, Asshole. I'll pull over right now and whip your ass on the side of the road."

Hardy laughed up beer in the backseat. Michael was glad. It was impossible to be serious with these guys. He didn't want to be serious. He felt like doing something physical. He felt like all his tension would go away with a game of tackle football or a fight with Simpson on the side of the road.

Michael smiled and pointed toward the woods on the far side of the car. When Simpson turned his head to see, Michael dumped his beer upside down in Simpson's lap. The brake pedal slammed to the floor and the car skidded to a stop on the dirt road. Before Michael could get the door open he could feel the hands grab at the back of his shirt. He could feel the adrenaline explode through his veins.

He could hear Hardy yell, "Kill 'em, pull his hair, pull his hair!" And then Michael was out of the car with Simpson half on his back and half straddled across the open door of the big red Chevrolet.

They were on the ground. First Simpson on top, then Michael gained the leverage to flip Simpson over. He held the larger man's shoulder against the ground. His energy seemed to run along a line the length of his body. It felt good to do something other than think.

Hardy was out of the car. Michael knew his advantage was only temporary. Simpson was stronger and bigger and, in his mind, had a lot more to lose. Michael made his break back to the car. When Simpson stood up, he could see the wet spot from the beer. All three of the men looked at once.

Michael shrugged his shoulders and said, "No big deal. It'll be dry by the time we get to the camp."

Michael kept Hardy between himself and Simpson. It took fifteen minutes to get back in the car and fifteen more minutes to get to the camp two miles away. Michael ended up running most of the second mile with the big red Chevrolet following right behind. Simpson's revenge was always two eyes for an eye. He liked to win.

## 4

Most of the guys were already at the fish camp when Michael arrived with Simpson and Hardy. They only expected seven or eight. Sometimes more would show up, sometimes less. When they made it down the dirt driveway, Michael saw Joey Brunson standing alongside the dock trying to sort out fishing poles. Joey was a serious fisherman. His father was a dentist. Joey was boring. Nobody really invited him. He always just showed up.

The fish camp was nothing fancy. When Michael's grandfather died, he and Phillip inherited the place. Michael got the little house where he lived with Suzanne. He was already living there when his grandfather died. It was good to have a house without a monthly payment. It was one of the reasons Michael was able to survive on so little income through the years.

The camp sat on the edge of the Tensaw River. It was secluded, surrounded by woods with no houses in sight. The men started drinking beer and whiskey as soon as they arrived, and Hardy sparked up the grill. Usually they ate sausage or steaks, smoked a few cigars, and sat around playing cards. That Saturday night, after some of the guys had gone to sleep, Michael sat on the back deck with Phillip and Simpson and Hardy.

Phillip was a successful lawyer. He had never been married. He started his own practice out of law school and now had six lawyers and five secretaries in his office. Phillip had an unnatural control over his intensity. He could always concentrate and focus completely on whatever was at hand. This gave him an advantage over most people in almost everything he did. Michael had grown up in the wake of this strength. In some ways, Michael's life had been a reaction to Phillip, and Phillip's life had been a reaction to the world around him. This left Michael once removed.

They planned to go fishing early the next morning. Mark Simpson and Hardy went to bed leaving Phillip and Michael alone on the porch. Michael had been wanting to talk to Phillip, but he knew their conversations usually deteriorated into jabs and side comments. The brown whiskey burned as it trickled down Michael's throat. His head was light when Phillip asked, "Is everything all right with you, Michael? You seem a little quiet."

There was silence. The men listened to the crickets and bullfrogs somewhere in the darkness making their noises. Michael finally said, "I don't know."

"Well, if you don't know, who does?"

It was the kind of response Michael expected, but didn't need.

Phillip added, "Why don't you get a job, Mike? There can't be much of Grandpa's money left."

They'd had this conversation before, and it always ended the same. Phillip leaned back in his chair. He was the picture of comfort wherever he was. He put his hands behind his head and stretched his back.

Michael said, "I never was very good at reaching other people's expectations, was I?"

"Who gives a shit about other people's expectations, Michael? Reaching other people's expectations doesn't get you where you want to be. It doesn't make you happier. It just makes them happier. Most people, underneath, really want you to fail anyway. It lets them feel better about themselves. It seems to me you've found some middle ground between doing what was expected of you and doing what you wanted. The middle ground is doing nothing at all."

Michael spoke without emotion, "Fuck you, Phillip. You've never had to worry about anything in your life. Everything's always been easy." The whiskey helped the words flow.

Phillip laughed. "You can't make me feel guilty for my success. You can't blackmail me with my abilities. Save that shit for Mom. I work hard, and I make good decisions. It's not a coincidence."

Michael wanted to believe his older brother was cold and lacked compassion, but in truth, Michael knew he was right. He knew Phillip's advice was the most compassionate of all because he presented a solution, a light at the end of the tunnel, instead of a good cry or a pool of warm pity.

Phillip continued, "You've got to see the world as it is, Michael, not as you'd like it to be. If you don't see problems as they are, you can never come up with the answers. You never give yourself a chance. There are things you can't control, and things you can. Every day that you don't do something about it, every day you don't choose, you in fact make a choice. You've chosen not to decide. It's the easiest thing to do. If the situation isn't bad enough to get off your ass and make a few changes, then it isn't bad enough to complain about. If you'd rather just complain, complain to somebody else."

When they were kids, Michael could never beat his brother at anything. He was smaller, and younger, and couldn't quite get it done, no matter what the sport. When Phillip was a senior in high school, and the star baseball player, Michael made the team as a freshman. He knew people believed he only made the team because of his brother. It made Michael try harder to prove they were wrong. He would show up early to practice and leave late. There was a part of him that knew he was the weakest man on the team. There was a part of him that believed maybe those people were right, but he put everything inside himself behind proving he belonged on the team.

One spring afternoon, in a practice game, Michael was playing left field. Phillip was up to bat. The pitcher was slow, and Michael knew Phillip would get around on the ball and pull it his way. Michael backed up a few steps and felt the butterflies touching the insides of his stomach.

The pitch came, Phillip took a full swing, and the ball cracked off the bat toward Michael in left. Michael turned to his right and took off at a full gallop. He knew the ball might make it over the six-foot wooden fence. He knew it would be close. Michael turned to see the ball in the air above. He stretched out his glove and positioned his right arm to feel for the fence. It was a chance to make a great catch. A chance to steal a home run from mighty Phillip, the king of the field.

The ball hit the leather glove. At full speed Michael crashed into the wooden fence. He felt his right knee explode in pain. The ball bounced from the glove and Michael never played baseball again. The pain in his knee was a regular reminder of that day.

"I didn't come here for another lecture," Michael said.

He turned up his glass and drank down the last warm swallow.

"I just can't figure out why you won't live your life. Do something, Michael, anything. Get a job with Simpson at the marina. Write. Have babies. How can you sit in that house every day watching the sun come up and go down out the window?"

"I can't see the sun come up from my window. I can only see it go down."

Phillip shook his head and leaned up in his chair. He said, "Maybe they'll put that on your tombstone."

Michael stood gingerly. His knee was stiff. Phillip noticed, and Michael saw him notice. Neither of them brought it up.

Early the next morning, Phillip and Hardy woke Michael to go fishing.

"It's the best time, Mike. Come on, get up."

He was tired, and the taste of whiskey was still hard in his throat. He washed out his mouth and followed his brother through the back door. Hardy was bent over a tackle box. His fat hands were busy adjusting a fishing knife to his belt. He was excited about catching fish. Everyone whispered.

"Mornin', Mike."

"Mornin'. What time is it?"

"Time to catch a whale, my boy." The English accent was still there. Hardy held the boat alongside the dock for the others to climb aboard. They went up the river to a place Phillip had fished before. When the engine was shut down, the cool morning silence was fantastic. Phillip was in the far back of the boat with Hardy in the middle and Michael half asleep in the front. Each of the men appreciated the quiet and sat for long spells without a word spoken.

Suddenly Hardy's line went tight and his reel squealed for an instant. Michael jumped to his feet in the little boat and then squatted back down as he realized where he was. The fourteen-foot aluminum boat rocked and steadied.

Phillip put his pole aside and turned to grab a net. They all knew Hardy had something big.

"Holy shit."

"Hold on, Hardy," Phillip said, "Hold on."

"I watched a fishin' show once. The guy caught a twenty-three-pound catfish in a place just like this." Hardy was talking fast-forward. The quiet was forgotten.

"Maybe it's a catfish. Maybe it's as big as a pig." Hardy wouldn't shut up.

Phillip positioned himself with a net. Michael sat back at the far end of the boat and watched.

"It's heavy, man. It's heavy."

The line was tight and the pole seemed bent down as far as it would go. Hardy stood. The line snapped and he fell backward onto the bottom of the boat on his side facing Phillip.

Michael burst out laughing. It was the first reaction. Even Phillip smiled as he relaxed against the side of the boat. Then something seemed very wrong. For a moment it was quiet and still. Hardy stayed on his side. His face was locked in a strange expression. Phillip reached out and nudged his shoulder. He pushed Hardy over onto his back, and from where Michael sat he saw the bright red blood in the grooves along the bottom of the boat.

"Hardy. You all right, Hardy?" Phillip asked.

Then Phillip saw the blood. He moved very quickly. He tore the clothes from the place soaked red. Hardy's fishing knife was buried deep into the flesh above the hip. The weight of the fall had sunk the knife up to the handle.

Michael watched. His hands were cold and he felt the juice from his stomach creep into his throat.

Hardy was breathing. He was in shock. The blood came from the hole, mixed with river water, and ran down to a dry rag in the corner of the boat. The rag seemed to suck the red wetness. Phillip started the motor and covered Hardy with a blanket. He looked to Michael at the front of the boat.

"Come here, Michael, and steer the boat."

To Michael it seemed the voice came from the sky. His head floated and he could feel his stomach start to heave.

"Now, Michael."

The voice was calm and sure. Michael stepped over Hardy and took the motor handle in his hand. He looked out over the water and tried to pretend nothing was wrong. The blood was the only thing he could think about.

Phillip rolled Hardy over and pulled the knife out of his side. He squeezed the hole closed and held it with his hands. Michael maneuvered the boat to the wooden dock. His hands quivered as he tied the rope. Phillip held the wound tight. The two men, along with Simpson and Joey Brunson, carried Hardy up to the house. Instead of waiting for an ambulance, Phillip and Simpson drove Hardy to the hospital in Bay Minette. Michael stayed at the camp.

Phillip and Simpson came back to the fish camp later. Michael decided to ride home with Phillip. He sat in the front seat of his brother's black BMW. It had been a long day, and it was only noon. Neither of the two men had much energy.

"I don't want to go home, Phillip," Michael said.

"Why not?"

Michael kept his eyes out the window. He wanted to tell his brother he couldn't go back right now to Suzanne in that house. He wanted to explain why he felt like crawling in the back of the hall closet and holding his arms around his knees. But at the same time he didn't feel like explaining himself.

"Never mind."

"You all right, Mike?" Phillip asked.

"Yeah, I'm fine."

They rode a long time in silence. Phillip turned into the driveway and Michael got out to gather his stuff from the backseat. He tried to hurry so Suzanne wouldn't have time to appear at the door. He wasn't fast enough. She stuck her head out and waved until Phillip waved back.

Michael threw his bag over his shoulder and started the long walk up the drive. When he stepped into the bedroom, she was in the same place he left her the day before. He dropped his bag and fell down on the couch.

Three weeks later Hardy was up and around like always. He couldn't remember any of the pain. He couldn't remember anything after the line snapped. But Michael couldn't forget. He couldn't forget how helpless he felt, and he couldn't forget his sickness at the sight of blood. It wasn't the first time.

## 5

The weeks went by. It was nearly fall. Mornings seemed to slide away into evenings with nothing in between until it was another Saturday morning and Jimmy Butler watched Michael Brace from across the room. To Jimmy, Miss Suzanne looked even more beautiful than ever before. From where Jimmy stood he could see her sitting in front of the mirror at her desk in the bedroom. She looked like a picture. He watched her stand and turn sideways to the mirror. Her hand rested on her stomach. At times Suzanne imagined she could feel her body swell with a child. Then she would know it wasn't true. On some mornings she'd remember fragments of conversations from her childhood. She'd remember pieces, and sometimes those pieces would fit together with other pieces.

Suzanne had been raised Baptist. She used to watch the people down the block dancing for hours. Her aunt would say, "They never caught God dancing." Suzanne would think about that for years and finally decide it was good. She would remember that statement in the middle of conversations where it did not exist or belong. It almost always made her happy. She felt less alone, like the conspiracy existed outside her own mind. Like God had something to do with it.

Jimmy watched Miss Suzanne walk across the room toward the porch where Mr. Brace sat in his chair looking for things across the bay. Jimmy wanted very much to see them talk to each other. From where he sat he couldn't hear a word they said, only mumbles.

"Michael."

The voice startled him, but he didn't show it. Suzanne sat down on the swing next to his chair. Sometimes she'd start a conversation as if they were the happiest couple in the world. He could smell her perfume, and she was close enough to touch.

"I'd like to ask you a favor, Michael."

He hated to want her. He hated the way it made him feel, weak and afraid of himself. She had always had a way of making him feel in debt every time she gave her body. He owed more than he got. It's like an addict who somehow can't help paying twenty dollars for a ten-dollar habit.

"Last month, when you went fishing, I was here alone."

Michael had no idea what she was going to say. She continued.

"I don't feel safe here by myself anymore. The Perrys were robbed last week, and I just don't feel comfortable about being here alone."

Michael held his face without expression.

Suzanne didn't wait for a response, "I think we should get a gun of some sort for the house. It would make me feel better."

Michael waited for a moment and then said, "What kind of gun?"

Suzanne's voice sharpened, "I don't know what kind of gun. That's why I'm asking you."

They had argued so many times it had become a way of communicating. Suzanne turned her head to look out across the bay in the direction Michael faced. She lowered the edge from her conversation.

"A pistol, Michael. Some kind of pistol."

Michael nodded his head in agreement. He could argue about the nice neighborhood, or the low crime rate in the town, or statistics, but it was easier just to agree. It was always easier just to agree. Michael had been worn down like a wooden floor in a busy doorway. "OK, Suzanne. I'll get a pistol."

They sat silent a few minutes. Jimmy Butler waited for the smile that didn't come.

Suzanne stood to leave and then stopped.

"Oh yeah, Michael, how's Hardy doin'?"

Michael's defenses were down. He answered the question the way a husband should answer such a question. "He's feelin' good. He's sitting around at home making up stories about the one that got away."

Before she turned to go, Michael asked, "Where you going this morning?"

Suzanne almost smiled. It was just enough to make Jimmy Butler think everything was all right on this certain Saturday in the Brace house.

"I've got an appointment with Dr. Riis."

Jimmy watched Miss Suzanne move across the room and pick up her purse. She was talking to herself, words Jimmy didn't understand, and then she went out the front door without saying good-bye. The boy could hear his mother washing dishes in the kitchen. He waited until Miss Suzanne's car drove away down the street before he went to the porch.

"Well hello, Mr. Butler," Michael said.

Jimmy smiled. He wanted to ask Mr. Brace about throwing the ball, but earlier in the morning, on the way to the house, Jimmy's mother told him not to bother the man with baseball or anything else. Sophie Butler had very clear lines drawn in her mind between different kinds of people. It was the way it always had been, and she didn't see it changing any time soon. Those lines weren't so clear to Jimmy. He just wanted to throw the ball in the backyard and hear another story.

Michael Brace said, "Jimmy, what do you think of a woman who walks around talking to herself, but won't even say good-bye to her husband when she leaves for the day?"

The boy answered, "I heard her talkin', but I couldn't hear what she said."

There was no hurry to the conversation. It flowed gently.

"Maybe she's talkin' to God," Jimmy said. "My momma sometimes talks to God."

"You ever hear God talk back?" Michael asked.

"Momma says He talks back, just not in words."

Michael looked out over the bay. He watched a sailboat drift and thought of the conversation about the gun. He hadn't heard about the Perrys being robbed.

The silence was broken by Jimmy asking, "What's that man there doin' all the time?" He pointed to Jerry coming up the sidewalk, moving at a steady, slow pace. He had his hands in his pockets and a white garbage bag sticking through his belt loop. He was barefoot and stopped every so often to pick up something off the ground or look up high in a tree.

"He looks crazy or somethin'," Jimmy said.

They sat on the porch and watched Jerry through the glass. He kept moving along the sidewalk until he was directly in front of the house. Jerry stopped, and then turned to look straight at Michael and Jimmy Butler. They were all three frozen still. No words were passed. Finally, Jerry looked away and began to walk again, stopping to pick up a red can.

There was a knock on the door. Jimmy turned and ran down the hall to his mother. Michael remembered his parents were stopping by. The door opened before Michael could get to it, and in came Ellen and Edward Brace.

"Good morning, Michael."

"Morning, Mom."

Michael's father was two steps behind. There was a tension between Michael and his father easily felt. Not even Ellen Brace could relieve the tension or pretend it didn't exist. It made her nervous. She had dedicated a piece of her life to supporting her youngest son. The toll was enormous upon her, but the effect on Michael was even more enormous.

Michael kissed his mother on the cheek and tried to get away to the bedroom to change clothes.

"Did you forget we were coming?" Edward Brace asked.

Michael didn't answer. Ellen Brace headed straight for the kitchen where Jimmy Butler and his mother would soon be wishing they'd left five minutes earlier. Michael's father went to the porch with his newspaper. He'd retired ten years earlier and looked forward to the local morning newspaper. Michael walked out to join his father.

"What's going on in the world today?" Michael asked.

Edward Brace was neatly dressed. Michael couldn't remember many times when he wasn't. As a child, Michael would go with his mother sometimes to his father's office. It held the place of a church in Michael's mind. He would sit on the other side of his father's huge oak desk and look around the walls at the framed certificates and photographs. His father was important, and his mother said so every day. He left home early in the morning with a word and a wave. He got back late at night after Michael was long since asleep. The competition for the attention of Edward Brace was fierce.

Michael found himself in the shadows early.

Edward Brace bent over the spread-out newspaper. "It says here Clark Peters killed himself down in Point Clear. I just saw him a few weeks ago at the bank. He looked completely normal. Where's your mother?"

Michael was trying to remember if he'd met Clark Peters. He didn't think he had.

"Says here the man left a note for his wife not to come out to the garage, to call the police. Says here he went out back with a pistol and knelt over a big tub of water. Shot himself and they found him with his head down in the water."

Michael's father was quiet a minute. Then he said, "I don't understand that."

Michael said, "Sounds like he hoped if the bullet didn't kill him, he'd drown."

Edward Brace looked up and then back down at the newspaper. He shook his head and read the article again. His mind stopped on certain words, then moved along down the page. With every word he could see Clark Peters bent over in his garage with his head in a bucket.

Ellen Brace came out of the kitchen with wet hands and her shirt sleeves rolled up to her elbow. Michael had once seen her wash the same dish five times, hold it up to the light, and then throw it away.

Ellen Brace leaned down to Michael and whispered, "What do you pay Sophie? When I first went back there she was fixing that boy a cheese sandwich."

Michael laughed, "Well, I hope you took it away from him."

Jimmy Butler wanted to leave. His mother was uneasy, and her uneasiness made him nervous. Before the white lady came into the kitchen, he was looking forward to a sandwich. Something about the way she looked at him made him afraid and angry at the same time.

The cheese sandwich sat on the kitchen counter. A fly stopped on the edge of the crust for a moment and then went away. Jimmy peeked around the corner and heard Mr. Brace laugh. He looked back at the sandwich on the counter. The fly had landed again. From across the kitchen he could see it was one of those big green flies. Jimmy's father had once told him big green flies mean business.

## 6

Suzanne sat in the lobby of Phillip Brace's law office and looked at a *People* magazine. She had made an appointment with Phillip through his secretary a few days before and hadn't given a reason. The women working in the office knew who she was and whispered. Over the past several months, Suzanne called occasionally and left messages for Phillip Brace. She never gave a telephone number.

Phillip spent more of his life between the walls of the office than any other place, and preferred it that way. He was driven by an unknown source. There were several times when he came back from court and found a message from his sister-in-law, with no number and no explanation. When he finally asked her about it, Suzanne had very little to say.

Phillip spent many hours through the years trying to understand Suzanne. He knew she was very smart, but he couldn't quite figure out exactly what she wanted, and Phillip was a man proud of his ability to analyze other people. It was part of his advantage as a lawyer, sifting through the layers and getting to the heart of a person, isolating their motivations and intentions. But Suzanne Brace remained a mystery. Phillip had forgotten about the appointment until his secretary buzzed him.

"Mrs. Brace is here to see you."

Phillip straightened the files on his desk into three neat piles, arranged in a fashion only important to himself.

"Send her in, Kathy."

The secretary walked around her desk and said, "Mr. Brace is ready to see you."

Suzanne, sitting in a burgundy chair, legs crossed, looked up from the magazine and said, "I bet he is."

Kathy let the comment linger. Suzanne stood and the secretary started to lead Suzanne down the short hallway to Phillip's office.

Suzanne said dismissively, "I know where his office is, thank you."

Kathy stopped, and Suzanne walked past her without looking back. Phillip stepped into the hall and met Suzanne at the doorway.

"Good morning, Suzanne. Come in."

After she sat down, Phillip left the door open, and Suzanne noticed. It was a lesson Phillip had learned from a wise old lawyer. Closed doors can sometimes invite unnecessary discussion and even more unnecessary speculation. They sat down across the desk from each other.

"What can I do for you today, Suzanne?"

They'd studied each other a long time. By now, Suzanne realized she couldn't intimidate Phillip with her long legs and air-tight smiles. It had always been a standoff between them, and Suzanne was intrigued by Phillip's strong will. She knew her strength with him was her unpredictability. It kept him interested.

Suzanne lowered her head and said, "I need to talk to you about Michael." Suzanne's hands fidgeted in her lap, and she stared at one particular finger.

There was a pause. Phillip didn't change expression at all. He was in his element, sitting behind his desk, surrounded by the trophies of his achievements. People came every day to tell him unbelievably crazy stories about themselves, and then at the end of the conversations, often paid large sums of money for his advice. He knew how to hold his face, how to shake his head at the right times, how to ask necessary questions.

"What about Michael? Is everything OK?" Phillip asked.

Suzanne had never talked to him about Michael, or their marriage, or any problems.

"First of all," she said, raising her eyes to meet Phillip, "I need to know our conversation is just between the two of us. I know he's your brother, but

I need to talk to someone, and I need to be sure it won't leave the room."

Phillip had no idea which direction Suzanne was going, but he believed she was sincere. Her eyes were powerful, they always had been. She had the ability to pull most people inside.

"If it's important to you, and in everyone's best interest, it will stay in this room."

As a lawyer, Phillip always left himself a way out.

"What's the problem?" he asked.

Suzanne lowered her head again. "Michael's drinking too much, Phillip. He just sits at home, day after day, doesn't work, doesn't do anything. He ignores me and won't go places with me. I don't know what else to do."

When she stopped talking, Phillip waited for her to start again. She looked up.

"I love him, Phillip. But I'm not sure he loves me anymore."

Phillip watched Suzanne's mouth move. Her big brown eyes filled up with sadness.

"Have you talked to Michael about this?" he asked.

Suzanne dropped her head again. For a second Phillip thought she might leave through the open door, but she said, in a low voice, "He hit me, Phillip. He hit me." She said it slowly, and then stopped. Suzanne raised her hand to her face and cried.

Phillip came around the desk and knelt down next to her chair. He wasn't sure what to say, so he didn't say anything at all. He held her hand between his hands.

The secretary appeared in the doorway. She saw Phillip rise to his feet and let go of Suzanne's hand.

"Mr. Brace."

"Yes."

"I'm sorry to disturb you, but Dr. Kennon is on the line. Line three."

Phillip looked at Suzanne. She kept her face turned away from the secretary. Kathy left.

"Suzanne, are you all right?"

She wiped her eyes again and nodded.

"Excuse me just one minute. This won't take long."

Phillip moved behind his desk and picked up the phone. He turned his back to look out the window and spoke in a quiet business tone. Phillip watched a squirrel dart to a spot in the grass, examine an acorn, and scurry back up a tree. When he hung up the phone and turned around, Suzanne was gone. He hadn't heard anything. He hadn't felt the movement behind his back.

The conversation bothered Phillip. His brother was a lot of things, but he couldn't imagine he'd hit Suzanne. There were times Phillip felt he knew Michael better than Michael knew himself.

Suzanne made sure Kathy saw her eyes were red. The telephone call came at a perfect time. On the drive home, Suzanne passed the old pawn-shop owned by Mr. Potter and saw Michael's car parked out front.

Michael had never bought a gun before. They felt heavy in his hand. He held almost every one in the glass case before he picked out a silver .22 caliber that somehow seemed more civilized. The handle was brown and the metal had clearly been shined by someone who cared.

The pawnshop looked exactly as it had twenty-five years ago. When Michael was a boy, he would sometimes stop by the place on his way home from school. It was filled with so many things he didn't see in regular stores: army surplus, big gold watches, and rifles. There was a glass case full of pocketknives. One knife in particular caught Michael's attention.

After school on Fridays he would stop by to look at the special knife. He saved every nickel his grandfather gave him until finally, after months and months, Michael had enough to buy it.

He felt proud when he went in the shop on the last Friday afternoon with a cigar box full of coins. Mr. Potter counted out the nickels one by one, and Michael watched every nickel slide across the glass, the man's big fingers pushing each one to a separate pile. He reached into the glass case and pulled out the knife. It was silver and red. The blade seemed sharper than a razor. It made Michael feel like a man to hold it in his hand. He had never seen anything like it.

Two weeks later, on a Friday afternoon after school, Michael went back to the pawnshop. There in the glass case, in the same spot, was another knife exactly like his own. It was as if he had never bought it.

"Mister."

"Yeah."

"How many knives like that you got?"

"Which one?"

"The red one here in the corner."

"I got a box full in the back. They been sellin' like hot cakes. Sold one today in fact."

All these years later he still felt the disappointment. Mr. Potter, the man who sold Michael the pocketknife, still owned the pawnshop. He spotted Michael near the gun case and headed over to see him.

"Michael Brace," he said.

"How are you this afternoon, Mr. Potter?"

"I'm fine, how 'bout yourself?"

"Ain't complainin', Mr. Potter."

"How's your momma and daddy?"

"They're both doin' fine."

The young lady who had allowed Michael to hold the different guns went to the far end of the counter to assist another customer.

Mr. Potter asked, "Can I help you find a gun?"

"I think I found one I like. This little .22."

"You sure you don't want somethin' bigger than that peashooter?"

"No, sir. I think it'll do."

Mr. Potter said, "I'll get you a box of bullets."

Michael watched him walk over to a separate cabinet and come back with a small box of bullets.

The old man said, "You're not gonna pay for all this with nickels now are ya?" He smiled.

"No, sir." Michael smiled back. It was a tired smile. Mr. Potter said something about the nickels every time the men saw each other.

Mr. Potter said, "You know you got to wait three days? It's the law. I'll hold the gun and bullets in this bag here."

Michael didn't know about the three-day wait, and he hoped Suzanne wouldn't ask him about the gun. She'd never believe there was a three-day requirement. She'd believe he just hadn't bothered to do what she'd asked him to do. Michael couldn't help but feel uneasy about bringing a gun into a house so full of anger and frustration.

## 7

The front door closed, and the sound woke up Michael. He thought he smelled breakfast, but the house was empty. He used to make fun of his grandmother living alone with seven cats. Now he understood. Now he wished a cat would jump up on his belly where he lay on the couch, circle around, and purr like she was glad to see him.

Out the window he could see Mrs. Forester in her front yard across the street planting pink flowers. She was out there almost every morning on her hands and knees. Her husband had his legs blown off in the Korean War, and he sat upstairs in his wheelchair watching his wife work in the yard below. Michael had never seen Mr. Forester outside, but one morning, a year or so earlier, Michael remembered getting up at five o'clock in the morning to go fishing and seeing the old man at the window watching him in his driveway. He didn't know whether to wave or not.

Michael put on the same pair of blue jeans he wore the day before. On his way to the car Mrs. Forester turned and waved. Michael waved back. He drove to the pawnshop and was glad Mr. Potter wasn't there. The plump lady from three days earlier gave him the small bag with the gun and the bullets. Michael carried the bag to the car. He took the gun out of the bag and set it on the front passenger seat like a baby. As he drove through town on the way home, he looked at the pistol like it was a separate person, a person he knew would do something bad.

Michael took a left on Magnolia Street, and when he stopped at the light, he could see Suzanne walking down the sidewalk a block away. When the light turned green, he pulled over in front of the bookstore and watched her stop and look in the windows of the dress shops along the street. To watch her from a distance made him feel strange. The connection between people can be gone in an instant. It is there, as strong as blood, and then it can be gone, in a single solitary moment, floating downwind with the flow of the next moment, or maybe no flow at all. The fibers of the connection do not exist without the touch of both ends, and cannot be held, or twisted to meet the next minute of this life.

Michael leaned up on the steering wheel and watched his wife in the world without him. He looked down at the small silver gun on the seat and his mind took a turn down a path purposefully left untraveled.

Suzanne walked through the door of the office of their family physician, Dr. Andrews. Michael waited a few more minutes, drove slowly past the doctor's office, and went back home.

He sat on the edge of Suzanne's bed and held the gun in his hand, pressing the cool metal against his skin. Michael took the pistol and small box of bullets and put them in an old cowboy boot in the closet. He stuffed them down as far as they would go and placed the boot in the corner of the closet.

On the way out the bedroom door, Michael noticed a book he hadn't seen before on Suzanne's bedside table. The front cover was dark blue with small white letters. *The Ride Through Life,* by Helen Kilgore Wills.

A slip of yellow paper marked a page in the middle of the book. Michael turned to the page and read the words:

> Are we born sinners or do we become sinners? If we're born sinners, then everything from then on is uphill. I believe we choose to sin. Some of us make very deliberate decisions to sin, and some of us, through poor choices or awkward circumstances, find ourselves in situations where sinning appears to be an opportunity, rather than a mistake. In these situations, weak people make weak decisions. Strong people climb over themselves to see not only where they stand now, but where they will stand tomorrow. A wish is an order, not a waste of time.

Michael put his finger on the place where he stopped reading. He looked up for a moment and then read the last sentence again. He flipped through the book and stopped on the final page. It ended, "Not only does the strong person recognize the difference between man's laws and God's laws, but he uses this difference to his advantage."

The title page had been signed by the author, and there were places with folded corners and sentences underlined. He was careful to replace the yellow paper between the pages. Michael set the book back on the bedside table exactly where it had been before.

He wondered if Dr. Riis had given her the book. He heard a car door slam in the driveway. Michael hurried from Suzanne's room and sat down quickly on the couch. The front door opened. Suzanne casually came into the living room and sat down in a chair. Michael remembered her at the dress shop window earlier. She never seemed to be unhappy except with him. No one else could see what he saw.

He didn't want her to speak. He didn't want her to move. Michael just wanted to drive naked with her around town in the Volkswagen Bug and to see her look at him again the way she used to, even if it hadn't been real then, or wasn't real now. They just sat in the living room silent for ten minutes. Ten minutes can be a very long time.

Finally Suzanne asked, "Do you love me, Michael?"

There could be a thousand reasons for a question like that. There could be a thousand wrong answers and a thousand more. Michael wasn't about to step into a trap as obvious as this. He had done it too many times before. But he also knew that no answer was just as bad. No answer meant "No." She would assume what needed to be assumed. She would actually play both parts in the argument until he couldn't stand it anymore and would end up trying to defend answers he never gave.

Michael stayed still. He didn't want to move, worried that if he showed any expression, she would use it against him. If he walked away, he would want to come back. If he yelled, she would yell back. If he tried to reason, she would say that love isn't something you reason with. If he changed the subject, she would change it back. If he kissed her, she would turn her face. If he packed up his things and moved, he would talk to himself and sit alone in another house.

Michael knew why he would never leave her, but he couldn't figure out why she would never leave him.

Suzanne waited for an answer. Michael didn't move. She knew what she was doing and liked it. It was more than a game. It was somehow appropriate even though it had been dulled through the years.

Suzanne smiled. Michael moved. She let him go. He relaxed.

"Do you know what February 3$^{rd}$ will be?"

Michael knew exactly what it was, but he didn't say.

"It's our fifteenth anniversary, Michael. We've been married for fifteen years."

It was strange for him to see Suzanne smile.

"I've decided to plan a party for our anniversary. A big party. Lots of people, and food, and cakes, and everything."

Michael laughed before he could stop himself.

"What's so funny? It's not funny. I think it would be wonderful."

Michael shook his head and said, "I don't understand, Suzanne."

"You don't understand what? What's there to understand? It's a party, Michael."

"OK, Suzanne, OK. We can have a party, if that's what you want," he said. Michael just couldn't figure it out.

"I want finger sandwiches and champagne. I want to have it catered and have the house and backyard decorated."

"You want to have it here?" Michael asked.

"Yes, I want you to wear a suit. I want your friends to wear suits. I want it to be perfect, no bullshit, with music, and maids, someone to park the cars."

Michael hadn't seen Suzanne act like this since the time she had a poem published in the local newspaper. After that day she spent weeks planning how she would write books and be famous and live in Europe. She wrote twenty pages and threw them in the fireplace on a Saturday afternoon.

"Michael, there's an insurance man who keeps calling here. He asked me if I have life insurance and I couldn't tell him one way or another. Do I?"

"We've both got small life policies," Michael answered.

"I've asked him to come by here on Monday morning. I won't be here. Could you talk to him? Get us a bigger policy, get one for both of us. You're good at things like that."

Michael smiled, "You planning on getting rid of me, Suzanne?" Michael thought about the little silver gun in the bottom of the boot in the bedroom closet. Suzanne hadn't asked about it since the day she first told him to buy it.

"Don't be stupid. I've been poisoning your coffee for years. You won't die," she said.

They laughed together for the first time in years.

Suzanne said, "I just want things to be better. We've got to think about the future. The man's name is Nick Crawford."

They sat quietly for a few minutes. There had been times like this over the past few years when Michael felt things would change. He closed his eyes on the swing and wished it would rain. His mother used to make chocolate-chip cookies every time it rained. There was safety in the confinement.

"What time is it?" Suzanne asked.

"11:15."

Suzanne jumped up from her chair.

"I've got to go. I've got to be at the church meeting at 11:30."

She took long steps across the hardwood floor and grabbed her purse off the table on the way out the door.

Michael said to himself, "Good-bye, Suzanne."

8

At 9:43 on Monday morning there was a knock on the door. Michael jumped up to see the numbers on the digital clock on the VCR under the television. He'd forgotten why he jumped up until there was a second knock on the door. Standing outside the screen was a man in a suit. The corners of his briefcase were worn and the handle fit neatly in his hand. Michael opened the door.

"Mr. Brace?"

A thought ran through Michael's mind, but he answered before there was time to really flesh it out.

"Yes."

"My name is Nick Crawford. I saw your wife last week, and she suggested you might be interested in getting some new life insurance or maybe expanding your present policies."

Michael scratched the back of his head and stretched out his knee. He started to correct the man and explain that this was his wife's idea and not his, but it seemed like a waste of time.

"Yeah. Come in."

Nick Crawford stepped through the door like an insurance salesman. Michael pointed toward the porch and said, "Have a seat. Give me a minute."

Nick Crawford sat down in Michael's chair and placed his briefcase on the table. He began to get his papers in order. Selling insurance was like having a conversation. He'd been doing it so long he didn't have to think about making a pitch or setting up a line. He just talked. It came out.

Michael stared into the mirror. Like a kid before school he looked around the bathroom for a diversion. Insurance salesmen and math teachers took up the same place in his brain. The water on his face was cold. There was a question about brushing his teeth and shaving. Michael walked out unshaven with a bad taste in his mouth.

"I hope I didn't wake you. I could come back later."

"No. No. This is as good a time as any, Monday morning, 9:43."

"OK. You sure?"

"I'm sure."

Nick Crawford leaned back in his chair. Instead of going into a spiel he waited for Michael. Mrs. Brace had told him that Michael already had some ideas in mind about what he was interested in.

Michael waited for the spiel. He didn't know much about insurance, so he thought he'd just let this man ramble for a while. Besides, he needed to take a minute to wake up. Neither man was really uncomfortable with the silence.

Finally Nick Crawford said, "Are you interested in life insurance for yourself or your wife or both? My file indicates you already have small life policies for both of you with the company. I believe they were with Paul Robinson before he retired."

"I'd like to increase the coverage for both of us if I can afford it," Michael said.

Mr. Crawford laid out the existing policies and Michael picked up the pieces of paper. He could see that each application listed the spouse as the full beneficiary. The two men talked about coverage amounts and monthly payments and circumstances in which benefits would and wouldn't be paid.

About midway through the conversation, Michael began to wonder why Suzanne had set this up. For a moment he could see her standing across the room by the door holding the gun at him. He could see the flash from the barrel and the reaction of her hands from the jerk of the gun. These images flashed in and out quickly, and he reminded himself life insurance was practical.

"I'll need to have you and your wife fill out these applications. Also, you'll each need to get a standard physical examination."

Michael turned his head and stared out across the bay. He was thinking about the first time he held Suzanne in his arms and remembered it as a gift. And now, years later, he sat across the table from an insurance man and questioned in his own mind her motives. He sat staring across the bay wondering if there was something wrong with him or if sometimes life can just get complicated by itself. She was so happy about the anniversary party.

"Are you all right, Mr. Brace? You don't look very well."

"Yes." Michael stuck his hand out to Mr. Crawford. They shook hands, and Michael began to gather up the papers he had been given.

Mr. Crawford wanted to go back over a few things before he left.

"This is the amount you owe per month now. This figure is the increase. You can either drop these forms off at my office, or I'll come by and pick 'em up in a few days. I've given you a copy of the terms of the policy and copies of your old policies as well. I'll check with you from time to time to make sure you're satisfied with the existing situation."

Michael's head still wasn't clear.

"Do you have any questions, Mr. Brace?"

"No, no." Michael thought a moment and said, "I'll have Suzanne fill these out, and I'll bring them by your office later in the week."

Mr. Crawford picked up the briefcase with the worn corners and left Michael alone on the porch. He watched a pelican dive into the bay and for an instant become completely submerged before bobbing to the top with a fish hanging from its bill. It reminded him of something he had written a long time ago.

Michael left the insurance paperwork and applications on Suzanne's bed along with a note letting her know about the physical examination. Michael had never been comfortable with doctors. He hoped to put off his physical as long as possible.

Three days later Michael found the insurance papers he had left for Suzanne in a stack on the coffee table. She had filled them out in detail and signed her name where it belonged. She didn't ask any questions or act like it was really very important. Michael's doubts from Monday felt far away. He rolled up the papers and headed for Mr. Crawford's office.

"Mr. Crawford, I've got the paperwork we talked about on Monday."

Michael called him Mr. Crawford. The two men were nearly the same age, but Michael felt no desire to be closer than strangers.

"Good, good. I've put together a packet of information I thought you might like. It goes over in detail the benefits of different types of policies we can offer. Please take a look at these and let me know if you have any questions."

Mr. Crawford talked as he looked over the forms Michael had handed him.

"Your wife seems to have dotted her i's and crossed her t's. You'd be surprised how many people can't figure these things out."

Michael got out his checkbook and began to fill in the date.

Mr. Crawford pulled the cap from his pen and went through the forms like he had done it a thousand times before. Out of the corner of his eye he could see Michael with his checkbook.

"Oh! There's no need for a check at this time, Mr. Brace. I'll need to send the applications to the home office and make sure they're approved before the additional cost will be added to your regular payment. Just let us know after the physical is complete."

Michael put the checkbook in his back pocket and the two men shook hands for the third time.

"I think you've made a wise choice, Mr. Brace. Insurance can provide a stability and a peace of mind that most things in life cannot. It's one of those things we hope we'll never need, but we're glad to know it's there. Kind of like a safety net."

Michael smiled. "Yeah, a safety net." He wanted to leave.

## 9

Dr. Andrews lifted the gown above Suzanne's shoulders and placed his fingers on the bruise on the ribcage underneath her left arm. "Does that hurt?"

Suzanne flinched with a natural pain that shot through the back. "Yes."

Dr. Andrews felt around the outside of the bruise. He watched Suzanne's face as he moved his fingers to a smaller bruise just to the right of her left breast.

"Is this still sore?"

Suzanne could feel him watching her.

"Yes," she said.

Dr. Andrews was a fifty-seven-year-old small-town doctor who over the years had seen everything from the birth of a cow to the newest, rarest, most devastating illnesses. He had patients from the poorest to the richest people in town. But Dr. Andrews had never had a patient like Suzanne Brace.

She had first come to see him almost fifteen years earlier. He felt as uncomfortable with her fifteen years later as he had that very first visit. Even though this was just a simple examination for her life insurance, he never performed even the smallest examination without a nurse in the room with them at all times.

"Suzanne, these are some pretty serious bruises." The doctor hesitated to ask the question on his mind.

Nurse Louise Ferguson ran her fingers gently across the purple and yellow marks.

Suzanne said, "How long will it take for them to go away?"

"A few weeks. Maybe a little longer. Is there something you need to tell me about how you got these bruises, Suzanne?" the doctor asked.

Suzanne made eye contact with Nurse Ferguson, and then looked away to the other side of the room. There was a picture of a bird with a light blue background. Suzanne stared at the picture for a count of three.

Then she said, "No, it was just an accident."

Dr. Andrews and Nurse Ferguson looked at one another.

"Suzanne, I'm going to give you a prescription for the pain, but if there's a problem, you need to go see someone who can help you. I've got names and numbers of people who can help."

Suzanne reached her right hand across her body and pulled the skin gently so she could see the bruises. She was sure to accidentally stretch back the gown enough to reveal the nipple of her left breast to the doctor, and only the doctor.

"You think they'll go away in a week or two, you say?"

Dr. Andrews instinctively looked Suzanne straight in the eyes and kept himself from drifting down to the edge of the gown.

"Maybe longer."

After leaving, Suzanne checked the date and the doctor's name on the papers and carefully placed them in her purse.

## 10

It was November, and the heat of the summer had given way to the waves of cold air from the north, separated by days of rain. Michael awoke to the sound of voices from the kitchen, the voices of Jimmy Butler and his mother. He was halfway between sleep and the new day. The voices seeped inside his mind like honey.

"But Momma, I brought my new football. Mr. Brace says it's football weather."

Sophie Butler was cleaning the kitchen. "Let the man sleep, Jimmy."

There was the sound of running water, and a piece of silverware fell to the tile floor.

"Shhh."

"Momma, why does Mr. Brace sleep on the couch?"

"I told you already."

"Why don't he sleep in the bed with Miss Suzanne like you and Papa?"

"People are different," Sophie Butler told her son.

"How's Mr. Brace different?"

Sophie was always very patient with her son. Her mother had always been patient with her, and Sophie believed this patience led to a gentleness. She believed this gentleness led to a peace in her heart.

She said, "My mother used to tell me, 'God made horses, and God made sparrows.'"

There was quiet again. Jimmy sat on the stool near his mother and held the new football he had just gotten for his birthday. His mother had told him before that God made everything, so he wasn't sure what horses and sparrows had to do with Mr. Brace sleeping on the couch.

"Momma, what does that mean?"

"It means that God knew what he was doing. He didn't make a world with only sparrows, or a world with only horses. He made a world full of different creatures, and different people. Horses can't fly, and sparrows can't pull a carriage. They can't do it now, and they won't ever be able to do it."

Michael thought of his brother's question, "Why won't you live your life?" Maybe the black lady in the kitchen knew the answer. Maybe Michael was born not to live his life. Born to sit and watch others. Maybe that's what a writer is, he thought. A person who writes about the world, instead of changing it. Today would be a good day to work on his novel, Michael thought.

The phone rang twice. Michael heard Sophie Butler say, "Hello." And then she said, "He's asleep. Yes, sir."

Sophie put down the phone and said to Jimmy, "Go see if Mr. Brace is awake. The man say he needs to talk to him."

Jimmy looked down the hall from his place on the stool. He could see the black umbrella next to the bedroom door, and Jimmy remembered the time he accidentally knocked over the umbrella. With the leather football in his hands the boy tiptoed down the hall and left a wide berth around the black umbrella. He peeked around the corner to the couch to see Mr. Brace with his eyes open.

"It's football weather, Jimmy," Michael said.

"There's a man on the phone for you."

Michael got up and picked up the phone in the living room. Jimmy started to run back to the kitchen and then stopped himself. He made another wide circle around the bedroom door and got back to the kitchen to tell his mother Mr. Brace had picked up the phone in the other room.

"Michael!"

"Hardy."

"Why don't you come over to the house? We've got football on all day. Alabama plays at three."

"Who's over there?" Michael asked.

"Phillip, and Rake, and me, and…Bridgette Pearson's over here sittin' on the couch in her underwear with those twirly things on her nipples."

Hardy laughed at himself.

"Come on Mike, Simpson's comin' over in a few hours. We've got beer fallin' out of the refrigerator."

"OK, OK, I'll be over there in a little while," Michael answered.

"Michael."

"Yeah."

"Bridgette Pearson isn't really here."

Hardy hung up. Michael smiled. Bridgette Pearson had been his prom date in high school. She was four feet seven inches tall and wore a size 38 double-D bra. After the prom he took her down parking by the big pier. It was their third date. Two months later she got engaged to Ray Baxter. Two years later she weighed 210 pounds. Michael always figured he got the best out of that deal.

It would have been a good day to write, but he hadn't hung out with the guys since the fishing accident, and he wanted to spend a day out of the house. He knew they'd probably end up in a poker game.

Jimmy Butler came back to the living room. "Can we throw the football?"

Michael stood next to the phone in his boxer shorts. "Let me see that ball, young man."

Jimmy held it out proudly. For a boy, there is no prize like a new ball.

"This is a beauty. Where'd you get it?"

"Yesterday was my birthday. I'm eight. My papa got me the football. It's real leather."

Michael held it to his nose and smelled the smell. It made him think about those games in the yard with neighborhood kids. The sense of smell is so tightly bound to our memories. Chocolate-chip cookies, burning leaves, grandfather's pipe, and the smell of a new leather football. Michael put on his pants and spent nearly an hour in the crisp November morning teaching Jimmy Butler to run buttonhooks and post patterns. Jimmy had already forgotten the conversation about horses and sparrows. It didn't matter anyway.

*

For Hardy, football was a religion. During the workweek his mind stayed occupied with the weekend football schedule. He could watch teams he'd never heard of and care which team won. When Michael arrived at Hardy's house, Phillip had already staked out the spot in the big brown chair. The fourth man in the room was Barry Prescott. Since the third grade Barry's nickname had been Rake. Some people didn't even know his real name. Rake was an appropriate name.

Michael enjoyed those Saturdays at Hardy's house. He wished they happened more often, but he suspected Hardy's wife kept them to a minimum. Kids occasionally would bounce in and out of the room.

Rake had a bag of Cheetos. His hands and lips were orange with Cheeto residue. He would stop sometimes and look down in the bottom of the bag as if one Cheeto was better than the other. He was Hardy's next-door neighbor, and somehow he ended up at the house most of the time.

"Rake, are those Cheetos good?" Hardy asked.

"Yeah, why?"

Rake was always afraid somebody was doing something to him they shouldn't be doing. He had good reason to fear. Hardy and Mark Simpson used Rake as the testing ground for practical jokes.

"No reason, Rake, no reason."

It was just enough to make Rake put down the Cheetos and look very closely into the opening of his beer can. He made small talk.

"Where you working these days, Michael?"

Phillip answered, "Michael doesn't work; he's independently wealthy."

Michael glanced at his brother and changed the subject. "How's the hole in your side?" he said to Hardy.

"Doctor says I'm almost completely healed. He says if I'd been fishing alone, and you guys hadn't been there, I probably would have bled to death in the bottom of that boat."

Rake saw Jerry walking down the neighborhood street outside. He pointed. "Look, there's old Jerry. I'm surprised he still comes down our street."

Michael looked out the window at the man in his short pants, barefoot in the cold.

"Why's that?" Michael asked.

Hardy smiled. Rake said, "They didn't tell you what they did to that poor bastard."

Michael asked, "What?"

"Just had a little fun," Hardy said.

"I saw it," Rake said, "Simpson took beer cans and made a trail from the front yard, around the side of the house, into the backyard. He put 'em about ten feet apart and waited for Jerry to come by."

Hardy smiled again and changed the channel to another game. The Alabama game hadn't started yet.

"Anyway," Rake continued, "that stupid bastard came walkin' down the street. We got up on the roof with Hardy's big mullet net. Jerry stopped on the street and looked over with those stupid glasses and saw the trail of beer cans. He must've thought he died and went to Heaven."

Phillip turned from the television and watched Rake as he spoke. Hardy could see the whole thing in his head, and he laughed out loud.

"Jerry picked up the first can and put it in his sack. He moved to the next, and then the next, like a fuckin' squirrel, until he was all the way around the house and next to Hardy's back door. We watched him go all the way around.

"When he picked up the last beer can, Simpson threw the net. It was a perfect throw. The stupid bastard was caught like a mullet."

Michael turned to Hardy, "Why the fuck you do that? What did he ever do to you?" The anger in his voice surprised Hardy. Phillip watched closely.

Hardy coughed up beer through his nose. He stood and went to the kitchen to get a towel, laughing the whole way.

Michael turned to Rake and asked, "What did Jerry do when the net fell on him?"

"That was the weird part," Rake said. "He just stood there. We thought he would scream and try to get out, but he just stood there and looked up at us. It was kinda weird."

When Hardy came back to the room he announced, "We need to make a beer run before the kickoff."

"I'll go," Michael said. He couldn't stop thinking about Jerry under the fishing net, looking up at the men on the roof, holding his sack of cans.

"I'll go with you," Rake said.

They got in Michael's car. Rake talked nonsense until Michael got to the closest grocery store. He drove past.

"Hey, you just drove by the store."

"I've got another store. The beer's cheaper," Michael lied. He wanted to go to Greer's grocery store just outside of town. The one where Laura Simmons worked. It just came to his mind. Rake talked more nonsense until they arrived.

As they pulled up, Michael felt butterflies in his belly. It was a feeling he hadn't had in many years. He wondered if she would be there. Would he see her when he walked through the door?

And he did. Laura smiled at him as he came in, like she was waiting to see his face, like she knew he would come on this certain Saturday.

She had first seen Michael Brace five years earlier. When she was a waitress. She couldn't hide the way he made her feel, and she didn't want to. Laura would get nervous just walking past his table. He was older, and seemed out of place somehow.

There were nights when Laura Simmons would spend long amounts of time thinking about Michael. In her mind she had been through a thousand scenes a thousand times. She saw him reach his hand across and rest it on top of hers. She could see them sitting together in a nice restaurant drinking wine and never wanting to spend a moment apart. She could also see the two of them in the dark, spending hours wrapped around each other's bodies. If she closed her eyes tight, she could almost feel his hands slide down her body perfectly. From a distance he could be everything she wanted. The fact that they were never together was the very thing that made him perfect in her mind.

Because Laura Simmons was simply a pretty woman, she had the opportunity growing up to learn the lessons of men as many times as she wished. In a small town, she had her choice of football players, college boys coming home for the holidays, and the rich young men who wanted her to stand nearby for their friends to see. But she wasn't stupid. She knew the reasons.

Michael and Rake stood in the back of the store in front of the beer cooler.

"It's the same price as the other store," Rake said.

"I guess so," Michael replied. He took two twelve-packs from the cooler. The timing had to be right. It couldn't be too obvious choosing her checkout line over the line with the fat old woman wearing a scarf.

Michael turned the corner. Laura's line was empty, but at the other end of the store he could see a lady with a grocery cart moving toward the checkout. Michael left Rake behind and picked up the pace.

"Where you going?" Rake asked.

"It's almost kickoff."

And then Michael was next to her.

"Hi," Laura said.

"Hi." Nothing else came out of his mouth. He didn't need to say anything else. Michael was nervous like a schoolboy.

"I haven't seen you in a while," she said.

Michael fumbled for his wallet and it fell to the floor. Rake threw a pack of cigars next to the beer Michael had placed on the counter.

They were so close to each other. He saw her hands. They were soft, without rings. Michael's thumb touched the underside of his wedding ring. It wasn't a conscious thought. He just did it.

She smelled clean.

"Bye," Laura said. She wanted to say more.

"Bye," Michael said.

The feeling was still in his belly when he got back to the car.

Rake asked, "Do you know that girl?"

"Not really," Michael answered.

They drove back to Hardy's house. Mark Simpson had made his appearance. The game was a good one, went down to the last second, and after it was over, they ordered a pizza. The poker table was yanked out of the closet and the five men sat around in different size chairs. The conversation was loose.

Phillip said, "I hear you've got an anniversary party coming up."

Michael cringed. "That's what I'm told."

"An anniversary party?" Mark Simpson said. "I don't believe Asshole's ever had a party of any kind in history. When is it?"

"February 3$^{rd}$."

"Why the hell don't you have any kids?" Simpson asked, out of nowhere.

Michael looked at his cards and took a sip of his beer.

"I was wonderin' that myself," Hardy said.

Since Phillip's meeting with Suzanne in his office, he'd been trying to decide whether or not to talk to his brother about what she said. He'd decided to wait. Phillip looked up from his cards at Michael.

"It just never seems like the right time," Michael finally said.

Hardy said, "There ain't no right time, Mike. There's always a new house to buy, or the next promotion at work, or in your case, the next book to write."

Rake asked, "You write books?"

Simpson said, "He talks about writing books, but I'm not sure I've seen one on the shelf at Wal-Mart."

Phillip said, "And when's the last time you looked at the bookshelves at Wal-Mart, Simpson?"

Hardy was half-watching another game on television. The men threw chips into the pile in the middle of the table.

"You need kids, Michael," Hardy said. "They'll change the way you see this world. Besides, you're gettin' older. Gettin' old is hard enough, you don't want to do it alone. How old are you?"

"I'll be thirty-eight in December."

"Thirty-eight," Hardy repeated. "That's about the age you figure out you won't live forever. You'll get old and die like the rest of us."

The men were all a little drunk.

Rake asked, "Phillip, why don't you have any kids?"

Simpson said, "Phillip's pecker got sliced off in a tractor accident."

Nobody laughed. "No shit?" Rake said. Then they all laughed.

"That ain't true," Rake said.

"No, Rake, it ain't true," Phillip explained. "I've still got my pecker. I just haven't found the right girl yet."

Rake said, "Maybe Michael could set you up with that girl at the grocery store. She was damn good-lookin'."

"The girl at the grocery store?" Phillip said. "What girl is that?"

Rake said, "She's young, now. She works at the grocery store outside of town."

Simpson said, "That wouldn't be Laura Simmons, now would it?"

Michael changed the subject quickly. "Why the hell did you throw the fishing net on Jerry? Sometimes you're a shithead, Mark."

Phillip didn't miss his brother's attempt to veer the conversation away from Laura Simmons. He knew who she was, but that was all. Michael's sensitivity to the subject left him wondering if the girl had anything to do with Suzanne ending up in his office.

Mark Simpson took a long sip of his beer. He genuinely liked to get people pissed off. It made the world a more interesting place in his opinion.

"Why do you care, Asshole? Jerry's a retard."

"Maybe it's you who's the retard, Mark."

It started to rain outside. They played poker until late and Michael drove home after midnight. He told himself he wouldn't go to Hardy's house again for poker, but he'd told himself that before, and he always went again.

Michael could see the light on in Suzanne's bedroom from the driveway. He walked around to the back of the house and stood in the bushes looking through the window.

Suzanne was writing at her desk. She would stop, read what she had written, and stare at the wall for a while before putting the pen back to the paper. Michael moved to another spot in the darkness to see. He wondered who she would be writing to? Why would the right words be so important?

Michael finally walked around to the front of the house and unlocked the door quietly. In the dark, with the buzz of a dozen beers in his head, Michael inched his way to the couch. He laid down in all his clothes and fell asleep. The rain still fell.

## 11

Suzanne sat in her room at the desk. The blinds were almost closed and the rain fell steadily outside. She held a pen in her hand and shifted her body so the light would fall onto the empty piece of paper and the envelope in front of her. Twice she moved her hand to the page and waited a moment. Twice she pulled it back and turned to watch the rain against the window.

It was dreary in the room. The bed wasn't made, and it looked tan and too warm. There wasn't enough light to show the colors of the pictures on the walls. There wasn't enough light to see anything much besides the desk, and the photograph, and the empty page.

Suzanne felt like the room. It was a lazy hatred. Too tired and too warm and too scattered out to concentrate. She started the letter.

The words were very important. In order to write them, she had to feel them. In order to feel them, she had to imagine what it would be like to be someone else. She had to imagine emotions she had never had. It reminded her of Michael's book.

The spoken word disappears as soon as it is heard. A letter has to stand alone through reading and rereading. It must make a circle from the last sentence back to the beginning because people will read it again and again. Suzanne leaned her head against her hand. The words started slowly and then began to flow like cool milk across the table.

The colors would have to be separated. The blue would need to be pulled apart from the green. Suzanne began to feel emotions she had only felt as a child. Her love for her father had been so simple, just as her love for Michael had been. How could he know?

Memories of her father Suzanne no longer knew she possessed sometimes came back to her. The night he brought home the dog. It was like a dream now, but Suzanne knew it wasn't a dream.

She was sitting at the dinner table with her mother and her little sister. He came through the front door with the dog in his arms. Not just a dog, a three-legged dog with thick mats of hair. As he got closer, the smell was unbearable. The dog's eyes were half-closed with puss.

Elizabeth said, "A doggie."

"This ain't a dog," Orin Manley said sharply.

Suzanne's mother said, "It looks like a dog."

"That's part of the beauty. It's part of the test. You didn't think God was gonna come down from the sky like a bolt of goddamned lightnin', did you? Hell no. Look at him."

Mr. Manley put the dog down on the floor next to the dinner table. It shook with fear, balancing on three legs, a nub on the back left. Mrs. Manley put her hand over her mouth and nose. Orin Manley lifted the head of the dog and pointed to the chest.

"You see that? You see the number seven in white on his chest? That's it. That's the sign. I seen it on the side of the road with my headlights. I seen it. And look here on his back. See here. The constellation of stars."

Suzanne looked at her mother. Mrs. Manley looked down at her food.

Mr. Manley said, "If I'd'a passed him up, if I'd'a drove on by, we'd all burn in the fire of eternal damnation." His face was so sure, so absolutely sure.

Suzanne, sitting alone at the desk, shook her head at the memory. She wrote on another piece of paper, "The mouse moves through the maze at a hurried pace. He takes wrong turns and comes to dead ends and turns and retraces his steps and moves along. He may make the same mistakes two, three, four times, but the pace is always the same, hurried. It keeps his mind off the ridiculous waste of time."

She tore up the piece of paper and threw it away.

She went back to the letter and wrote:

*"Dear Phillip,*

*"Seeing you tonight was like touching the sun. I think of you every minute of every day."*

Suzanne read the few sentences she had written. A smile came to her face when she thought of them reading the words out loud.

She continued, *"Just the few moments we can spend together are the reason I can get out of bed in the morning. A phone call, lunch, the afternoon in your car down by the old ferry landing."*

Suzanne started from the beginning and read it all over again. Each phrase had to be broken apart in her mind, the way they would be later.

*"Sometimes Michael will look at me like he knows. I am afraid what might happen if he does.*

*"I'm not sure I can make it through our anniversary party tomorrow with you across the room.*

*"When you tell me you love me, it makes me feel like everything will be OK.*

*"I will love you forever.*

*Suzanne"*

Suzanne thought about the gun in the closet. It hadn't taken her long to find it. It seemed small, like a toy. She walked to the closet and pulled the gun from the bottom of the boot. She held it up in front of the mirror. She smelled the metal and ran her fingers across the barrel. When she was finished, Suzanne put the gun back in the boot exactly as she had found it and sat down again at her desk.

Her father had said, "His name is Abraham. He eats with us now. Our home is his home."

Orin Manley took Suzanne's plate of food from in front of her and placed it on the floor for the dog. They watched the animal eat the mashed potatoes. Mr. Manley continued to kneel between the dog and the dinner table. Suzanne lowered her hand to touch the dog on his head. With a swift inhuman force, Orin Manley backhanded his oldest daughter across the side of her head. She saw black instantly and the chair crashed backward to the floor. The hungry dog barely looked up from the warm mashed potatoes. Suzanne awoke in the hospital, her mother at her side.

Suzanne closed her eyes and felt the side of her head where she remembered the pain. There was still a small scar near her temple she believed was left by her father's wedding ring.

It had been a very long time since she remembered the dog. Suzanne read the entire letter addressed to Phillip from top to bottom. It was only the first draft. She would rewrite the final copy with new ink on February 3, the night of the anniversary party.

## 12

On a breezy Wednesday morning in early December Phillip walked across the street from the courthouse and found himself a table in the corner of the restaurant. It was a local home-style restaurant. Nobody pretended it was anything more. Good food, friendly people, and red curtains on the windows. Phillip was in Mobile for the day, scheduled to argue motions in the morning and spend the afternoon at a deposition not far from the courthouse. It was nearly noon, and eating lunch alone would give him a chance to look over his file.

From where Phillip sat he could see the front door of the restaurant. It was a habit. He had been in his chair less than a minute when Suzanne walked inside. She came across the room without hesitation and sat down in the only other chair at Phillip's table.

She smiled and said, "What are you doing here, Phillip? I thought you mostly stayed on the other side of the bay."

Phillip didn't have much time to hide his disappointment. He liked Suzanne, but he had an important deposition in less than an hour, and with Suzanne at the table, he'd probably never even get the file out of his brief-case. Besides, he didn't want another conversation like the one at his office. He smiled and stood and invited her to sit down with a polite sweep of his hand. Phillip was almost always polite to women.

"I drove all the way over here because I knew you'd be eating lunch in this exact spot," Phillip said.

Suzanne pretended to blush and leaned over just enough to set her purse under the table. She watched Phillip's eyes to see if they would drop to the edge of her dress that opened up across her breasts. They didn't, and he noticed her watching. It was a game, and Phillip didn't lose many games.

"Can I join you?" Suzanne asked. She almost whispered.

"Yes," Phillip whispered back, "if you promise not to tell my wife."

Suzanne smiled. Phillip had never been married. There was no time. He came close once. In college. They talked about it. But then there was law school, and bar exams, and life dangled before his eyes like a carrot on a string.

Suzanne's dress was dark blue and cut from her shoulders across the brown skin of her chest. The fabric slid down and pulled comfortably tight around her hips. Every man in the restaurant had watched her for at least one of her steps as she walked from the front door to Phillip's table near the back.

A black woman stood and recited the daily menu. Suzanne ordered a vegetable plate, and Phillip had the Wednesday special.

For twenty-two years Morris Greene had owned and operated "The Kitchen." His wife and fat sister cooked the meals, and there were enough children in the family to keep from having to hire many outsiders. Phillip's grandfather had helped Morris get out of jail more than thirty years ago after a downtown barroom brawl. Morris Greene had never forgotten and always made a point of coming over to Phillip's table when Phillip was in the restaurant.

"How ya do, Mr. Brace? How ya do today?"

"I'm doin' fine, Mr. Greene. I'll be doin' better when your wife's home-cookin' gets out here."

The two men shook hands. Mr. Greene put his hand over his heart and stepped back a step from Suzanne.

"And who is this intoxicatin' woman?" Morris Greene asked.

Phillip laughed and Suzanne smiled like a girl. She wanted to reach out and hold the man's hand across the table.

"This is Suzanne, my sister-in-law. Suzanne, this is Mr. Morris Greene, the owner of the best restaurant east of the big river."

Morris smiled.

"Sister-in-law?"

He shook his head from side to side.

"I think I could do without the temptatin', if you know what I mean?" Mr. Greene said as he turned to wink at Phillip. Suzanne never said a word.

After Morris Greene left, the two sat in silence.

Phillip finally said, "I don't mean to be rude, Suzanne, but would you mind if I looked over a few papers?"

"No, no. Not at all. Go ahead, please."

For most of the lunch Phillip pulled and pushed papers in and out of his briefcase. At every moment he was aware of Suzanne sitting across the table. It wasn't uncomfortable, but it wasn't easy either. He could hear her eat, and he wondered if she was there by accident.

The young girl with braids stopped by to refill the iced tea glasses. She picked up the empty plates and put the bill down between Phillip and Suzanne. The girl continued to clean up the table. Suzanne reached her hand out and pushed the bill toward Phillip. The girl looked over and smiled.

Suzanne said, "That's what men are for." They smiled at each other and the girl disappeared into the kitchen.

Phillip paid the bill and they walked out together. He recognized four or five lawyers sitting around the restaurant. They nodded at one another. Suzanne's high-heel shoes stung the floor step by step across the room, and one of the women in the back spent a few seconds feeling bad about herself.

Suzanne and Phillip said good-bye on the corner across from the courthouse. It was uneventful, even boring. Phillip walked toward the law office for his one o'clock deposition. About a block and a half away from the courthouse, he turned to look back. Suzanne stood in the same place he had left her minutes before. She watched him and waited until he turned away. She watched him walk out of sight. Phillip would remember for the rest of his life seeing Suzanne that day, standing in the cold on the sidewalk, watching him. He would remember feeling something was wrong.

Phillip spent the next several hours thinking about Suzanne's strange behavior. During a break in the deposition he called his office.

"Kathy, I'll probably get out of here about four or four thirty; do I have any messages?"

Kathy read each message carefully. After four years of being Phillip Brace's secretary, she knew how important it was to take good messages. She also knew how important it was to seem uninterested in the private life of Mr. Brace.

"And the last message is from Suzanne. She called at two fifteen and said to tell you 'Thank you for the wonderful lunch.'" Kathy read each message with the same professional tone. She waited on the other end of the line for some reaction out of the ordinary. There wasn't any.

"Thank you, Kathy. Don't forget to get that Henderson letter out this afternoon. It's got to go in today's mail."

"Yes, sir."

Phillip hung up the phone. He thought about Suzanne's message for a moment and then spent the next hour and a half in the deposition asking questions that built a castle.

After the lunch in Mobile, Suzanne drove home across the old causeway. She stopped and bought a pack of cigarettes. It had been more than ten years since she smoked a cigarette, but on this particular day she drove around with the windows down smoking one after another. The air outside was cold and the chill dug deep into her skin.

She felt useless and pretty and strange and alone. Down the four-lane she pulled up at a red light next to a college kid in a pickup truck. While the light stayed red, she watched him watch her out of the corner of her eye. She watched him keep his young blue eyes on her for every second until the light turned green, and she bolted away. He had seen Suzanne's nipples pressed out hard against her dress.

## 13

It was Michael's birthday, two days before Christmas. He was thirty-eight. His mother and father invited him to their house for dinner. He lied and said Suzanne wasn't feeling well. He hadn't seen her all day. She was gone when he woke up. She still wasn't home when Michael's mother called with the invitation, and Michael had no idea where his wife had gone.

He drove to his parents' house alone. It was the same house he called home all his life. His old room had been transformed into a sewing room, even though his mother didn't do much sewing. Phillip was at the table with his father having a bourbon when Michael let himself in the door.

"It's the birthday boy," Phillip said. He was still wearing his shirt and tie. A suit jacket hung from the back of the dining room chair.

The Christmas tree was over ten feet tall. It was decorated with the same ornaments Michael had seen since the first Christmas he could remember. Through the years new ornaments had been added, but their newness faded away and they soon became part of the old. But the old was good. His Christmas memories were strong and bright. Michael stood in front of the tree and took it all inside himself, the evergreen smell and the tiny white lights.

Michael's father asked, "Should we expect Suzanne tonight?"

"No, Dad. She still doesn't feel too well." Michael lied again.

Edward Brace said, "Your mother thinks Suzanne's pregnant. Of course, she thinks that all the time."

With his back still to the dining room table, staring at the tree, Michael said, "She's not pregnant."

Before long, Ellen Brace served a wonderful meal: fried catfish, cheese grits, and butter beans. Michael knew these were the people he loved. He knew he came from his mother, and he knew his father's blood moved through his veins, but there were times Michael saw his parents as strangers. They had followed Phillip's life, living again through his eyes, but Michael's life had been harder to follow. There was less to see, and more to watch. The time would come soon, Michael knew, when he would ask them for money again. There were other options, but somehow those other options seemed harder to select.

Ellen Brace knew the longer they sat at the table together, the greater the chance her husband would step across one of those lines between himself and his youngest son. She knew all the men at the table, their strengths and weaknesses. She knew her husband, even on Michael's birthday, could not go much beyond his second glass of wine without asking, "Tell me about your job prospects," or "You must be finished with that novel. When can we see it?," or "It's about time you paid off that loan, don't you think?"

She served the key lime pie quickly. Ellen Brace had prayed for a daughter. She loved her firstborn, but he was bullheaded and aggressive like his father. She wanted purity, and pink dresses, and ribbons. Instead she got another boy, but this one was different from the first. He could sit and look at people's faces for long periods of time. He thought too much and did too little. The world was a hard place for a boy like that, so Ellen Brace draped herself around him. She did it out of love, but it just made things worse. He never learned to fight.

Before the men could finish their dessert, Ellen Brace set the birthday present down in front of Michael. He tore off the paper to find a book: *The Moviegoer,* by Walker Percy.

"It's a first edition," Ellen Brace said. "I know you like him."

"Thank you, Mom," Michael said. He hugged his mother.

Edward Brace started to make a comment, but he stopped himself. Instead, he lifted his second glass of wine and took down the last sip. Ellen Brace watched her husband put the wineglass back down on the table.

Michael said, "Thank you for the nice dinner and the book. I've got to go home and check on Suzanne."

"I've got to go, too," Phillip added. "Thank you, Mom."

The boys each hugged their mother and shook hands with their father. They walked out together.

Phillip said, "Hey, before you go home, let me buy you a birthday beer."

The men looked at each other. The night was fairly warm for the time of year. A front was pushing through and rain was expected. Michael didn't want to go home.

"OK."

"I'll drive," Phillip said.

They pulled in front of a bar in a little town next to Fairhope called Montrose. The bar had been there a long time and Michael knew several people by name. The walls were covered from top to bottom with ceramic whiskey bottles and horseshoes and signs with stupid little bar slogans.

> I DON'T HAVE A DRINKING PROBLEM.
> I DRINK, GET DRUNK, AND FALL DOWN.
> NO PROBLEM.

> THIS AIN'T MY BELLY —
> IT'S A SHRINE.

Michael sat on the stool and slowly picked at the label on his beer bottle. There were about fifteen or twenty people total around the bar area and in the back room with the pool tables. Michael was thinking about nothing. He had peeled off almost the entire corner of the label and bits of balled-up paper lay around the base of the bottle.

"Is there anything you need to talk about, Mike?"

Phillip had his sleeves rolled. Michael was always amazed how comfortable his brother could be in so many different settings. Michael continued to pick at the place on the bottle where the label had been. There was hard glue on the brown bottle.

"I thought Dad was pretty good tonight," Phillip said. "Of course, Mom had us outta there before the old man had time to think of anything to say."

Laura Simmons appeared from the back room and walked toward Michael on the way to the bathroom. She was wearing a pair of blue jeans and a white T-shirt, and Michael saw her coming before she saw him. He turned his head back to the bottle of beer. Through the years Michael Brace had become very good with mirrors. He knew where every mirror was located in the bar, and he knew how to watch someone without ever looking in their direction.

"Wasn't that the Simmons girl?" Phillip asked.

"Where?"

"The girl who just went past. The one with the wonderful blue jeans."

"I don't know. I didn't see her," Michael said.

"Liar."

"Are you finished with your beer? I need to go," Michael said as he stood up from the barstool.

"No, I'm not finished," Phillip answered. "What's your hurry?"

Michael sat back down on the barstool. A few minutes went by. Phillip turned his head around to see Laura Simmons come out of the bathroom and walk their way. She spotted Michael and immediately got the feeling she would get, the lightness in her legs, conscious of her breathing.

"Aren't you Laura Simmons?" Phillip asked before she could get by.

"Yes, sir."

"Sir? Please, don't call me 'sir.' Hell, I'm only old enough to be your brother."

"I'm sorry." Laura blushed and tried not to look beyond Phillip at Michael who kept his head down, still scratching at the label on the beer bottle.

"Don't be sorry," Phillip said. "Instead, have a seat, and I'll buy you a beer."

"No," Michael said. He said it without thinking. It just came out. He rose up from his chair as he said the word and put his hand on Phillip's arm.

Michael stood still a moment, and then said, "I told you, I've got to go home."

Laura Simmons could tell that something was wrong. The tone of Michael Brace's voice was just below angry. It was less a demand and more of a warning of some sort.

The bartender looked up from the drink he was pouring.

Phillip pulled his arm away. It was just a reaction to the challenge of a little brother in a public place.

"Hey!" The bartender made sure his voice would be taken seriously. "If you two can't get along, take it outside."

Phillip looked from the bartender to Michael. The alcohol and the situation made him say, "What the hell's the matter with you? You don't have anywhere to go, except maybe back home to knock your wife around the house a little."

Everybody stood still. It was one of those moments.

Michael's anger took a wild swing at Phillip and missed his jaw by inches. The bartender was on the other side of the bar before another punch could be thrown. It was quick. The brothers' arms were tangled around each other. For a few seconds they grasped for leverage and then separated with a push.

Laura Simmons backed away and stood by the wall. She couldn't believe it could be true.

Phillip was immediately sorry he had said it. He couldn't take it back, and he knew it would be impossible to explain away. How could he tell his little brother that his beautiful wife had sat in his office with tears in her eyes, and told him that Michael had hit her? How could he tell him that Suzanne showed up for lunch out of nowhere, and called his office and left messages regularly?

When Phillip finally got out of the barroom, Michael was gone. They were miles from home, but Michael was nowhere to be seen. Laura Simmons was left inside with no explanation of what had just happened.

It started to rain. At first it was a light sprinkle with flashes of lightning off to the west far across the bay. Phillip sat in the car, the radio off, the raindrops rolling down the windshield reflecting the streetlight. He tried to put himself in Michael's place. Phillip could remember places, events, people, episodes, in Michael's life, but he couldn't put them together. He couldn't see how they were important or unimportant to Michael. It was like having a road map with all the locations, and cities, and lakes, and rivers, marked clearly, but without any roads or streets or highways that connect all these places.

Phillip had no idea where Michael would go in the rain in the middle of the night in December. He had no idea. He stood by the car and looked across the road before he drove home and went to bed.

Michael stood in the edge of the woods off the road. He watched Phillip sitting in his car, and then watched him drive away. The rain fell steadily. Michael pushed his hands into his pockets. He thought about cutting through McLean's woods to the bay and then making his way down the shoreline to his house. It was dark, but Michael had been through these woods a thousand times as a kid.

In the middle of those small-town southern summer nights Michael used to sneak out the bedroom window. He would crawl across the rooftop to the big oak tree that hung over the house and then drop down to the ground behind the toolshed. Sean Simmons, Laura's older brother, and Mark Simpson would be waiting in the shadows. Michael was eleven, Sean was ten and a half and Mark was twelve and a half. Michael was the rich kid.

Each Saturday during the summer months the boys would spend their days walking up to town and back, riding their bikes through the dirt trails, playing baseball, and shooting squirrels with Sean's Daisy BB gun. Fudge Hardy, Billy Hadley, and Tony "Mule Boy" Crosby were three others from the neighborhood. Nobody could throw a baseball like Mule Boy Crosby. He once threw a fastball that stuck in the wooden door the boys used as a backstop behind home plate.

Saturday night was adventure night. Almost every adventure night centered around McLean's woods and the railroad tracks that ran through the middle. There were stories about men who lived on trains. Men who set up camp in those woods and sat in the dark smoking cigarettes and drinking whiskey. Men who came from places like New York, and California, and Mexico. Men who killed boys for sport and buried them under the railroad tracks late in the night.

Simpson would take the point position and circle down Fels Avenue toward the bay. He would stop outside the Hadleys' house and tap three times with the end of his pocketknife on the metal fence post. A few minutes later Billy Hadley came charging around the back of the house, wide-eyed and out of breath. The boys carried a flashlight, a pocketknife, a glow-in-the-dark watch, and a pocket full of kite string. They wore blue or black

T-shirts, blue jeans, and tennis shoes rubbed brown with dirt to cover the white. Michael could feel the fear the minute he left his window. He wondered if Sean or Mark or the other boys felt the same fear. He wondered when they finally reached the edge of McLean's woods if anyone really knew what waited for them in the darkness at the railroad tracks.

Michael waited in the rain with his eyes on the door of the old bar. He decided to count to thirty slowly, and if Laura didn't come out the door, he would walk home through McLean's woods. He slowed down at twenty. At thirty he disagreed with himself. Just as Michael turned to leave, the door opened, and Laura Simmons walked out into the same rain he felt. He stepped out from the woods across the street.

Laura smiled. Michael could see it under the streetlight. She stopped, hesitant, and then asked, "You need a ride?"

Michael nodded his head, "Yeah, I do." He walked across the road and climbed into the passenger side of an old red pickup truck.

Laura cranked the truck. "Did your brother leave you?"

Michael had his hands deep in the pockets of his jacket. He could feel the cold rain trickling down his face.

"Is this your truck?" he asked.

"It used to be my brother's," she said. "I can't seem to get rid of it."

Michael thought about Sean's funeral. He died three years earlier in a car accident up near Birmingham. He was a passenger in a car blindsided at a light. Sean was crushed to death.

"I miss him," Michael said. The words surprised him. He hadn't thought about Sean much. They hadn't seen each other for years before the accident. But he did miss him. He missed being a boy with Sean in Fairhope on those Saturday nights, and those summer days at the baseball field, and sitting in the woods pretending they were hunting bears when there were only squirrels and blue jays.

Laura drove from the parking lot. She took a right and then a left.

"Do you know where I live?" Michael asked.

Laura looked over at him. She wasn't embarrassed.

"Yes," she said.

The windshield wipers repeated themselves. The truck tires touched the wet pavement. Laura Simmons and Michael Brace went down streets they'd been down a thousand times before, just never with each other. They were only two blocks from his house. The rain stopped.

"I didn't hit my wife," he said.

"I know," she said.

Laura pulled up in front of Michael's house. He got out of the truck and stood at the door. They looked at each other.

"How do you know?" Michael asked.

Laura smiled again. "There's some things I just know about other people. There's some things we can't hide, no matter where we go."

Michael wanted to get back in Sean's truck and ask Laura Simmons to drive him away, anywhere, just away, with her. But he closed the door of the truck and walked up his driveway. He listened to Laura drive away behind his back and then remembered he'd left his car at his parents' house.

Suzanne's car was in the driveway, but the house was completely dark. He decided to walk down to the Fairhope pier. The rain was gone and the night was still warm. Michael knew the cold front wasn't far behind. He sat for hours down at the pier and felt it get colder and colder. Later, he went back home and fell asleep next to the front door.


Jerry sat in the darkness. He liked to walk to town very early in the mornings. The world seemed to be his own. He had taken his usual path from Church Street to Fels Avenue and down to the bluff overlooking the bay. Some mornings he would sit for a long time listening to nothing and smoking cigarettes on the bench under the trees. He would usually leave when the light in the upstairs bedroom of Mr. and Mrs. Forester came on. It was the first sign the rest of the world would wake up soon and spoil the silence.

At 5:00 A.M. sharp the light flicked on in the upstairs window across the street. Mr. Forester rolled his wheelchair to the window and looked out from his house. As daylight broke and cleared, Mr. Forester could see Michael Brace asleep beside the front door. He could see it clearly.

## 14

When Michael was a boy, he began to believe there were too many people in the world. He believed there must have been a time when one person could make a difference. There must have been a time when everyone was accounted for and no one fell between the cracks.

Michael felt as the population of the world exploded through the nineteenth and twentieth centuries, something began to happen to people. As the population multiplied to five billion and beyond, the people who were affected most were the people like Michael Brace. At least that's what he believed.

There just wasn't enough time anymore for everybody. Even the small towns like Fairhope grew to the point people didn't really know their neighbors.

Michael read once that rats do well in a confined space in certain numbers. Two in a cage will thrive. Three in a cage will have no problem. Four in a cage, or five, or six, and the rats still maintain a sense of community and order. But when you add the seventh rat, all seven will begin to attack one another. Even if food and water are plentiful, the sheer lack of space will send the animals into a frenzy.

Michael believed it was the same with people. The overpopulation of the planet is the cause for the worldwide increase in violence, immorality, and even natural catastrophes. People have lost their identities in the masses.

Unlike rats, human beings don't always react to this with violence. Some people just disappear.

Michael Brace waited for his wife to go to bed. He drank half a bottle of whiskey, smoked seventeen cigarettes, and decided to leave. There just wasn't enough space inside the house. The car started on the first turn of the key. Michael backed out of the driveway with the lights off. He took back roads crisscrossing through the farm country in the heart of the night.

At 2:45 A.M. Michael Brace was driving down old Highway 31 with the radio off and the windows rolled up tight. He wanted to be able to leave this place. He wanted to be able to drive to a new place, far away, where no one knew he was the only person who knew.

For no real reason, Michael Brace started to cry. And for the first time since he was a child, he didn't try to make himself stop. The tears rolled down his cheeks, and he didn't wipe them away, or try to think of something nice, or turn up the radio. Michael's body rocked slowly as he held the wheel with both hands.

The houses went by, and the fences, and the trees. The gas stations went by, and a church, and a field of wildflowers in the dark. Michael Brace cried. He turned around and drove back home before the sun came up.

## 15

By the middle of January Suzanne had the entire anniversary party planned down to details. It was almost the only topic of conversation between Michael and his wife.

On a beautiful early Saturday morning Michael woke up with Suzanne sitting next to him by the couch. She had a pen and pad in one hand and a cup of coffee in the other.

"Good morning," Suzanne said.

"Good morning."

Michael watched her without moving. He didn't know why she was there, but he did know it had something to do with the anniversary party. For the first time in years Suzanne seemed to be excited and interested. Michael had stopped trying to figure it out months ago. He just enjoyed seeing her the way she used to be.

"What time is it?" Michael asked.

"It's 7:30. Wake up. Mrs. Forester's been working in the yard across the street for two hours already, and you're still asleep."

Michael lifted himself against the pillow but didn't make any attempt to crawl out of the sheets.

Michael said, "If God had intended people to be up that early, he would have made it light outside."

"How do you know what God intended?" Suzanne snapped.

Michael wished he hadn't said anything. Suzanne's tone was a punishment. She let it linger for a minute and then moved along.

"Here's the list so far: your mother and father, Phillip, Betty Riis and her husband, Hardy and Phyllis, Grace, Lisa, John Mateland and his bitch wife, Pat, Mrs. Forester, Lynn and Tony."

Suzanne skipped down her list a few names. She looked up at Michael. His eyes were closed.

Before she could yell, Michael asked, "Who's Lynn and Tony?"

"You know Lynn and Tony. Lynn's father owns the fabric shop. Tony used to play on your softball team."

Suzanne was already tired of this. She had forty-seven names on the list. It didn't make any difference whether Michael approved of them or not. The invitations were already sent.

"Never mind. Get up. There's some things I need you to do in the yard."

Michael started to put up a fight, but it wasn't worth the aggravation. He crawled off the couch and pulled on a pair of blue jeans. Out of the window on the way to the bathroom he could see Suzanne already out in the yard with a trash can full of rakes and hedge clippers.

Michael whispered to himself, "The party's three weeks away. It's 7:30 in the morning."

Michael walked down the outside steps. He started to tell Suzanne their anniversary was more than three weeks away, but Mrs. Forester was walking across the street with her gardening gloves and dirty knees.

"Good morning, Mrs. Forester," Suzanne said.

"Good morning. Isn't it just wonderful out here? It's enough to make an old woman feel frisky again."

Suzanne laughed. Both women turned to Michael as he walked over from the house.

"Good morning, Mr. Michael," Mrs. Forester said, "rise and shine."

Suzanne shook her head in a pleasant, wife kind of way.

"I just can't seem to get this old man movin' in the morning, Mrs. Forester. And look at those hands."

Suzanne held Michael's palms up.

"Look at these hands. They haven't touched the Earth in I don't know when."

Mrs. Forester peeked over at Michael's clean hands and gave him a little wink that Suzanne didn't see.

"Michael, you oughta be ashamed of yourself. I've been out in my garden or working in my yard almost every morning for the past seventeen years. And every morning I look over here expecting to see you out churnin' up the dirt." She smiled.

"Yes, ma'am," Michael answered.

Suzanne said, "If you ever see this sleepyhead up and out early in the morning you better take a picture. On second thought, you better not, it probably means he drank too many beers with those lousy friends of his playing poker the night before, and I wouldn't let him in the house."

Mrs. Forester looked up to her husband in the window. She waved and he waved back. Suzanne and Michael did the same.

"Oh, yes. Mrs. Forester, did you get your invitation for our anniversary party on February 3? We'd very much like it if you would come. It'll be on a Saturday evening, here at the house."

"I did get the invitation, and I certainly will be here. Congratulations, you two. It's nice to see a young couple stay together these days. So many people seem to have forgotten that a marriage takes hard work. It isn't easy," Mrs. Forester said.

"No, ma'am," Michael said.

Suzanne's eyes were fixed across the street on Mr. Forester in the upstairs window. Mrs. Forester finally walked away and left Suzanne and Michael standing in the yard alone.

"I didn't hear Mark Simpson's name on that list," Michael said.

"It's on there," Suzanne answered. "Here's the list, why don't you take a look at it yourself."

Suzanne pulled the pad of paper from her back pocket and handed it over.

Michael went down the list. There were forty-seven names and not a single member of Suzanne's family. From no origin in particular, and for no reason Michael could identify, a feeling rose inside of him. A feeling of anger and frustration, from his chest. For the first time in his life, standing in the front yard, Michael had an urge to hurt Suzanne. He wanted her to feel the same kinds of pain she'd been making him feel for years.

Suzanne was down on her knees stacking red bricks in the small garden area around the shrubs in front of the house. Her black hair was in a ponytail. Pieces had pulled loose on the sides and hung down around the frame of her face.

Michael said, "Why isn't Elizabeth's name on the list?"

Suzanne turned to look at him. There was dirt on the end of her nose. He'd expected her eyes to be full of vengeance, but they weren't. They were soft and alone, and Michael immediately wished he hadn't said it. He wished he could take it back, pull the words from the air and put them where they belong, inside himself, to be dealt with, but it couldn't be done.

As they stared at each other, Michael's regret began to change very slowly. He could see the pain he had caused in her eyes. He could see the same fear and frustration he saw in the mirror, in his own eyes, and Michael began to like what he had done. He began to understand what Suzanne had always understood. The change passed between them, and Michael finally spoke, "I left my gloves inside. I'll be back in a minute."

Michael walked through the front door and hurried into Suzanne's bedroom. He opened the closet and took out the old cowboy boot in the corner. Michael shoved his hand inside and felt the gun, exactly where he had left it before.

## 16

Jimmy Butler sat down in the chair farthest away from the man sleeping on the couch. It was Saturday morning, one week before the big party his mother talked about. It was very quiet. The door to Miss Suzanne's room was closed, but Jimmy could see light underneath the crack between the door and the floor. He wanted to lie down on the floor and peek his eye to see what he could see. He was afraid the door would open while he was lying on the floor with his top eye closed. He imagined Miss Suzanne stepping on his face with those high-heel shoes.

Jimmy Butler would be directly in the line of sight of Mr. Brace if he were to open his eyes. This fact made Jimmy squirm in his chair with anticipation. It was so quiet. He wanted Mr. Brace to get up before Miss Suzanne. It was always easier that way. When it happened the other way around, sometimes it ruined everything.

Suzanne sat in her bedroom looking into the mirror. She looked closely at the lines in her face. Where had they come from? Had they always been there? Had she just overlooked the lines before? Each line was like a road she had traveled. They started no place and ended alone. She put her hands on the side of her face and pulled the skin tight to make the lines go away. She thought it was a sad compromise. The lines were all gone, but her face was ugly and distorted.

Jimmy Butler grew tired of sitting in the chair. He walked down the long hall to the kitchen where his mother was cooking a pot of gumbo. He sat on his favorite stool and smelled the smell of his mother's gumbo. Jimmy heard the bedroom door open. Suzanne Brace walked past the hall and out the front door. She stepped with purpose. Jimmy leaned up on his tiptoes to see out the kitchen window above the sink. He saw Suzanne Brace climb into the car, back out the driveway, and drive toward town. The coast was clear. The boy ran down the hallway, his tennis shoes slapping on the floor. He stopped at the edge of the wall and peeked around the corner. Michael Brace had one eye open and one eye closed.

"Ladies and gentlemen," Michael announced, "from the University of Alabama—starting in the Super Bowl at running back—James Butler."

Suzanne pulled into the church parking lot. It was Saturday, but today was the last day to sign up for the church trip to Atlanta, which was scheduled for February 17th. She closed her eyes for a second when she thought about the ride to Atlanta on the bus.

"Hello, Suzanne!" Mrs. Welch yelled.

"Hello, Mrs. Welch," Suzanne answered with a smile.

The short, fat lady sat behind a desk. She had a clipboard that held the list of people who would be going to Atlanta. Suzanne wrote her name on line number twenty-seven and pulled out her checkbook. The entire time Mrs. Welch spoke happily without interruption.

"Will Michael be joining us on the trip? I do wish he would come with you. I always thought you two made the nicest little couple. I saw Michael last week at the grocery store. He looks like he's gained a little weight. I like it. You can't trust a man who's too skinny. Have you ever been to Atlanta? Reverend Edwards has each day planned. My pantyhose are making me crazy."

Suzanne nodded her head at the right times and wrote a check to the church for the cost of the trip. She carefully wrote at the bottom, "church trip—Feb. 17th—can't wait." Mrs. Welch took the check and placed it in the envelope with the others.

## 17

On Monday morning Suzanne found Michael asleep on the couch. His breathing was deep with the alcohol he had poured into his body the night before. Suzanne sat down on the chair next to the couch. The room was very quiet. It was a cloudy, cold day that offered little motivation for the lazy. She held the manuscript of Michael's novel in her lap. Suzanne looked long at Michael's face and listened to his deep, slow breathing. How could a man so quiet be responsible? Who did he think he was to write the words he had written?

Even though she had only shared bits and pieces with Michael through the years, she wished she had kept it all locked away inside. He couldn't change any of it anyway, and now she felt violated by this man asleep in her home. This man who had stolen her words.

Suzanne slid the manuscript gently back under the couch as she did each time, always careful to place it exactly the same way. Michael's wallet lay on the floor next to his shoes. She took out all the cash, forty-three dollars, and shoved the bills to the bottom of her pocket.

Suzanne moved across and sat on the edge of the couch. She was careful to sit slowly. Her fingers reached out and touched the hair of this man who once had seemed to be the white knight who could carry her away from all the bad things. He looked like a little boy. A scared, lonely, crazy little boy given a grown man's job with no way to recognize the futility. He looked like her father. Suzanne leaned her face down and kissed Michael's cheek with the tenderness of a child. She closed her eyes and bit down hard on the skin of his face.

Michael screamed like an animal.

"Jesus Christ, Suzanne! Jesus Christ!"

He bolted from the couch with his hand on his face. There was no blood, but the teeth marks could be seen clearly by Suzanne from across the room.

"Are you insane? Jesus Christ, you bit me. You bit a hole in my fuckin' face."

Suzanne sat without expression. She did not smile. For a moment Michael actually thought he was having a dream, one of those real dreams. The kind we can't be sure about until reality sets and hardens like cement.

Suzanne said, "I need you to do me a favor."

"A favor?" Michael yelled. "You just woke me up by biting my face."

Without expression or emphasis on any particular words, Suzanne said, "It's not even bleeding. I need you to go up to the hardware store. The anniversary party is only five days away and we still have lots of work to do in the yard. We need a shovel. The handle is broken on the old shovel."

Michael listened very carefully to what she said. He still wasn't completely awake. Somehow it didn't seem real.

"A shovel?"

"Yes, a shovel."

"What time is it?" Michael asked.

"It's 8:30."

Michael sat down with his hand still holding his cheek. The teeth marks were blue and clear. With his other hand he reached for his wallet. The night before seemed disjointed. Michael was not surprised to find his wallet empty.

"I don't have any money," he said.

Suzanne hesitated as if she was thinking.

"Write a check," she said.

In her mind she actually pictured the check being signed by Michael, handed to Mr. Borden, sent to the bank with the regular deposits, and becoming a permanent business record. Michael could only think about that certain day in the next few months when the money would finally run out. It weighed on his mind. The checkbook was a daily reminder. He put on his shoes, brushed his teeth, and started to the car.

On the way out the door Suzanne said, "And I need some rags, please."

During the drive to the hardware store Michael thought about rags. What color? What size? What are they for? How many?

He parked his car in front of the old local hardware store in downtown Fairhope and went inside.

"Good morning, Mr. Borden."

"Good morning, Mr. Brace. What can I help you with this morning?"

"I need a shovel and some rags," Michael said.

"What kind of shovel?" Mr. Borden asked with interest.

"The kind that digs," Michael said. Neither man laughed. They were only a few feet away from each other.

"Looks like somebody bit you on the cheek, Mike." Mr. Borden squinted through his glasses. Michael put his hand up to his face. He had almost forgotten.

"So what?" was all he thought to say.

Mr. Borden handed Michael Brace a shovel and a bag of yellow rags. They walked together to the cash register up front. No one else was in the store.

Michael wrote a check. Mr. Borden looked at Michael's cheek again, and Michael could feel the stare. The receipt was put in a small bag with the rags, and Michael carried the shovel out to the car. He sat behind the wheel and looked at his face in the rearview mirror. The individual teeth marks could be seen in the circle of indentions. Past the mirror, in the hardware store, Michael saw Mr. Borden standing at his cash register watching through the window.

## 18

Suzanne sat in her usual chair in the office of Dr. Riis. She looked around the room at the certificates and diplomas on the wall. What were they good for? Dr. Riis must not have been listening in class. She must not have paid attention in those fancy seminars in New York City and Miami. She couldn't tell the real tears from the unreal. There had not been a single occasion during all these sessions that Suzanne felt the woman break through the outer layer into the abyss. Maybe there was something Suzanne had missed. She doubted herself for a moment, and then Dr. Riis stepped into the room.

"Good morning."

"Good morning."

Suzanne could smell the smoke on the clothes and hair of Betty Riis.

"Well, tell me how things have been at home, Suzanne."

Dr. Riis got comfortable in her chair and turned to look Suzanne Brace in the eye. There were times in her relationship with Suzanne when she would get a certain feeling. The feeling was hard to describe. Something just wasn't quite right, and Dr. Riis simply was not equipped to take apart the pieces of this strange feeling and rip the roots from the black soil.

"Betty, I don't want to sound too dramatic." She stared out the window over Dr. Riis' shoulder. Tears pooled in the bottoms of her brown eyes.

"Something bad is gonna happen. I can feel it. We had a fight yesterday.

A bad one. Michael was drunk. He came into my room while I was asleep."

Suzanne's words caught up in her throat. She stopped and held her fingers against her closed eyes. The pressure squeezed tears down her face. Dr. Riis handed her a Kleenex.

"What happened, Suzanne?" She was genuinely concerned.

"He came into my room when I was asleep. He climbed on top of me, pulled off my panties. At first I didn't know what was happening. His whole weight was on top of me. His face was pushed up against my face. I bit him. I bit him on the face as hard as I could bite."

"Good, Suzanne," Dr. Riis whispered. She leaned forward in her chair and touched Suzanne's arm.

"If something happens to me Betty, I have a sister named Elizabeth. She lives in Pensacola. We haven't seen each other since we were kids. Would you tell her about me?"

"Suzanne, don't talk like that. You've got to make the decision to get out of there. You've got to decide to get away from him now."

"I can't."

"Yes, you can."

The women were silent for minutes. Betty had seen it so many times, the circle of abuse and control. Many women just can't imagine a life without the abuse, without the control. Their helplessness is pounded into their heads over and over and over again until they completely believe they are helpless, even deserving of the violence. Betty knew that breaking the cycle is difficult. The more dependent the victim becomes upon the abuser, financially, socially, emotionally, and otherwise, the more impossible it seems to the victim to have a life apart. It's like imagining living on another planet, far away, with different air.

Betty felt her own brand of helplessness in her inability to free Suzanne. She often wondered if maybe Suzanne had suffered abuse as a child, but she just couldn't crack the woman's strong, hard shell of survival. Betty had to remind herself constantly that she was only the therapist and couldn't live Suzanne's life for her. Suzanne would have to decide to free herself or the freedom would never be real.

Suzanne sat up straight and patted her cheeks. She looked Betty Riis in the eyes.

"We're having our fifteenth wedding anniversary party at the house on Saturday, February 3. Please be there. We've got champagne, and balloons, everything. Please tell me you'll be there."

Betty smiled at the strange enthusiasm. She had received her invitation in the mail weeks earlier.

"I'll be there, Suzanne. I'll be there."

When the session ended, Suzanne glanced up and down the street. It was a beautiful cool blue day. People were walking with their children, or shopping, eating lunch with their husbands and wives. Suzanne drove home to an empty house. She made sure Michael wasn't home before she walked to the mailbox.

The envelope she had been waiting for was wedged between the phone bill and a shoe catalog. Suzanne walked back inside and locked the door behind her. She held the envelope carefully by the edges and opened the end with a kitchen knife. She pulled out Michael's bank statement with a pair of tweezers and was careful not to touch any part. The savings account was down to $1,100. She knew there was nothing left when this was gone.

Suzanne placed the bank statement back into the envelope addressed to Michael L. Brace. With the tweezers holding one corner she put the envelope inside the pages of the big dictionary along with the receipt from Dr. Andrews, the receipt from the hardware store, and the first draft of the letter to Phillip.

There were only a few days left until the anniversary party. Suzanne unlocked the door, sat on the porch, and went through her checklist for the party:

*invitations sent*
*yard ready*
*wine*
*dress*
*balloons*
*hors d'oeuvres*
*champagne*
*trash bags*
*ice*
*plates*

*glasses*
*caterer*
*napkins*
*music*
*cake*
*photo album out*
*peanuts*
*bourbon*
*bartender*
*paper towels*
*Michael*

On Friday night, the night before the party, Suzanne walked back and forth through the house going over each detail in her mind like a teenage girl. She didn't notice the red pickup truck drive past the house.

Since the night at the bar, Laura Simmons hadn't been able to stop thinking about Michael Brace. She had seen something in his face she couldn't describe, and she couldn't forget. He needed something. She had driven around town alone in no hurry. Eventually, Laura knew her truck would pass slowly by Michael's house like it had so many times before. She looked for cars in the driveway as she went past, not driving too fast or too slow. The living room lights were on, and Laura saw Michael's wife walk by the window. She was surprised to feel no hatred or jealousy at the sight of the woman.

Mr. Forester sat in his wheelchair in the dark at the window across the street. From the second floor he saw the truck below pass the house and stop at the stop sign at the corner. His legs were useless, but Ed Forester had twenty-twenty eyesight and could hear a whisper from two rooms away. He knew his body had compensated somehow for the loss of his legs by actually improving his eyes and ears. He was a man who chose to limit his world to a view from the window of his bedroom. It was not a compromise.

*

Phillip was home alone. He hadn't talked to Michael since the night he disappeared in the rain. Phillip was a solver of problems, other people's problems, but he couldn't get his mind around Michael and Suzanne. He had a hard time believing what his sister-in-law said to him, but Michael's reaction at the bar and the possible involvement of Laura Simmons left Phillip unable to isolate or dissect the situation. The anniversary party added to the confusion. There was no way for Phillip to know his life was on the verge of change. Change beyond his control. Something new to Phillip Brace, the king of the baseball field.

Betty Riis was anxious about attending Suzanne's party. She tried to keep a safe distance between herself and the people who came to her office. They shared secrets and fears with her, but when they walked out her door, Betty simply switched to the next set of secrets and fears, the next face in the chair. But she felt herself being pulled by Suzanne Brace. Pulled in a direction uncertain.

By 11:30 P.M. the Brace house was completely dark. Michael could only hear the low hum of the living room ceiling fan. It was February, and cool outside, but he couldn't sleep without a ceiling fan. It was the night before his fifteenth-wedding-anniversary party, and he was alone on the couch looking up in the darkness. He listened for a sound from Suzanne's bedroom, any sound.

Michael had resigned himself weeks ago to the fact that he was simply unable to figure out this anniversary party. He worked in the yard, he ran errands, he put stamps on invitations. He went down with Mark Simpson and Hardy to the store and brought home champagne, and wine, and bottles of liquor. He washed windows, and washed cars, and washed dishes. And while Michael did all these things, he couldn't stop thinking about how unbearably miserable he was.

Thoughts ran through his mind. Maybe Suzanne was really trying hard to make things better. But why had she bitten him? Michael touched the side of his face in the darkness. He could still feel a sensation of pain at the touch. The mark was almost completely gone. Maybe there was something wrong with Suzanne beyond anything he had imagined. But maybe, just maybe, the anniversary party would be a new start. A beginning.

The lights from a vehicle shined in the living room from the outside street. Michael didn't know they were the headlights of the red pickup truck. Laura Simmons drove back past the house one more time. She saw the lights were out and both cars were still in the driveway. The yard was perfect, and the streetlight revealed a recently power-washed house, neatly trimmed hedges, and a few new plants and flowers. Laura took a long last look. She drove down the bay on her way home, passing Jerry sitting next to the fountain. The clear water flowed to a lighted holding pool and sparkled in the lights. Jerry looked down at the pennies people had tossed into the water along with their hidden wishes. Wishes of all shapes and colors, some destined to come true, and some not worth the corroded penny at the bottom of the water.

Michael followed the lights across the white walls. He hadn't spoken to Phillip since he came so close to hitting him in the old bar. They would see each other the next night, he knew, and he wondered why his brother had said what he said. Michael had never laid a hand on his wife. He had always swallowed the anger and melted away into himself. It had always been that way for as long as he could remember. With Suzanne, with Phillip, with his father, with writing and working, and even with living.

The hum of the fan eased the pain. Michael's eyes closed slowly and he felt the warmth of sleep pulling his mind gently away. The world dissolved into a dream and Michael saw himself standing in a field of yellow sunflowers with Laura Simmons. He was holding her hand.

# PART II

*Two Days in February*

1

Jimmy Butler and his mother arrived at the Brace house early on the morning of February 3. Aside from this early arrival, it was just another Saturday for Jimmy. They entered the back door, and Sophie Butler was quick to remind her boy to be quiet until Mr. and Mrs. Brace were awake.

Jimmy watched his mother in the kitchen for as long as he could. He listened for any sound from the other parts of the house.

"Momma, can I go out to the porch to look at the water?"

Sophie cut her eyes at the poor excuse. She made sure her son understood she knew he really wanted to go see if Mr. Brace was awake.

"Be very, very quiet."

Jimmy started down the long hall. Each hand reached out to touch the walls. His little brown fingers slid gently against the clean white paint on both sides. Between every step Jimmy would listen for a sound. He always had to pass the door of Miss Suzanne's bedroom on the way to the living room.

The door on the right to Miss Suzanne's room was open just a crack. Jimmy leaned his head toward the wall at his left hand. The light was on inside. Jimmy took one more step with his eyes held to every detail through the crack. He saw Suzanne Brace at the door of the open closet. Her hair was in a ponytail.

Jimmy knew what his mother would say. She would say, "Go boy. Go past the door. Don't stare inside. Go to the porch and look out at the bay."

Jimmy stood still, frozen with curiosity. Suzanne Brace bent over and picked up a cowboy boot. She turned slightly sideways and Jimmy could see the edge of her face. He watched her reach her hand into the boot. He watched her pull out a little silver pistol. It looked like a toy.

Jimmy leaned a bit more to his left so he could see the handle of the little silver pistol. The hardwood floor under his feet made a tiny creak. Suzanne turned slowly toward the sound and looked Jimmy Butler straight in his eyes. Without hesitation her hands gently placed the gun back in the boot while her eyes remained fixed on the little boy in the hall. Jimmy backed away out of sight and ran to the kitchen.

Suzanne dropped the boot back in the closet. She put her hand up to her eyes and tried to rub the pain away. It was the wrong day for a headache. She had to focus on the preparations. Every detail needed the proper attention. There were forty-seven people due to arrive in less than twelve hours. Jimmy Butler was eight years old, and he hadn't seen anything that couldn't be explained.

Suzanne's head hurt from the base of her skull to a point directly behind her eye. The pain was slow, simple, and constant. She knew if she made sudden moves the pain would pound with her heartbeat and then go slowly back to the simple and constant ache she was accustomed to.

The first thing Michael saw when he opened his eyes was a handwritten list hanging over the corner of the coffee table next to the couch under his wallet. He felt his knee beneath the sheet, stiff and dull. For a moment he forgot it wasn't just another Saturday. For a moment he forgot it was his wedding anniversary.

Suzanne reached under her bed and pulled out the small locked metal box. She spun the numbers under her finger until they showed 239. The money in the box was neatly stacked. Suzanne had saved every penny she could over these months knowing she couldn't count on Michael to help pay for the party. She put the bills on the marble-top bedside table and closed the metal box. She purposely didn't scramble the numbers.

Throughout the day Suzanne and Sophie Butler cleaned and vacuumed, dusted, sprayed, sorted, and washed. They set up the bar, perfectly positioned the stereo speakers, and put dishes of mixed nuts in exact locations.

Suzanne marked off the parts of her list one by one. She tried to focus around the pounding in her head. She narrowed the pain into certain locations and prayed the way only people in pain can pray.

When Michael left the house with his list, Suzanne handed him a stack of five- and one-dollar bills. No words were exchanged. Michael wondered where the money came from. He hoped she hadn't taken it out of the account. The electric bill was overdue.

After Michael picked up things and dropped things off, he wanted a drink. He was glad Simpson and Hardy and some of the other guys would be at the party. His mind searched for places to hide. Suddenly seven o'clock was only three hours away.

Suzanne sat down at the mirror to put on her makeup. Sophie Butler and her son left through the same back door they had entered hours earlier. They would be back by 6:45 to serve food and then clean up after the rich people.

Michael and Suzanne were left alone in a house that had been buzzing with sounds and people since morning and would once again be buzzing with sounds and people in just a few hours. Michael was tense, waiting for the time to pass. He stalled. Michael didn't want to get dressed too early. He'd learned as a teenager being dressed too early for a formal occasion leads to sitting around sweating and worrying about dust balls and wrinkles and other specks of insignificance.

Suzanne sat alone at the mirror with her medicine. Through the day she'd tried every trick that had ever worked to slow the pain in her skull. She stood in the shower with cold water pulsing against the top of her head. She sat alone in the dark for thirty minutes and concentrated on breathing deep into her lungs. She took medicine, drank black coffee, and ate sesame seed bread. Finally, she began to feel the numbness that usually led to the end of the pain.

2

At 6:40 Suzanne walked out of her room. She wore a long black dress with a gold necklace and high-heel shoes. Michael sat with his back against the wall in his suit and tie. For a moment Suzanne didn't see him as she stopped to look at herself in the mirror behind the door. She was gorgeous. Suzanne's body held a presence all its own for Michael. And in the quiet of the moment he felt his breath go shallow.

Suzanne turned her head to look directly at Michael against the far wall. They looked at each other for too long, like two strangers across a crowded restaurant who both think they've known the other before, but can't place the face.

"Are you ready?" Suzanne whispered.

Michael wanted to say, "Ready for what?" Instead he whispered back, "Yes."

The back door opened and they both knew Sophie and Jimmy Butler were in the house again, but neither turned away from the stare until Suzanne smiled.

Phillip knocked on the door. He was early. Phillip never paid attention to those rules about arriving fashionably late. Suzanne opened the front door and gave him a kiss on the cheek. There was no reason to linger. There was nobody to see.

"Wow! Look at this place. All fancy, with balloons, and decorations. Did you do all this yourself, Michael?"

"Of course he did," Suzanne laughed as she headed down the hallway to the kitchen.

When Michael saw her leave he reached down to pick up the glass of bourbon behind the leg of the chair. He took a long sip and let the ice touch against his teeth. Both men were very aware of the last words that passed between them weeks earlier at the bar.

Phillip said, "I hope that's your first drink, big boy, or it's gonna be a long night."

Michael didn't answer. He took another sip and put the glass down where it was before.

There was another knock. Phillip opened the door to see his parents.

"Mom, you look splendid," Phillip said as he hugged his mother and shook hands with his father at the same time.

Michael stood back and watched his parents. They were perfectly dressed. Phillip and his father were both tall. Michael looked more like his mother. Ellen Brace immediately turned toward the kitchen and left the men alone in the room together. The bartender, a slightly built older black man, came from the kitchen and took his position behind the bar. Michael had seen him at other people's parties before, but he couldn't remember his name.

"Congratulations, Michael," Mr. Brace said. "Fifteen years is a long time in this day and age."

The three men sat in the room with peanut dishes and jazz music. They sat in their suits, among balloons, and clean curtains, and white napkins. Each of the men, individually, hoped for a knock at the door. When it came, the sound was sharp and loud. Sophie hurried from the kitchen to greet the party guests. The door swung open and a large couple entered Michael's home. He had never seen them before.

"Hey, Mike," the big man said.

"Hey," Michael answered. He found nothing recognizable in the man's face.

And then there was another knock. Michael retreated to the porch. More well-dressed people arrived until the house slowly filled with voices. Bits and pieces of conversations shot around the room as one group would laugh and then become two groups, and three.

Betty Riis roamed around the house scouting out the rear door. She looked forward to the opportunity to step outside and smoke a cigarette. On her way through the house she took efforts to learn things about Suzanne and Michael she could never learn through her sessions with Suzanne. She watched Michael across the room talking with his friends and asking the bartender for another drink. Michael watched Betty Riis watch him and imagined the two ladies sitting alone the next day sorting out his behavior.

Mrs. Forester had a lovely time. She didn't go out often because she hated leaving her husband behind. Mr. Forester would never allow himself to be wheeled around through all these people. He sat in his window across the street and watched the cars pull up. Several times he could see his wife at the front window waving to him. He made an effort to think through his loneliness and just be happy she was having a good time.

Michael and Simpson and Hardy stood by the bar. As the evening progressed, their collars and ties loosened as they pulled and stretched like little boys in church.

"Who the hell are all these people?" Simpson asked to no one in particular.

"I'm not sure," Michael answered.

Hardy said, "I don't want to know most of them, but I wouldn't mind knowing that blonde in the red dress. Watch her eat that cracker. Look. Look."

Each of the men turned to see. They watched the blonde in the red dress take a Ritz cracker and put the correct amount of blue cheese on top. They watched her lift the cracker to her red lips and push it inside.

Two old ladies broke Michael's focus. The fat one said, "Congratulations, Mike. How on Earth did you keep a wonderful woman like Suzanne for fifteen years?" She giggled and Michael remembered she taught Sunday school at the church. Her name was Edna Townsend.

From out of nowhere Suzanne appeared. Her eyes were red. She was crying.

"Please, Michael. Please don't drink so much," she said.

Edna Townsend was embarrassed. Her friend turned away. Michael stood transfixed with a glass of bourbon in his hand. There was no time to prepare. No time to adjust to the attack.

Suzanne said, "Not tonight, Michael. Please don't ruin this for me."

Michael said, "What? I haven't done anything wrong." He was angry before he could think. His voice was louder than hers. A man behind Suzanne turned around. Mark Simpson instinctively put his drink behind his back, and Hardy looked like the kid on the playground who turns to see the teacher.

Everyone was uncomfortable except Suzanne. She closed her eyes, took an obvious deep breath, and went away toward the kitchen. Edna Townsend followed.

"What the shit?" Michael said, "I haven't even done anything, yet."

"Man, you better go see about her," Hardy whispered. "She's pissed off."

Rake walked up with a handful of candy-covered almonds and a little plate of food. Simpson stole a meatball from the edge of his plate with his fingers.

"Hey!" Rake said.

As he chewed the meatball, Simpson said, "Rake, have you told Asshole about your little hobby you had when you were a kid? Tell him."

Rake shook his head. Hardy laughed and a little bit of gin and tonic shot through his nose. Suzanne's tirade had no noticeable effect on Simpson or Hardy or Rake.

Rake said, "No. Michael doesn't want to hear about that. This is his anniversary party."

"If you don't tell it, Rake, I'm gonna tell it for you."

Michael was face to face with Rake. He had missed most of the conversation, but there had been so many conversations like this before that it didn't matter. He just wanted to think about something else besides his wife's stupid comments.

"Tell me the story, Rake," Michael said.

Rake began, "It's not really a story, really."

"It's not the story about Annie Tillman again is it?" Michael asked.

"Oh, no!" Hardy said, "But it's equally deranged. Our little friend Rake has big problems."

"What kind of problems?" Michael asked.

"OK, OK, I'll tell it. It's not such a big deal." Rake swallowed the last cracker and put the clear plastic plate on top of the TV. He wiped his hands on his pant leg.

"When I was a kid, I used to keep a journal. Every day I'd write down the time and place I peed. I kept it every day from the seventh grade until I was out of high school. I never missed one pee. Not one."

Michael wrinkled up his face. He tried not to laugh.

"Why, Rake, why? Why would you keep a journal about pissing?" Michael asked.

Rake licked something off his finger. "Well, where's the weirdest place you ever peed? Do you know? I bet you don't even know."

Hardy held his belly with his hand. He laughed so hard he had to hold himself. Simpson just liked to watch Rake's expressions while he defended his hobby.

"Yes, I do know," Michael said.

"Where?"

Michael said, "When I was eight years old, I peed on the devil, Rake." Slowly he said again, "I peed on the devil."

Rake squinted and turned his head slightly to the side. Hardy's face was red from laughter. He had to wipe his eyes under his glasses to keep a tear from rolling down his cheek. He felt a pain from the scar on his hip.

Rake finally asked, "The devil?"

Michael laughed out loud. It felt good to laugh. For a moment it was like they were alone watching a weekend football game with no one else around. But there were lots of other people around. Ladies from the church, Suzanne's psychiatrist, people he didn't know, and Phillip.

Phillip looked at Suzanne's arms for bruises. Her dress was sleeveless, and he could see no bruises anywhere. He didn't realize it seemed to other people like he was staring too long at his sister-in-law. He didn't realize until Suzanne turned from across the room and looked him dead in the eye. She walked past Mrs. Forester at the window and went directly to Phillip. Suzanne smiled the entire way. She put her hand on Phillip's arm and whispered into his ear.

Phillip noticed Mrs. Forester turn and watch them. He saw Edna Townsend looking from across the room.

Suzanne whispered, "Don't you want to put your hand under my dress?"

And she walked away.

It felt like to Phillip every one in the room heard. It seemed for a moment her whisper was on a loudspeaker. She left Phillip transfixed. He hoped she was just drunk. It would be the easiest explanation. The other possibilities were far more complicated.

Throughout the night, no matter where Phillip drifted in the house, he would find himself catching the eye of Suzanne, or bumping into her, or being led into conversations.

On one occasion Phillip went into the kitchen alone. Sophie Butler was making her rounds through the living room and Jimmy was watching TV in the spare bedroom. Suzanne saw Phillip go down the long hallway. She would not miss the opportunity. Sophie Butler would only be out of the kitchen a few minutes at the most.

Suzanne snuck up behind Phillip at the kitchen sink.

"Boo!"

Phillip jumped, "Damn, Suzanne! What are you doing?"

"What are you doing?" she asked playfully. Suzanne's ears were pinned to the sound of footsteps coming down the hall. One step, two steps, three steps and the moment was perfect.

Suzanne said, "Kiss me, Phillip. Michael is too drunk to know."

Sophie Butler stepped around the corner of the hallway to see Suzanne Brace pushed up against Phillip Brace with her mouth to his mouth. She had heard the words. She had seen the act. Sophie Butler turned her face away, but the fire of sin had entered her eyes and ears and she would see it and hear it for the rest of her life.

"Suzanne!" Phillip said as he turned his mouth away and pushed Suzanne from his body.

He saw Sophie. He saw the look on her face.

"What the hell is the matter with you?" he asked.

Sophie Butler hurried back down the hall to the living room. Without pause, Suzanne turned and followed Sophie out to her waiting guests. She left Phillip in the kitchen wiping lipstick off his lips.

## 3

Phillip went home. Rake and Simpson left. Mrs. Forester walked across the street to her husband, and Betty Riis went home to her four cats. Sophie Butler stood at the kitchen sink handing glasses to Suzanne. Suzanne placed the glasses neatly in the dishwasher. The women had removed their rings and stood side by side washing dishes. Suzanne's shoes were off, and the cool tile of the kitchen floor felt good on her bare feet. Neither woman spoke.

Michael Brace sat alone in his favorite chair on the porch looking out the window across the dark bay waters. It was like sitting in an empty gymnasium after a basketball game. The stillness was a pleasant gift.

At 12:55 A.M. the house was as clean as it needed to be. Sophie Butler softly woke her boy and held his hand as they slipped out the back door to the car. Without a clear, conscious thought, Sophie Butler hoped the sin from the house hadn't gotten inside her child like a nasty little virus. She decided she would never go back again to the house of Michael and Suzanne Brace. She would just have to do without the extra money, she thought to herself.

Suzanne checked the clock. She looked out the kitchen window at the Foresters' dark house. She walked quietly down the hallway to the living room. On the porch she could see the back of Michael's head in the chair. She leaned over and switched off the last lamp in the room. The only light in the house now came from the moon and the streetlight at the corner.

Suzanne Brace felt spectacular. She eased up behind Michael and placed her warm hand on his shoulder. He didn't move. The bourbon dulled his reaction to the point where he actually had time to decide not to react. He imagined himself floating on the waters of the bay. Suzanne leaned down and placed her face against the side of his face. Michael closed his eyes.

The song on the stereo was Van Morrison's "Moondance." It was gentle, and easy, and made Michael forget and remember all at the same time. He let himself smell her hair and felt it on his skin. He let himself believe.

Suzanne took Michael by the hand and eased him up from the chair. Michael's jacket was off, and his tie was on the floor. They stood face to face, in the dark, alone. Suzanne put her arms around the back of Michael's neck and pulled his head down to her shoulder. She leaned her body against his body, and they slowly began to dance. Their eyes were closed and they moved only with each other.

Suzanne kissed her husband. She kissed him slowly, and elegantly. And then she kissed him with passion. As they stood, she could feel him against her waist. For a wicked little moment she knew it was the right thing to do. Suzanne took her husband by the hand and led him to her bedroom.

Michael was afraid to say a word or move. It seemed any little thing could make it end in a horrible way. He sat on the edge of the bed and watched his wife take off her clothes. He realized how long it had been, and how he had taken her body for granted when it was his to enjoy. The black dress dropped to the floor. Suzanne reached around to remove her bra. It was dark, but Michael used every tiny piece of light from the window to see her breasts. He could see the black panties against her skin slide to the floor. Michael refused to lift his hands.

Suzanne unbuttoned each button of Michael's shirt. She pulled it away. Michael's face was against her skin. He closed his eyes and wished to taste her. It was like the smoke of opium floating all around his mind. It was more than just skin, and breasts, and soft smells. His pants were off, and she was under him. They hardly moved at all.

Suzanne Brace bent her neck back. She felt the fullness. There was brutality in the refusal to break the silence or give in to the temptation of motion. They barely moved, but each movement was together. The tenderness was exact. The purity was precise. They kissed, and kissed again, and the movements became like one person, alone and perfect, waves and touches, quiet and captured, lifting and falling into each other.

Suzanne clenched her teeth. Michael buried his face in Suzanne's neck and prayed. He prayed the world would end, and he would be captured for eternity in the arms of Suzanne Brace. And then she felt the completeness. She felt the force, and the grasp, and the ease of the tension of the muscles, and they held on, in the dark, in silence, until Michael began to breathe deep, and Suzanne let him fall asleep at her side. She glanced at the clock. It was 1:42 A.M. There was much to do.

4

S uzanne removed herself from the bed. She quickly put on her panties and took the robe from the closet. It was quiet, and Michael was sleeping soundly. Suzanne knew he wouldn't wake up. She clicked on the lamp on the desk and sat down. The fat red dictionary was hidden in the back of the bottom left drawer.

Suzanne opened the dictionary to the papers and envelope inside. She first removed the letter she had written to Phillip months before. In the last week she'd taken the time to read the letter over and over so she wouldn't have to read it again on this night. Suzanne rewrote the letter on a piece of stationery. She tried to write at a natural speed, not too careful or too exact.

*Dear Phillip,*

*Seeing you tonight was like touching the sun. I think of you every minute of every day. Just the few moments we can spend together are the reason I can get out of bed in the morning. A phone call, lunch, the afternoons in your car down by the old ferry landing.*

*Sometimes Michael will look at me like he knows. I am afraid what might happen if he does. I'm not sure I can make it through our anniversary party tomorrow with you across the room. When you tell me you love me, it makes me feel like everything will be OK.*

*I will love you forever.*
*Suzanne*


Suzanne folded the letter and placed it neatly in the matching envelope. She wrote "Phillip" on the outside, sealed the envelope, and placed it gently between the mattress and the box spring on the side of the bed closest to the desk. Michael slept on the far side of the bed next to the nightstand. He felt nothing.

Next Suzanne removed from the dictionary the bill from Dr. Andrews. She opened the top right drawer of the desk and placed the old bill between the electric bill and her credit card statements. She wrapped a rubber band around the small bundle and placed the bundle back in the drawer.

Besides the hardware store receipt for the shovel and rags, the last document in the dictionary was the envelope containing the bank statement of Michael's account. Suzanne was careful to pick up the envelope with the edge of her bathrobe. She never let her fingers or skin touch the paper. She walked softly around the bed to the other side where Michael slept. Michael's left hand rested on the outside of the covers. Suzanne inserted the envelope between his fingers. From experience she knew Michael was a deep sleeper, and she relied on the bourbon to take away any risk. Suzanne pushed Michael's fingers and palm against the envelope. She was sure to get his index finger pressed against the little cellophane address window.

Suzanne picked the envelope up again with the edge of her bathrobe. She held the open end of the envelope down and shook gently until the statement inside stuck halfway out. Suzanne slipped the end of the statement between Michael's fingers and again pressed them against the paper. She turned the envelope upward, shook the statement back inside, and walked into the living room. Suzanne bent down and pushed the envelope underneath the couch next to the manuscript of Michael's novel.

Suzanne went back to the desk. She picked up the old first draft of the letter to Phillip and took it to the bathroom at the far end of the house. She turned on the light, tore the letter into tiny pieces, and flushed them down the toilet. She flushed again to make sure every piece was gone away forever.

Suzanne returned to the bedroom. The clock showed 3:05 A.M. She was in no hurry. The list was in her mind.

Suzanne stood next to the bed. She reached up with her left hand and took hold of a clump of hair on the back of her head. She purposefully did not jerk. She pulled hard in a fluid movement to be sure the roots came out clean. Suzanne's eyes watered, but she made no sound. She dropped the hair on the bed between Michael's head and the other pillow.

Suzanne sat back down at the desk. Her mind raced. She opened the bottom left drawer again and put the dictionary back where it belonged. She removed the yellow rags Michael bought at the hardware store. She took the silver razorblade from the top drawer where she'd hidden it the day before. Suzanne lifted her foot up to chest level. She rested her heel against the desk and with the sharp blade she slowly made a cut between her second and third toe. The pain was almost friendly. The cut was deep enough to deliver the right amount of blood but from a wound that would close fairly quickly. Suzanne dabbed the yellow rags on the drops of blood and held the last rag firmly against the cut until the bleeding stopped.

Jerry noticed the light still on in the house of Michael and Suzanne Brace. He noticed lights on inside houses like he noticed the light in the bedroom of the Foresters'. He had no idea what time it was when he saw a figure move slowly from the front door of the Brace house. From across the street on his bench he saw a woman carrying something to the car in the driveway. He couldn't hear the key in the trunk, or the snap of the lock as it opened, but when the little light came on he could clearly see Suzanne Brace quietly place a shovel in the trunk of Michael Brace's car. He could see her throw a yellow rag on top of the shovel. Then she turned, took something from her hand, and tossed it in the bushes. Jerry watched her shut the trunk without a sound.

Suzanne opened the door of the car. She pulled the map of the county from the glove box and shoved it under the driver's seat. She folded up the hardware store receipt and dropped it on the floorboard. She closed the door silently and moved across the yard, back through the front door. Jerry turned around to the bay and lit another cigarette.

Suzanne went to the back bathroom. She washed her hands under the cool water in the sink. She could feel the wetness of her panties. In the mirror she caught a glimpse of her face. The years had actually made her more beautiful than she had ever been before. For some reason she thought of her father. It always went back to him. Everything always ended with Orin Manley, the same place it had begun. She couldn't make it stop.

Suzanne lifted her hands. She traced her fingers from her eyes slowly down to the edges of her mouth. Her hands moved together on each side of her face touching. It was 4:30 A.M.

Suzanne opened the kitchen window above the sink. It was cool outside, but not too cool to have a few open windows. She went to the living room. Her bare feet were light on the hardwood floors. She opened the window in the living room where hours earlier Mrs. Forester had waved to her husband across the street.

Suzanne went back to the bedroom. Michael had rolled over, and his face was now turned toward the center of the bed. Behind his head was the night table. If he opened his eyes he would see across the empty pillow to the desk and the little lamp. Suzanne opened the bedroom window six inches. She opened the closet door and removed the boot from the floor. She pulled out the little silver pistol and put the boot next to its mate. She noticed the razorblade lying on the desk top.

Suzanne had wiped the blood from the blade on the yellow rag before. She put the blade back in the sewing kit next to the desk with the thread and needles. She had removed one bullet from the box the day before, making sure not to touch it directly. She placed the bullet in the gun the way she learned from the book in the library. One bullet, no more.

Suzanne wiped the gun clean, every inch, with her bathrobe. She hung the bathrobe back in the closet and stood in the room with only her panties on. There were bruises on her rib cage. The clean gun lay on the top of the desk. With the sharp point of the scissors Suzanne punched a hole in the lace fabric of her panties. With her finger inside the hole she tore the edge of her panties on the left hip. The rip was three inches long and a thread hung loose. Suzanne placed the black umbrella against the wall outside her bedroom door. She stood silently in the room until the clock behind Michael showed 4:56 A.M. The time had come.

## 5

Suzanne purposely left the lamp on. It was the only light in the house. She left it like that for two reasons. She needed to see what she was doing.

Michael's body remained as it had before. Lying on his left side, his hands resting in front of him like a man boxing. The sheet covered his naked body below the waist. Suzanne picked up the clean gun from the desk top with a piece of tissue she had brought from the bathroom. She laid the gun gently in the bed pointing at herself six inches from Michael's right hand.

Suzanne climbed into the bed and maneuvered slowly onto her right side facing Michael. With the tissue she pushed the gun under the palm of the limp right hand of Michael Brace. She pressed his fingertips down on the metal silver surface.

Suzanne had lived this moment in her mind a thousand times. The light was always on. She was always in her black panties on the clean white sheets. Suzanne kept the tissue between her skin and the gun. She gently placed her husband's right index finger through the trigger hole of the pistol. They were face to face only two feet apart. If Michael would open his eyes he would be looking into the eyes of his wife with a gun in his hand.

With her left hand Suzanne felt the rip in her panties. She moved her left hand back to Michael's right hand, which rested on the gun. She moved her right hand underneath with the tissue wrapped around and now held

Michael's hand and the gun between her two hands. Suzanne kept the small piece of tissue between. Their skin never touched, and her skin never met the cool metal of the little pistol.

With the barrel still in her direction, Suzanne slowly lifted Michael's hand and the gun from the sheets. She placed her thumb on top of his index finger on the trigger and held his fingers tightly wrapped around the handle of the gun as they would if he held the gun awake. Without a thought, Suzanne pulled the trigger back and blew a bullet into her face and out the back of her head.

The silence exploded. Michael was literally thrown backward by his reaction to the sound and cracked his head on the marble top of the night table behind. Suzanne's face was a churn of blood and bone. Her brains were sprayed across the white wall above the desk and within seconds the pillow beneath her head filled with rich, dark blood.

When Michael reacted backward, the gun was thrown with him off the bed onto the floor next to the base of the night table. Suzanne's hands fell together. The sound of the shot echoed through the open windows. Mr. Forester's alarm clock went off at 5:00 A.M., and the light came on in his upstairs window. Jerry heard the noise as he bent down to pick up a Coke can under an azalea bush. Michael Brace lay on the floor with his hand on the back of his head feeling for the blood he was sure would come. For the moment, his own pain was his only thought. He had no idea.

Michael rolled over on the floor onto his back. He realized he was naked and for a moment couldn't remember where he was. Out of the corner of his eye, eight inches away, he noticed something. He turned his head to see a silver pistol on the floor under the table. Michael reached his hand over to touch the gun. He held it gently and wondered where it belonged.

From the floor there was no way for Michael Brace to even imagine what he would see. His head pounded as he used his arms to pull his back up against the far wall facing the bed. He sat with his knees pulled up and his hand on the back of his head. The world changed in a single second.

Michael saw Suzanne's face.

He was perfectly still. She was perfectly still. Silence was back. There was no explanation. The gun was by his side, but he didn't know why. Shock turned to panic, and Michael began to breathe quickly. He stood up too fast.

His bad knee buckled and he fell back against the wall. He saw his pants on the floor and put them on with his eyes turned away from the body in the bed. The blood made him weak.

The noise startled Paul Cooper next door. He got out of bed and looked out his front door to see if maybe it was the backfire of a car. He woke up his wife, and she told him to go back to sleep. Something about the sound made Mr. Cooper uneasy.

Michael stood in the bedroom bare-chested, breathing hard. He tried to remember the sound before the crack of his head on the marble table. He tried to remember the bedroom, and Suzanne, and the night before. Nothing he remembered made sense with the blood in the bed. He smelled his right hand and smelled the sweetness of gunpowder.

Instincts circled around fear. Michael thought of putting the body in the car before it got too light. He ran to the window in the living room and looked outside. Mr. Forester sat across the street in his wheelchair looking out. He had not heard the sound of the shot. His clock showed 5:05 A.M.

Mr. Cooper couldn't stand it anymore. At 5:06 A.M. he picked up the phone and called 911. He told the operator he heard a sound like a gunshot from the direction of the house of Michael and Suzanne Brace.

There was no way Michael could get Suzanne's body in the car without Mr. Forester seeing. Michael tried to think. There was no explanation. Reason crept in among the panic. How could he explain something he didn't understand? The image of Suzanne's face made Michael bend down and heave inside. Nothing came up.

Michael went back in the bedroom. He approached from behind Suzanne and saw the three-inch rip in her panties. He just wanted to touch her hair. He just wanted to tell her he loved her.

Michael thought of the gun. He stepped across to the other side of the bed and sat down on the edge of the mattress. He picked up the gun from the floor. Michael heard one car door slam and then another through the open windows. Michael held the gun in his hands. He heard footsteps come up the front path. He thought about the future and the blood. There was a knock on the door. Michael lifted the gun to his head and pulled the trigger. Click.

Officer Marty Draper knocked again. Michael dropped the gun from his hand and it bounced on the hardwood floor. Officer Draper heard the sound and checked the door. It was unlocked. He opened the door a crack and called inside.

"Hello! Fairhope Police. Is anyone home?"

Michael lay down on the bed where he had rested before the night was split in half by a bullet. He rolled up in a ball with his eyes closed and his heart hidden deep inside.

"Fairhope Police. Is everything all right? We're coming inside."

The officer opened the door slowly. He could smell the odor of a fired gun. Both police officers pulled their weapons from their holsters and moved into the living room. They listened for the smallest sound. There was none. Blood dripped through the mattress next to the envelope. It dripped from the bottom of the box spring to the floor below and pooled in the cracks of the hardwood floor.

Officer Draper peered around the doorframe. He saw a naked dead woman with her underwear ripped. He saw a gun on the floor and bits of bone and brain splattered across the bedroom wall. He saw blood, and hair, and a house full of evidence to explain the rage it takes to shoot a person in their face. And then he saw Michael Brace, rolled in a ball, crying, and shaking, and wishing again the world would come to an end.

## 6

Investigator Tim Tuberville got a Sunday-morning telephone call. He tried not to wake his wife while he fished around the closet for his shoes and shirt. He was fifty-two years old, and even after twenty-five years working in law enforcement he never got comfortable with the early-morning ring of the phone. His friends called him "Tubbie." Everyone else called him "Chief."

He knew the way to the house of Michael and Suzanne Brace. Tim Tuberville had known the Brace family all his life. He made up his mind early to play this one by the book. He had a respect for Phillip Brace, and he knew Phillip had an equal respect for him. They were friends. They had battled in courtrooms, but outside of court they had crossed the line into friendship. Phillip had eaten at the Tuberville home. They went to baseball games together at the high school.

When Chief Tuberville pulled up to the house, there were five police cars and one ambulance. Neighbors stood in their yards. Some wore robes and pajamas. Mrs. Forester was already dressed for yard work. She held a brown pair of gloves in her hand. The neighbors would talk about this morning for the rest of their lives.

Tim Tuberville was the chief investigator of the Baldwin County Murder Task Force. When it was formed eleven years earlier, he had been unequivocally the best choice for the job. The task force consisted of

Tuberville and three other investigators and was given jurisdiction anywhere in the county over a murder investigation. Only a man like Chief Tuberville could avoid the usual squabble between the city police and other agencies over who would take the lead in an investigation like this one.

"What we got, Ernie?"

"It's bad, Chief. Suzanne Brace in the bed, a bullet through the face, panties ripped, gun on the floor. Michael was lying in the bed next to her. He hasn't said a word. He's in the back of the car over there."

The chief listened and said, "Don't take him yet. Walk me through inside. Has anybody called his brother?"

Investigator Ernie Watson responded, "I don't think so."

"Have someone call Phillip."

Tim Tuberville walked through the front door. Several officers strung yellow police tape around the edge of the yard. Suzanne Brace's body was still in bed. Two paramedics were in the room.

The chief said, "Is the coroner on his way?"

"Yes, sir."

Investigator Earl Grimes arrived next. He carried rubber gloves and plastic evidence bags. He knew his job and immediately cleared out everyone who didn't need to be in the house.

"Ernie," the chief said.

"Yeah, Chief."

"What caliber gun?"

"Twenty-two. I checked, it's registered to Michael. He bought it several months back. There are no more bullets in the gun."

The chief looked puzzled. He said, "How many shots you think?"

"Just one," Ernie said.

"Who called 911?"

"Neighbor. Paul Cooper. He heard one shot. He says around 5:00 A.M."

The chief asked, "Who was first on the scene?"

"Draper. Fairhope officer. Says he and his partner knocked on the door, got no response, heard a noise inside, door was unlocked, drew their weapons, looked in the bedroom, and saw the woman with half a face and the man curled up in the bed crying. They had to pick him up to get him out of there. Draper says he smells like alcohol, and he's got a goose egg on the back of his head. He's also got what looks like a bite mark on the side of his face."

The chief asked, "Got any idea what caused the bump?"

"Not yet."

"Make sure they get a picture of the bite. What else you got so far?"

Earl Grimes started taking photographs. He stood next to the bed and snapped pictures.

"Looks like a wad of black hair in the bed. The bullet is stuck in the wall just above the desk. Looks like it went through her left eye socket and out the back. We've got some brain matter on the wall you can see. They had some kind of party here last night. I bet we've probably got some semen in the woman's panties. She was dead in a heartbeat. There's a black umbrella you might have seen leaning against the door. It hasn't rained in a few days."

The chief scratched the top of his head.

"You think maybe the umbrella caused the bump on the back of his head?" the chief asked.

"I don't think so," Ernie said.

"Cover that woman up after you get the pictures, Earl." The chief pointed and said, "Phillip will be here any minute. Earl, we ain't gonna get any gunshot residue off the hands from a .22 so don't worry with that, but I want a blood sample from Michael for alcohol. Get Danley on the phone. Wake his lawyer ass up and tell him we need a subpoena to get a blood sample. I don't want to piss around with this case and lose anything later."

The chief walked outside. It began to rain lightly. He wanted a word with Michael Brace before Phillip showed up. He put his hands in his pockets and headed to the police car. The back door was open and two police officers stood on each side of the car. Tim Tuberville leaned inside.

"Michael, you all right?"

Michael Brace had his eyes closed and his chin to his chest. He didn't hear anything. The chief didn't try again. He didn't need to.

"Boys, the newspaper should get here soon with their cameras. Take Michael to the hospital for the bump on his head. I want three of you with him every minute. Don't talk to him. Don't take him from the hospital until you hear from me."

Across the street Chief Tuberville saw Jerry dragging his garbage bag of tin cans. Something made him watch Jerry for an extra second. He lost his train of thought. Phillip came across the yard.

"Tubbie, what in hell is going on? Where's Michael?"

"Hold on, Phillip. They're taking him to the hospital. He's got a knot on his head."

"Is he under arrest?" Phillip tried to push past the larger man.

"Yes."

"For what?" he barked.

"Come inside, Phillip."

The two men walked together. Phillip took the moment to gather himself. He had to start thinking. He turned to see the police car with Michael pull away. Phillip wore blue jeans and a sweatshirt. His head was heavy from the bourbon the night before. He hadn't slept well.

"Did he say anything, Tubbie?"

"Not a word to anybody. I told the uniforms not to speak to him."

"I got to get someone up there with him," Phillip said out loud to himself.

Phillip pulled a cellular phone from his pocket and called one of the young associates from his office. He turned his back to Chief Tuberville and gave orders for the young lawyer to go to the hospital and sit with Michael.

The chief heard, "And don't let him say a goddamned thing to anyone."

The chief led Phillip through the front door. They walked across to the bedroom and stood at the entrance. Suzanne's body was covered, but the blood was everywhere.

"Jesus Christ," Phillip whispered.

"It's bad, Phillip. Real bad. I'm goin' by the book. There ain't no corners to cut on this. It looks like Michael shot her in the face. It's gonna be a long road."

Phillip's eyes searched the room. He saw the pattern of spots on the wall, the blood on the pillow. He saw Earl Grimes pick up the little gun gently from the floor and place it in a plastic evidence bag. He saw the hair in the bed, and the tissue.

"What time did it happen?"

"About five o'clock this morning. Neighbor heard a shot."

The two men stood side by side without speaking for minutes.

Finally Tim Tuberville said, "Phillip, I'm gonna have to ask you to leave now. We've got a crime scene to work."

Without a response, Phillip turned and walked back to his car.

## 7

At the hospital a young doctor looked at the knot on the back of Michael's head. There was a small amount of matted blood. Two uniformed officers stood in the room. One stood outside the door. The young lawyer sat nervously watching the doctor. Even on Sunday morning he wore a shirt and tie. Nothing in law school had prepared him for this situation.

District Attorney Albert Danley had received a call shortly after getting out of bed. He telephoned half his staff to let them know what was happening. A subpoena was prepared ordering blood to be drawn for an alcohol analysis before the evidence dissipated. Judge Eugene Fields drove to his office in the courthouse to sign the order. The paperwork was taken by Investigator Eric Anderson to the hospital. It was delivered to the doctor.

Phillip was at the hospital. His instincts told him to fight the judge's subpoena, but he knew the effort would be wasted. Blood would be drawn from Michael even if they had to use force. The fight against the subpoena would have to be later in the courtroom. Phillip stood next to his brother while the doctor inserted the needle into his arm. Michael didn't flinch.

At the house, Chief Tuberville walked slowly from room to room. The body had been removed and taken for autopsy. The house now belonged to the Murder Task Force.

Phillip walked with his brother from the hospital room out to the waiting police car.

"Michael. Listen to me. Don't speak to anyone except me. Don't say a word to anyone at the jail. Wait for me to get up there so we can get some privacy. Do you hear me?"

Michael walked straight ahead. He didn't acknowledge anything.

Phillip turned to the young associate and said, "Go up to the jail. Sit with him while he's booked in. Don't let him speak to anyone. Don't leave the jail until I get there. Do you understand?"

"Yes, sir. I understand."

Phillip got in the car and drove to his office. He called his parents. He was glad his father answered the phone. With very little emotion, Phillip gave his father enough details for his father to understand the seriousness of the situation. Phillip's mind had moved from anger and confusion into a very calm, lawyerly mode. The first twenty-four hours would be vital to Michael's defense, and there simply was not time for wasted emotion.

Investigator Ernie Watson knelt down next to the bed where Suzanne's body had rested. His eyes searched for anything. He pulled the rubber glove tight on his left hand and lifted the pillow. He lifted the mattress from the box spring and saw an envelope. He gently pulled the envelope from its hiding place.

"Chief. I think you need to come in here for this one."

Chief Tuberville stood in the living room. He cringed at the words of Ernie Watson. He knew the tone of voice.

"What is it, Ernie?"

Ernie Watson turned the envelope up so the chief could see the name written on the front.

The chief said one word, "Shit."

Ernie Watson opened the unsealed envelope and removed the letter. Investigator Earl Grimes stopped what he was doing to listen. When Ernie Watson had finished reading the letter addressed to Phillip, Chief Tuberville shook his head. Things had changed.

Phillip sat in the lawyer room at the jailhouse. It was small, with a heavy metal screen between the lawyer's chair and the chair for the inmate. Michael was led into the room with his orange jumpsuit and handcuffs. The brothers were alone. They sat silently. Michael stared at the floor.

"Michael. Michael, are you listening to me?"

There was no answer.

"Michael. This is as serious as it gets. I need you to talk to me. I need you to hear what I say."

Michael looked up into his brother's eyes, but his face held no emotion.

"Michael. Suzanne is dead. We're alone. I need you to tell me what happened. Tell me what you remember," Phillip whispered.

There was nothing.

A guard knocked on the door. Phillip yelled, "Come in."

"Mr. Brace? There's a call for you in the docket room. It's Chief Tuberville. He says it's important."

Phillip leaned his face to the screen and whispered, "I'll be back in a minute. Don't say anything to anyone."

Phillip walked through the jail like he owned the place. He took the phone from the wall.

"Phillip?" the chief asked.

"Yeah."

"This ain't easy, Phillip," Chief Tuberville said.

"You're goddamned right it's not easy. What is it now?" Phillip demanded.

"Phillip, we found a letter under Suzanne's mattress."

"A letter?" Phillip asked.

"It's addressed to you. From Suzanne."

"What kind of letter, Tubbie? I don't know anything about a letter." Phillip's mind was reeling.

Chief Tuberville tried to listen for hesitation and emphasis in Phillip's voice. His instincts never left him for a second.

"Phillip, the letter talks about how she loves you. It talks about places you meet."

Phillip lost his mind before he could stop himself.

He screamed, "That's bullshit, Tubbie. That's a bunch of bullshit."

The men stopped speaking and let a period of time pass.

"Phillip? You there?"

"I'm here."

"I'll show you a copy of the letter, but before you step in there and talk to Michael as his lawyer, you need to think. You can't represent him. You can see where this is going. Think about Michael."

Phillip kept the phone to his ear and rested his head against the wall. His free hand rubbed the eyes that wanted to cry. He knew Tubbie was right. For the first time in many years he couldn't clearly see the line between himself and the law. Phillip hung up the phone.

Earl Grimes bent down with his flashlight to look under the couch in the living room. He pulled out the bank statement and manuscript, placing each in separate evidence bags.

Ernie Watson opened the desk drawer and removed the rubber band from the bundle of bills. He wrote down the name of Dr. Andrews and placed the bills in another evidence bag. The bag was placed in a box that contained the gun, the tissue, the life insurance paperwork, checking account statements, the manuscript, the clump of hair, and other items.

The house was dusted for prints in various locations around windows, on doorknobs, and all over the bedroom. Samples of the brain matter were scraped from the wall for analysis. The box of bullets was found in the very back of the closet in a shoebox. The empty metal box under the bed was tagged and taken. A small blood sample from the top of the marble bed table was lifted.

Michael Brace's car keys were found on the floor next to the chair on the porch, next to his tie and jacket. Chief Tuberville himself walked out to Michael's car. He looked through the car and found a hardware store receipt from five days earlier and a map. Next he opened the trunk.

"Earl! Can you come out here a second. Bring some of those plastic bags," he said loud enough for the men to hear inside.

Earl Grimes stepped across the yard to the back of the car.

"Earl, does that look like blood to you on those yellow rags?"

Earl Grimes kept the rags out of the light rain.

"Yeah. Looks like it. Not much. But looks like blood."

Earl placed the map in an evidence bag and the yellow rags in separate evidence bags. He tagged the shovel.

Chief Tuberville walked around outside in the yard alone for a long time. He tried to stop his mind from piecing together the story. It was too early. There were lots of witnesses to talk to and scientific tests to be performed. He knew he needed to call Albert Danley to talk about whether there was evidence to bring a capital murder charge. The image of Michael sitting in the electric chair passed through his mind. He took a long, slow, deep breath.

At 11:50 P.M. on the night of February 4th, Phillip Brace sat alone in his office. The day had lasted forever. He poured a glass of bourbon and worried.

Michael lay awake in his new place. It was loud, but he heard nothing. All he could see, every minute since it happened, was Suzanne's face.

Tim Tuberville and his investigators sealed the house, left an officer to guard the door, took their boxes to the station, and went home to their wives and children.

Suzanne's body lay naked and cold on a metal table in a forensics lab. Her face was still. Down the line of her frame, arms and legs were straight, flattened breasts led to a smooth stomach and then upward to hip bones, knee caps, and feet pointed to the ceiling. Red toenail polish added color to a colorless scene.

# PART III

*After*

1

On Monday morning Michael woke up on the bottom bunk of a jail cell. For a time, just a few seconds, he wondered where he was. But then he knew. When the moment was gone, Michael realized it would be the last time in his life his mind would be free of the reality of the death of his wife.

District Attorney Albert Danley sat in the conference room in his office. In the room with him were Chief Tim Tuberville, Investigator Ernie Watson, Assistant District Attorney Rebecca Mann, and a young research attorney. The purpose of the meeting was to discuss the evidence and make decisions on the warrants to be signed before the case could be presented to the next grand jury. A bond hearing was scheduled at 3:00 P.M. in front of Circuit Judge Cornett Lofton. Albert Danley hadn't slept much. He was totally aware of the fact that this case, and this case alone, could dictate the rest of his political career. His dark suit and tie were perfect, but the bags under his eyes gave away the strain of the hours spent sitting in his chair in the dark.

Rebecca Mann was the most capable trial attorney in the District Attorney's Office. At thirty-five she had ten years of courtroom experience. In the beginning she used hard work, preparation, and sheer willpower to compensate for the inexperience. Sometimes it had been enough; sometimes not. At this point in her career she had reached a strong balance of ability and personal commitment. She was difficult to beat.

When the door was closed, Albert Danley stood to pace the room. He said, "At three o'clock we have a bond hearing set. At four thirty I have a press conference downstairs before the five o'clock news. Obviously, the first decision to be made is how to draft the warrants on these murder charges. As we all know, if this is capital, we can ask the judge for no bond. The next grand jury doesn't come into session until two weeks from today."

They'd heard speeches like this before. Danley always paced back and forth and tried to keep his hands in his pockets. Chief Tuberville waited.

"Tell us what you got so far, Chief. I know it's early in the game, but let's put what we've got on the table so we can sort this out."

Chief Tuberville opened his notebook. He put on his reading glasses and spoke like a cop.

"At approximately 5:00 A.M. Sunday morning, Suzanne Brace, the wife of Michael Brace, was shot once in the face with a .22 caliber pistol. The pistol was fired at close range, maybe a foot away would be my guess."

Everybody in the room knew the Brace family in one way or another. They were able to picture Suzanne's face before the shot.

"A neighbor called 911 at 5:06 A.M. Officers arrived a few minutes later. They found Suzanne Brace dead, her husband Michael was rolled in a ball in the bed, and the gun was on the floor. He was arrested without a fight and hasn't spoken a word."

Rebecca Mann asked, "Who interviewed him?"

Chief Tuberville answered politely, "No one. He wouldn't speak at all. He was sent to the hospital because he had the back of his head busted. We don't know how. We found a little blood on the night table on the other side of the bed. We think it might be his. It was sent to the lab."

Chief Tuberville looked back down at his notes. He was surprised at how few times the lawyers had interrupted him so far.

"The dead woman's panties were ripped. I think we're gonna have some semen. We'll know more from the rape kit and the autopsy. They had an anniversary party the night before. I'd imagine they both had a few drinks. You know we got the subpoena for Michael's blood, and it was pulled at the hospital by the doctor. Of course, Michael's DNA will be compared with the semen in the panties and the blood we found on the night table. I think it'll probably match on both. We also took photographs of what looks like a bite mark on Michael's face."

Rebecca's mind shifted in different directions. She was able to see how each piece of evidence would play to a jury. Albert Danley was able to think only of the bond hearing and the news conference.

"With a .22 caliber pistol we won't get any gunshot residue on the hands because it's a rimfire cartridge instead of a center-fire. A copper-coated bullet was used. Grimes and Anderson dug what's left of the slug from the wall. It looks like it went through her left eye socket and out the back of her head. I was a little surprised a .22 caliber would make it out, but it did.

"We've got a clump of hair in the bed we sent to the lab. I think it's gonna be hers. We've got a piece of toilet tissue in the bed we sent to the lab. Fingerprints were lifted from the gun and various locations around the house. There was no sign of forced entry, but the front door was unlocked when the officers got there."

Albert Danley asked, "Were there any other guns in the house?"

"No. The .22 caliber was bought by Michael at a pawnshop several months ago. It's the first and only gun ever registered to either Suzanne or Michael Brace. I think you're gonna find his prints all over the thing. I think the blood tests are gonna show he was probably more than a little drunk. I don't know what to make of the bite mark yet. It doesn't look recent. She also had visible bruises around the rib area.

"And believe it or not, it gets even more interesting. We found life insurance papers in the house. It looks like Michael increased the life insurance on his wife about the same time he got the gun. We found a bank statement under the couch in the living room. We can't be sure he doesn't have assets somewhere else until we subpoena all the records, but his bank account was almost all gone."

Rebecca Mann wrote herself a note to send subpoenas for bank records, tax records, and anything else she could find about Michael Brace's finances. She could smell blood in the courtroom before the first break of the skin.

Ernie Watson spoke up. "We found a shovel and some rags in the trunk of Michael's car. There were spots on the rags that looked like blood. We sent them off to the lab. We also found a receipt from the hardware store downtown. The shovel and rags were bought last Monday."

The room was quiet. The young research attorney was mesmerized.

Chief Tuberville got to the end of his notes. The last entry concerned the letter written to Phillip found under the dead woman's mattress. He hesitated.

"And there's one other thing. We found a letter, in an envelope, addressed to 'Phillip.' It was under the mattress. We sent it to the lab to compare to other samples of Suzanne's handwriting."

Albert Danley asked, "Phillip Brace?"

"Yes."

Danley continued, "Does the letter say 'Phillip Brace'?"

"No. It just says 'Phillip,' but it talks about him being at the anniversary party. It also talks about Phillip and Suzanne having an affair."

To Albert Danley, this information, and the power it would hold, was unclear. It could complicate a conviction, or it could add a new ring to the circus. Maybe both.

To Rebecca Mann, this information meant that Phillip Brace wouldn't be against her on the other side of the courtroom. But the existence of the letter complicated the motive. Did Michael kill her for the money, or in the act of rape, or in a fit of jealousy? Rebecca knew that in Alabama Michael could be charged with capital murder if he killed for pecuniary gain. He could also be charged with capital murder if he killed during a rape. But if Michael Brace killed his wife in a fit of jealousy, he could be spared the death penalty.

Albert Danley said, "What do you think, Rebecca? I'm leaning toward two warrants, one for capital murder based on pecuniary gain, and one for capital based on rape. We could get no bond, keep his ass in jail, get back the test results, autopsy, whatever, and clean up the charges later if the evidence changes."

Rebecca Mann thought about it a few seconds and said, "And maybe we could go ahead and draw up a warrant also for heat of passion murder."

"Not now," Albert Danley said, "We can do that later if we need to. In the meantime, work with the chief to get those subpoenas and draw the warrants. We've got two weeks until we go to the grand jury."

Albert Danley looked at the research attorney.

"Go down to the library and make sure we don't have any extra hurdles for a man raping his wife. And make sure the life insurance policy doesn't have exclusions we need to know about."

Albert Danley had one question left to ask.

"Tubbie, is there any chance this was a suicide?"

The thought hadn't even crossed the mind of Rebecca Mann.

Chief Tuberville answered, "No."

"What makes you so sure?" Danley asked.

"I've seen a lot of suicides. Women don't shoot themselves. No disrespect to Ms. Mann, but they like to look pretty when they're dead. She wouldn't shoot herself in the face. Besides that, Anderson talked to a lady from Suzanne's church. Suzanne was planning on taking a church trip to Atlanta in two weeks. She already paid the money to go."

"Good," Danley said.

The meeting was over.

2

Phillip Brace stayed awake all night thinking about the letter, and the kiss at the kitchen sink, and the day Suzanne showed up for lunch. He wanted to see the letter. The District Attorney's Office maintained an open-file policy on all capital murder cases. If Michael was charged with capital murder, Phillip knew Michael's lawyer would get a chance to see all the evidence quickly.

The question remained, "Who would represent Michael?" Phillip knew his entire office would have a true conflict of interest. Michael's attorney would have to be connected, and capable of fighting the real fight. The attorney would have to be a bulldog with a personality. Through the years Phillip had learned that many of the older, established, criminal defense attorneys just coasted. They flew by the seat of their pants in and out of the courtroom. The finer points of preparation passed them by. He also knew that a young lawyer, without enough experience, would be crushed under the weight of this case.

Phillip decided on David Bailey. David Bailey was thirty-nine years old. He was a sole practitioner because that's exactly what he wanted to be, his own boss. He made every business decision alone. He turned down more cases than he took, and worked each case like it was the last one he would ever have. He'd moved to Fairhope from Georgia, straight out of law school, without knowing a single person. Every ounce of respect from the judges, cops, lawyers, and clients was earned. He could fight like an animal and then charm a favor from the devil's wife. Almost everyone liked him for one reason or another.

While the district attorney met with his people in the courthouse, Phillip sat down in the Baldwin County Jail with David Bailey, Michael Brace, and Eddie Creel. Eddie Creel was a crusty retired cop who worked as an investigator. He was loyal and honest and went back with the Brace family to the days of Phillip's grandfather.

"Michael, we've met before, I'm David Bailey. Your brother called me to ask if I'd represent you in this case."

Michael nodded.

David Bailey continued, "It needs to be your decision, Michael. I don't really care who signs the check that pays my fee. This is your life. You need to be comfortable with the person who represents you through this. You can't have doubts."

Michael spoke for the first time since he had fallen asleep in the arms of his wife.

"I trust Phillip."

The other men in the room were relieved to hear Michael's voice.

David Bailey said, "At three o'clock this afternoon there will be a bond hearing. I expect Mr. Danley will draft at least one capital murder warrant based on what Phillip has told me so far. The judge is Cornett Lofton. He's the best judge in this county, but I think you can expect he won't set you a bond. At least not yet. These judges have to run for office. This case will be high profile. Anything out of the ordinary would make it appear you're getting special treatment because of your name, your family."

Michael listened carefully. David Bailey continued, "The next grand jury meets in two weeks. I'll file a motion for a preliminary hearing. At the preliminary hearing we'll at least get a chance to ask Tuberville questions and root out some information early. Again, realistically, I think you need to expect the case will be bound over to the grand jury, and you'll be indicted for the murder of your wife.

"Michael, this process is going to be slow. You're going to have to be patient, whether we can get you out on bond or not. I'm not going to rush this case to trial in three months when you face ending up on death row. You know Eddie Creel. Eddie will be investigating everything right alongside Tuberville and his boys. He'll be interviewing witnesses, copying files, and sitting with us almost every time we meet. As soon as we leave here we'll be going over to the D.A.'s Office to learn everything we can learn before the hearing this afternoon."

Michael asked, "Will Phillip be with us in the courtroom?"

Phillip looked at David Bailey. His look was the only explanation necessary. Phillip Brace hadn't told his brother yet about the letter.

"Michael," Phillip said, "I won't be at the table with you, but I'll be in the courtroom."

David Bailey and Eddie Creel went to the District Attorney's Office to get copies of preliminary police reports and anything else they could have. The two men sat in David Bailey's office through lunch reading and reading again every detail they could consume. The case against Michael began to take shape like the foundation of a building. Walls connected with other walls, and David Bailey's eyes searched for the weak spots. He could imagine the rise and fall of the jurors with every piece of evidence.

At three o'clock the circus began. Newspaper reporters and TV cameras lined both sides of the courthouse hall. Michael was led in shackles up the stairs and into the courtroom. It was still not real to him. All eyes watched every step as if he might suddenly scream and turn against the crowd. He sat down in his chair and stared straight ahead at the judge. Behind Michael sat his mother and father and Phillip. There were dozens of police officers, and investigators, and lawyers. Every chair was full.

Michael Brace was formally charged with killing his wife for pecuniary gain and/or killing his wife during the commission of rape in the first degree. In the quiet courtroom the words echoed gently and clung to Michael's memory.

The judge ordered Michael detained without bond in the Baldwin County Jail. A preliminary hearing was scheduled for the Friday before the grand jury would convene. As Michael stood from his chair, he turned to his parents. His mother was crying. His father stood strong. In the back row Laura Simmons wore a blue dress and smiled a smile Michael didn't see as he was led away in his handcuffs and orange jail suit.

## 3

It was a cool, cloudy day when Suzanne Brace's body was laid to rest at the local cemetery. The mood was strange. People seemed to stand alone in different spots, nodding or speaking only when spoken to. Sophie Butler prayed to her own God. She grasped the handle of her purse with her arthritic hands and knew that Heaven existed. She hadn't told Jimmy what happened. He didn't know his friend, Michael Brace, was in jail.

Mr. and Mrs. Brace struggled for three days with the idea. Each day they swung from the thoughts of guilt to the obligation of eternal damnation. They stood far enough away to show respect, but close enough to hear the words spoken by those that speak the words in times of sadness.

Phillip's eyes searched the crowd. He looked for signs of every human emotion. He could not seem to turn away from Suzanne's sister, Elizabeth. In her face he could see nothing. She never cried or smiled. She seemed to have very much to say, but no space to speak. Every person was a stranger to her, including the body in the box. Her imagination was unfriendly.

Edna Townsend and the ladies from the church were eager to succeed. They rose to these occasions. Each flower must be perfect. Each spoken word must be contained in the sanctity of the Lord. They were displeased at the presence of the family of Michael Brace, but required to understand.

Jerry stood across the street with a Marlboro cigarette hanging from his mouth. He could not hear the words of the preacher and did not care. His feelings didn't take the shape of words. They were round, and clear, and floated on the smoke that rolled from his nose as he stared at the casket.

Betty Riis cried. She cried mostly for herself. She chose to believe her weakness forged the result. She could have said more, done more, forced the issue, drained the pool, saved the lonely spirit of Suzanne Brace with a swift kick in the ass or a paper airplane. Failure breeds failure, and Betty Riis would doubt herself each day for the rest of her life.

There were people at the funeral whom Phillip had never seen. He wondered if they had come from far away to say good-bye to someone they had once known, or if they existed somewhere in Suzanne's life in this little town. Phillip began to taste doubt. Doubt in what he saw in others, and doubt in what he expected from himself. It was an actual taste, dull and dry. He swallowed.

Michael sat alone on his bed and tried to dull the edges of the image of Suzanne's face on the pillow. He decided that each day he would concentrate on blurring one tiny piece of the picture. Over a period of years he figured the sight would no longer exist in his mind. It would be like a photograph out of focus, only a reminder of something he would never forget. He knew today was the day of Suzanne's funeral. Michael thought about the night they had driven around naked in that old Volkswagen. Suzanne's laugh was alive.

The casket was lowered into the hole in the Earth. She would never be touched again. The disgusting hands of a man, any man, would never strike her flesh. Dirty fingers would never seek shelter in the warmth of her soul. Freedom is complete, or it isn't freedom at all.

## 4

Two days before the preliminary hearing David Bailey sat in the jail with Michael and Eddie Creel. David wanted to wait as long as possible before he asked Michael the necessary questions. From experience David knew the importance of this first real interview. If Michael admitted he had killed his wife, a strange moral dilemma would instantly be created. Technically, a lawyer cannot call his client to testify in a criminal trial if he knows the client will commit perjury. Technically, the attorney cannot concoct a story for his client that neatly fits into the facts.

"Michael, we need to talk about a few things. First, remember that this preliminary hearing serves two purposes and two purposes only. We'll get the opportunity to learn, and we'll get the opportunity, if we're lucky, to get Tuberville to say some things that will be preserved in the transcript, and can be used to our advantage later. In a preliminary hearing the judge will allow hearsay testimony and other information that may never be allowed at trial. I expect they will only call two or three witnesses. The judge won't give us a shot at all the witnesses because the D.A. only has to prove probable cause. If the judge finds probable cause you committed the crime, he'll simply bind the case over to the grand jury. We can call witnesses if we want."

Michael listened carefully. He wondered why Phillip was not in the room.

David Bailey continued, "You won't testify at the hearing. We won't have to show any of our cards. But I need to ask you some very specific questions about certain evidence. You've had some time in here now to think about what happened."

Eddie Creel pulled a notepad from his file.

"First, where and why did you buy the gun?"

Michael thought about the little silver pistol on the car seat.

"I bought it at the pawnshop. Suzanne said she wanted a gun. She said she didn't feel safe because some neighbor down the road got robbed. So I bought the gun."

David Bailey spoke, "Why did you buy that particular gun?"

"I don't know. I just picked it in the glass case. I don't know a whole lot about guns."

"Where did you get the bullets?"

"Mr. Potter sold them to me when I bought the gun."

"Why did you get that particular type of copper-coated bullet?"

"I don't know. That's what he gave me."

David Bailey thought about the next question.

"Tell me about the increase in the life insurance on Suzanne. Why did you do that?"

"Suzanne told me we needed more life insurance. She told me a man would come by the house. I'd never met the man before."

David Bailey and Eddie Creel tried not to look at each other.

"How much did you have to drink at the party?"

"A lot."

"How much is a lot?"

"Maybe seven or eight."

"Seven or eight what?" David asked.

"Seven or eight glasses of bourbon," Michael answered.

"Michael, tell me what happened."

Michael rubbed his forehead with his fingers. For days he'd let those hours run through his head like a man on the edge of a river sifting for gold in the sand. There was just nothing to hold on to.

"I don't know, David. The party ended. Sophie went home. It was just me and Suzanne. For the first time in a long time it was nice."

Michael felt like he shouldn't be telling strangers the details of his wife.

It felt like a betrayal. David Bailey sensed the hesitation.

"Michael, I've got to know everything. If you leave anything out, and I have to learn it in the courtroom, I'm going to look like an idiot. But you've got to realize, when this is all over, one way or the other, I'm going home. Eddie's going home, the judge is going home, Albert Danley is going home. You may never go home again."

David Bailey finished, "Tell me everything you remember."

Michael took a long, slow look at David Bailey and said, "She took me in the bedroom. We had sex for the first time in years. I fell asleep. The next thing I remember I'm lying on the floor with my head split open next to the bed. The gun was on the floor next to me."

Michael stopped.

"Go on."

"The lamp was on at the desk. When I got up off the floor, I saw Suzanne. That was it. The cops were there in a few minutes. I put on my pants."

Michael decided no one ever needed to know he held the gun to his own head. Why would anyone need to know that?

"Michael, are your fingerprints on the gun?"

A moment passed.

"Yes."

"Why?" David Bailey asked.

"I picked it up off the floor."

"Why?"

Michael came out of his chair and yelled, "Goddamn it, David. I don't know why. It was just lying on the floor. I picked it up. I dropped it when the cop knocked on the door."

Eddie Creel wedged his words between the two men.

"Mike, they found a clump of hair in the bed. Do you know anything about that?"

Michael sat back down. "No."

Eddie Creel continued gently. "Suzanne's panties were ripped. Do you know how that happened?"

The image formed in Michael's mind like one of those photographs that develops slowly before your eyes.

"I saw that. I don't know how that happened. Her panties were off when I fell asleep. I saw her take them off. I remember that."

David Bailey asked another question, "Did you ejaculate?"

He waited for the answer.

"Yes."

Eddie Creel said, "Tell me about the shovel and the rags in the trunk of your car."

Michael looked puzzled. "We had a shovel. I bought it at the hardware store. And the rags. But they weren't in the trunk of the car."

Eddie Creel said, "That's where they found 'em that morning. And they sent the rags away to the lab to test the blood spots. They also found the receipt in your car. The receipt where you bought the shovel and rags five days before the anniversary party."

For the first time, Michael's mind took a turn toward Suzanne. The only person who knew where the rags were, or knew where to find the receipt, would have been Suzanne herself, Michael thought.

"I don't know anything about that, Eddie."

"What about the pictures they took of your face? It looks like a bite mark on your cheek."

Michael thought about the morning she bit him. It seemed so long ago, so far away from where he was now.

"She bit me," he said. "Don't ask me why. She bit me while I was sleeping. It was the same morning I bought the stuff at the hardware store. Mr. Borden saw the bite mark."

Eddie said, "Was there any violence between the two of you? Besides the bite?"

"No," Michael said. "I never touched her."

David Bailey said, "They found a bill from Dr. Andrews. Do you know why Suzanne would have been going to the doctor? We haven't seen any of the medical records yet."

"I know she had to have a physical for the increase in the life insurance. Dr. Andrews was her regular doctor."

There were many more questions to ask, but today was not the day for most of them. However, David Bailey could not fail today to ask perhaps the most difficult question of all.

"Was Suzanne having an affair, Mike?"

Michael said slowly, "I don't think so."

"They found a letter, under the mattress of the bed, written by Suzanne to Phillip. I've got a copy."

"Let me see it," Michael demanded.

The letter was pushed under the metal screen across to Michael. He read the words. He recognized the handwriting.

David Bailey wanted to be the first to speak.

"Phillip says it's not true, Michael. He says it's not true, but he knows how it's gonna look. That's the reason he can't have anything to do with your defense in the courtroom."

Michael finished reading. He folded the copy of the letter and placed it in his shirt pocket. He stood and walked to the locked steel door. He knocked three times. The door opened and Michael was led back to his cell. He left the two men alone in the room.

David Bailey and Eddie Creel had been lied to more times than they could ever count. Neither of the men could decide what was going on inside the mind of Michael Brace.

It all began to form in Michael's mind. The time alone, and now the letter, crystallized pieces of Suzanne. Michael remembered the morning when Suzanne was standing at the window across the room when he awoke on the porch. He remembered her slow, even turn, as she looked him in the face, the papers in her hand. She said nothing. She didn't need to. She simply walked across the room and handed him the four chapters of his book. The way she looked at him, he knew something had broken inside his wife. After that, Michael hid the manuscript under the couch.

The hatred was deep. There had been signs, but he'd lost perspective. Michael's love for her had displaced his ability to recognize the imbalance. Her bitterness had eaten away her tiny foundations of sanity.

Alone, in his jail cell, Michael played with the epiphany. Suzanne's remaining stability must have become her mission to avenge. Her focus turned to the one who knew, the one who had taken the place of the one she could never really force to confess, or pay the price of pain.

Michael's thoughts turned to words, and for the first time in a long time, Michael needed to write.

## 5

On the morning before the preliminary hearing Tim Tuberville sat in the conference room of the District Attorney's Office going through his file with the prosecutors one more time. He reviewed the witness statements out loud while Rebecca Mann jotted notes on her yellow pad. Tuberville had no doubt the case would be sent by the judge to the grand jury, but in capital murder cases there is no room for even small mistakes. Rebecca Mann was more than prepared. Albert Danley would allow Rebecca to ask most of the questions at this stage of the show. He knew it would give him a chance to digest the evidence and carefully weigh the strengths of the case.

Michael Brace was brought up the back steps of the courthouse in his shackles and handcuffs as the newspaper reporters and television cameras took their positions in the hall outside the courtroom. At least one cameraman was prepared to miss the shot of the defendant entering the courtroom in exchange for the spot at the door that gave him the best view through the little window of the defense table. Michael's parents and Phillip sat in the second row. Laura Simmons sat alone in the back.

Judge Cornett Lofton was a big man. He was the only black Circuit Judge in the history of Baldwin County. The respect for Judge Lofton in the legal community, from both sides, came from his extraordinary patience and his record of fairness. He walked with a limp from a bullet he had taken in the leg in Vietnam when he was nineteen years old.

The court came to order. Investigator Tim Tuberville was called to testify. He went through the crime scene detail by detail, and by the allowance of hearsay evidence, he was able to tell everything done by each of his investigators.

The forensics report on the blood, semen, hair, and other items was not back from the lab yet. The autopsy report had not been completed, although Suzanne's body had been buried ten days ago. These reports were not expected for several more weeks. Fingerprints had been lifted and compared.

Rebecca Mann asked, "Were you able to lift some usable fingerprints from the house?"

"Yes, we were," Tuberville responded.

"What locations?" she asked.

"We lifted good prints from the doorknobs, a lamp, and other places through the house. We also lifted usable prints from the gun."

"Were you able to compare the prints lifted from the gun with the fingerprints of Michael Brace?"

"Yes, I was."

"And did they match?" Rebecca Mann asked.

Objections were repeatedly made by David Bailey throughout the testimony and objections were repeatedly overruled by the judge. Testimony was provided to prove the training and experience of the investigators as well as the reliability of the method of fingerprint comparison. The legal dance was a formality.

"And did they match?" Rebecca Mann asked again.

"Yes. The fingerprints and palm print on the gun matched the fingerprints and palm print of Michael Brace. There were no other prints found on the gun. There's no way to determine the age of fingerprints," Tuberville explained.

Michael listened very closely to every word.

"We also found Michael's prints throughout the house, which would be expected, of course, because he lived there," Investigator Tuberville added.

This was the first time many of the people in the courtroom, including Michael's parents, Laura Simmons, and the press, had been able to hear the evidence against Michael Brace. Tim Tuberville testified about the life insurance, and the ripped panties, and the purchase of the gun, and the shovel and rags. He testified about the bank statement with Michael's fingerprint on the envelope found under the couch, and the hair found in the bed, and the apparent semen stains. Michael's mother dropped her head halfway through the hearing and never lifted it again. Laura Simmons sat still and looked straight ahead.

Rebecca Mann asked, "What evidence are you waiting for?"

Tim Tuberville reviewed the notes from his file.

"We've sent subpoenas for Michael's financial records to verify he was nearly out of the money he inherited from his grandfather years ago. We're waiting for the DNA results on the semen and also the blood found on the night table across the room from where Suzanne Brace's body was found. We're waiting for DNA tests on what looks like blood on the rags in the trunk of the car. And we're waiting for the autopsy report. We also issued a subpoena to Dr. Andrews, Suzanne's doctor, for medical records."

"Was blood drawn from the defendant the morning he was arrested?"

"Yes. We got a court order and blood was drawn at the hospital at 7:32 A.M., approximately two and a half hours after the shot was heard by the neighbor."

Rebecca Mann asked, "From that blood sample of the defendant, was a test performed to determine the amount of alcohol in the blood of Michael Brace?"

"Yes."

"What was the result?" Rebecca Mann asked.

Again David Bailey made the proper objections, and again the judge eventually overruled the objections. Introducing this evidence into the actual trial would be much more tedious and exact, but in this preliminary hearing, hearsay was allowed over the most convincing objections.

"What was the blood alcohol level of Michael Brace at 7:32 A.M. on the morning of February 4?" Rebecca Mann was allowed to ask again.

".14 percent."

"Is that over the .08 level established to prove driving under the influence of alcohol?"

"Yes. Nearly double. It's impossible for us to tell when he had his last drink. It's also impossible for us to know exactly how much the level dissipated from the time he had his last drink until 5:00 A.M., or how much it dissipated from 5:00 A.M. until we were able to get him to the hospital, get a court order, and get the blood drawn by the doctor. We can come up with some estimates," Tuberville explained.

Rebecca Mann asked, "Was there any alcohol, or a glass, found in the bedroom?"

"No. We found a glass on the porch with Michael's fingerprints. It still contained what we believe is a small amount of watered-down whiskey."

The newspaper reporters frantically jotted down every interesting tidbit for the morning story. The television reporters half-listened and wrote down oddly chosen facts to report in their thirty-second evening spots.

"Did you interview witnesses to various incidents?"

"Yes. We interviewed Edna Townsend, who was at the Brace house on the night of February 3 for the anniversary party. She saw an argument between Michael Brace and his wife about Michael drinking too much. She said Suzanne cried and went off to the kitchen. Michael kept drinking.

"We also interviewed Betty Riis, Suzanne's psychiatrist. She told us Suzanne was afraid of Michael. He was drinking too much and physically abusing her. Dr. Riis saw a burn mark on Suzanne's hand at one point, and Suzanne told her about an incident a week before the murder where she had to bite Michael on the face to get him off her. She said he tried to rape her.

"At the time of the arrest, we took a photograph of what appeared to be a bite mark on the cheek of Mr. Brace. One of the reasons we've subpoenaed the medical records of Dr. Andrews is to determine if Suzanne Brace had any signs of physical abuse. There were some noticeable bruises on her torso, around her rib cage."

Rebecca Mann knew there were many cards she didn't need to play yet. One of those cards was the letter to Phillip. She knew the investigators had interviewed witnesses who placed Phillip and Suzanne together at lunch in Mobile. She knew Phillip's secretary had admitted seeing Phillip holding Suzanne's hand in his office. She knew Sophie Butler had reluctantly described Phillip Brace and Suzanne Brace kissing in the kitchen the night of the party. She also knew David Bailey had absolutely nothing to gain by exploring this avenue in front of the world. He could learn all this information from the "open file" of the District Attorney's Office. The questions were never asked, and Phillip sat, unable to swallow, for the entire two hours of Tim Tuberville's testimony.

After four witnesses, as expected, Circuit Judge Cornett Lofton found probable cause to believe a crime had been committed, and that Michael Brace had probably committed the crime. The case was ordered to the grand jury, which would be empaneled on Monday. Court was adjourned.

Phillip stepped up to the table to whisper to Michael before he was led down the hallway amid the scurry of reporters and rude questions. Albert Danley waited for the proper time to move into the hallway for his appearance in front of the cameras. Tim Tuberville stepped out also into the frenzy. He sat down with his file on a bench next to Earl Grimes. There were lawyers, and cops, mixed with curious bystanders. Phillip avoided the scene and sat inside the courtroom with his parents. Albert Danley talked with one camera crew only ten yards away from David Bailey speaking to another.

Almost every day Jerry made his routine walk through the courthouse. On this day he was barefoot as usual and checked for change in each candy and Coke machine in the building. His eyes never met the eyes of the people he passed. The only people who paid attention to him at all were those who seldom visited the courthouse. Everybody else just passed him by. Most of the time, we only see what we want to see. We only notice the people we want to notice. Jerry was nobody.

Albert Danley, in the middle of his press interview, decided to share some glory. He turned and saw Tim Tuberville and Earl Grimes on the bench.

Albert Danley said, in his TV voice, "And these are the men who deserve the credit. Tim, you and Earl come over here a minute, please."

The men got up only because they had to. Good investigators rarely seek the spotlight and Tim Tuberville lumbered over to the pretty girl holding the microphone.

"Are you the lead investigator on this case, Mr. Tuberville?"

"Yes, ma'am," he said.

"Do you believe the DNA tests will show the semen belongs to Michael Brace?" she asked.

Earl Grimes stood next to Albert Danley and Tim Tuberville. It seemed strange to imagine watching the six o'clock news and hearing the word "semen." Tim Tuberville thought about his answer carefully. As he thought, and the camera rolled, Jerry picked up Tim Tuberville's file from the bench, walked down the back staircase, and left the courthouse.

When the interview was over, and the bright light was turned off, Tim Tuberville rolled his eyes at Earl Grimes and walked back to the bench to sit down. The hallway was almost empty after just a few minutes. Tim Tuberville noticed his file was missing. He looked under the bench, he looked on the other side of Earl Grimes.

"Earl, you seen my file?"

"It was here a few minutes ago."

They went back in the courtroom and looked. They looked under the bench in the hall again. Tim Tuberville began to try to remember the faces from the hallway ten minutes earlier. Lawyers were always accidentally leaving their files or picking up the wrong files. Maybe Rebecca had taken it back to the D.A.'s Office? There was no reason for the defense team to take it. There was nothing in Tim Tuberville's file that wasn't in the D.A.'s open file, except for some of his own notes and diagrams.

Earl Grimes and Tim Tuberville looked in every room in the courthouse and asked everyone they could remember being outside or inside the courtroom. The file was never found.

## 6

Michael Brace lay awake in his top bunk. It was Wednesday. In the month since his arrest, Wednesdays had become the only day for Michael to look forward to. On the first Wednesday after he was taken to jail, a guard grinned and told Michael he had a visitor. Michael walked down the long gray hallway in the direction of the visitation room. For a few seconds a strange thought invaded him. Was it Suzanne there to visit? Was it all just a dream, like the dream of the field of sunflowers? Was he somewhere in that place between sleep and seeing Jimmy Butler's face?

Michael walked through the door into the visitation room and saw Laura Simmons. He just stood and stared to make sure. That Wednesday was the first of many. They would sit alone and talk about everything except Michael's case. It was the only time his mind was free. They would laugh, and Michael would ask Laura to tell him every detail of her week. Her eyes were bright. They talked about each other in pleasant circles, never really crossing certain imaginary lines.

On one Wednesday Michael noticed Laura looking at his left hand. Before that day he hadn't realized he still wore the wedding ring his wife had slipped on his finger fifteen years ago. He hadn't thought about whether it was wrong to still wear the ring that symbolized a marriage that didn't exist. Later he lay awake and decided to wear the ring as long as he wanted.

*

The legal battle continued. David Bailey filed motions to exclude evidence. He filed a motion for a copy of the transcript of the preliminary hearing and a transcript of the grand jury proceedings. He filed a motion for the court to reconsider the denial of bond and a motion attacking the DNA procedures. The motions would all be argued in a single hearing at the end of April.

As expected, the grand jury returned an indictment with two counts of capital murder. One count was based on murder for pecuniary gain, the insurance proceeds. And one count was based on murder during the commission of rape in the first degree. A third count of noncapital murder was added. A conviction in either of the first two capital murder charges would carry a mandatory sentence of life in prison without the possibility of parole, or the death sentence. A conviction on the murder charge without the aggravating factors would carry a sentence of twenty years to life. Under Alabama law the jury would make a sentencing recommendation to the judge if Michael was convicted of a capital crime. Judge Cornett Lofton would then make the ultimate decision of life or death without being bound by the jury's recommendation. The trial was scheduled for the jury term in August. If Michael was still in jail, the case would have priority over all other cases on the docket.

Phillip Brace was drinking almost every night. He would have his first sip when the office closed at five o'clock in the afternoon. The weight was more than he had ever carried. His mind could focus on nothing else. Clients would sit in his office telling their stories, and Phillip wouldn't hear a word. In the courtroom his arguments tailed off and ended in a whisper.

Phillip drove to his brother's house and used his spare key to enter the back door. The yellow police tape had been removed along with the bed and various pieces of furniture. There was a feeling of emptiness. Guilt hung like an old overcoat around the shoulders of Phillip. For the first time in his life since he was a child, Phillip felt helpless. The fact that Suzanne had accomplished this goal was clear to him, but why was another matter. The events of the meetings with Suzanne at his office and the restaurant played over and over. The kiss in the kitchen held a place in every waking thought.

*

Michael didn't think about getting out of jail. He stayed to himself mostly and thought about things he didn't seem to have time to think about before. Over the past several years loneliness had done strange things to him. He realized how he had been afraid every single day of what Suzanne might do, and what she might not do. He was afraid he might never write again. And he was afraid if he did, he might not like what he would find out about himself.

An old man named Virgil shared the cell with Michael. He had arrived two weeks earlier and slept on the bottom bunk below Michael. Virgil was comfortable in jail. He acted like a man in his own living room.

"Michael, you awake?" Virgil asked. It was Wednesday morning.

"Yeah."

"Today's the day your girl comes."

"Yeah."

Michael liked the old man. He told stories that passed the time.

"Michael, you need to be careful with women. I don't suppose I need to tell you that, though, do I?"

Most of the inmates had seen Michael Brace on television and knew who he was.

Virgil continued, "Every day, at least once a day, I take the time to thank God I don't have a vagina."

Michael smiled in his top bunk.

Virgil said below, "It seems to be the cause of the problem. I ain't no doctor or nothin'. Certainly not a philosopher. But I was married six times. I still don't understand it."

Michael tried not to laugh.

"You awake, Michael?"

"Yeah, Virgil, I'm awake. I'm listening."

Virgil was quiet a few moments as he recaptured his train of thought.

"You know what I think? I think it's like a boat. You have to have a rudder. It gives you balance. Women go through life without a rudder. They seem to get tossed around by any wave that comes along. Any little squall can send 'em off in the wrong direction. It's emotions. They're blessed with emotions, but at the same time, those damn emotions cause all sorts of problems."

Michael noticed that since coming to jail, he seemed to listen differently. He seemed to hear words he hadn't heard before, and use the words differently in his mind. For all the bad things jail could be, it had become for Michael Brace a place of solitude. Before, there was a low noise in his head like the buzz of a fly. Always there, always present. The noise had been around so long it ceased to be a noise itself, and had become part of the background of life. Now the sound was gone, and Michael could think clearly over the jailhouse clatter, intercoms, screams, TVs, and endless voices.

Virgil said, "That all probably sounds like a bunch of shit to you, but I believe it."

Michael fell asleep.

## 7

The days passed slowly, at an even pace. Michael received visits from his mother and father. Phillip would always come with them, but never alone. The meetings were stiff and unbalanced. They talked about people and things that were meant to be light and casual. Michael's mother was unsure how she made it through each day. The people in town sometimes looked at her differently, and when they didn't, she thought they did anyway. She took a little yellow pill for her nerves. Some days she took two.

Edward Brace felt a responsibility to be strong. It was so deeply ingrained that the man didn't need to think. As life got harder, Edward Brace got taller. He hoped his unbreakable presence was enough, the stiffness of his collar, the sturdy step, the conversation, safe, above surface.

Hardy and Simpson came to visit once. They didn't seem to know what to say. The purpose of the visit existed in the visit itself, but the distance between the men made it seem like Hardy and Simpson were yelling down a well to a man trapped below. They could hear each other, but not really well enough to talk in full sentences. Michael thanked them for coming, and both promised to be at the trial.

Michael had purposely not told his family or David Bailey about the visits from Laura Simmons. He was afraid they would stop her from coming because it would hurt his case if it seemed he had another woman. Laura

Simmons was not another woman. She had always been a tiny corner of Michael's world where he could rest. For him, now, the rest was not a luxury.

At least once a week Michael received a fat envelope from David Bailey with copies of motions, or documents of evidence. On this particular day Michael received a copy of the autopsy report of Suzanne Brace compiled by the Alabama Department of Forensic Sciences. He sat on his top bunk with his back against the wall in the empty room to read the six-page report.

"This is the examination of the body of a thirty-five-year-old woman, 67 inches long and 122 pounds." The cold words of the report gave Michael a vivid image of his wife's body, face up, on a smooth metal table. "Her only clothing is a pair of black panties with a three-inch tear on the left hip. The panties contain what appears to be a significant semen stain in the crotch with no visible signs of bleeding. The panties were removed and bagged as evidence for further analysis.

"The body is that of a typically developed white female consistent with the stated age. Black hair appears on the head and the pubic region of the subject." Michael could see in his mind the flat stomach that rose slightly to the mound below the hips and then led between the thighs. At this stage of the report he saw her face perfect and peaceful.

"The external genitalia are without note. There are three healed scars, each two to three inches long, on the outer sections of the right leg. The first scar is approximately 10 inches from the heel up the leg. The second scar is approximately 10 inches above the first, on the outer side of the thigh. The third scar is approximately 10 inches above the second located on the outer portion of the hip. A single small scar appears on the left temple area." Michael remembered the story Suzanne told when he first felt those scars in the darkness. He remembered her words of one of the few stories she ever shared about her childhood.

She had said quietly, without emotion, "I was a little girl. Maybe eleven or twelve. I woke up at night. My mother and father were fighting. I heard glass break. I got my little sister and we ran out the back door into the field. It was pitch dark. You couldn't see your white feet in the black dirt. We couldn't tell, but we were running alongside the barbed-wire fence where Mr. Cates kept his cows. I ran down the side of the barbed-wire and felt each rip of the skin up my right side. It felt like fire."

"Internal examination notes healthy internal organs. The subject is not pregnant. Evidence obtained includes autopsy videotape, 35 mm photographs, tissue, blood, urine, gastric contents for toxicology, vaginal and anal swabs and smears, scalp and pubic hair, bilateral nail clippings, tape lifts from both hands, tape lifts from entry and exit wound. A rape kit has been performed on the subject.

"It is noted that on the back of the subject's head there appears to be a small section of thinning hair. The bottoms of the feet are lightly soiled. The subject is wearing no jewelry items. A small cut between the second and third toe on the right foot is noted without the presence of blood."

Michael could see the man open the toes one by one looking between. He tried to read the words for clues, but it wasn't possible to separate himself from her. She was on a cold table, naked, with her breasts and belly open to strangers. Strangers who counted hairs and measured scars. Strangers who couldn't know how she had laughed the night they drove around in the Volkswagen.

Michael had purposely skipped over the page titled "Evidence of Injury." He wanted to try to see her face the way it had been for a few extra minutes. He went back to the section.

"Penetrating gunshot wound through the left eye socket. Entry 4¼ inches from the top of the head. Outwardly radiating perpendicular lacerations range to 0.2 inches. Internally the wound passes through the eye into the brain with a slight angle upward and through the skull. There is an exit wound with dried blood and brain matter. Fresh blood is associated with the wound track. Dried blood issues from each ear with spots of dried blood located on other facial regions."

In only a few minutes the body of Suzanne Brace in Michael's mind had gone away. It was a mound of flesh and meat surrounded by men with rubber gloves. He skipped the detailed sections of internal examination.

"It is noted that there are several light yellowish bruises on the upper arms, left rib cage, and left thigh, which appear not to be recent. More recent bruising appears in the rib area."

After reading the report again, it was impossible to put the pieces of her body back together in his mind. He kept reading the parts about the missing hair, the rip in the panties, and the bruises. He took the copy of Suzanne's

letter from his pocket and remembered her sitting at the desk in the bedroom writing the words. He thought about the piece of bathroom tissue
found in the bed mentioned in the police report, and the one bullet in the
gun, and the bank statement Tim Tuberville said had been found under the
couch with his fingerprints. He thought about their argument at the party,
and the life insurance, and the shovel. Michael remembered that Mr.
Forester woke up every morning at 5:00 A.M. sharp. And then he thought,
for the first time, about spending the rest of his life on death row waiting for
a day marked in red on the calendar.

8

April dragged. Michael was taken along for the ride, but each day he felt himself grow stronger. Judge Lofton denied the new motion to set a bond. It was clear Michael would remain in jail until the trial at the end of the summer. The envelopes from David Bailey continued to arrive, and the evidence piled up in a brown file Michael kept in his cell.

The conversations between Michael and Phillip on the telephone were awkward. Michael knew the day would come when Phillip would talk. The day came in mid-May. It was already very hot in south Alabama.

Phillip sat in the little room across from his brother. The metal mesh screen separated the men. Michael noticed how bad Phillip looked. He was pale, and the dark rings under his eyes were easy to notice. There was the faint smell of whiskey from his body.

Phillip started.

"Michael, I swear to God I never touched Suzanne. I swear to God I never got a letter from her, or snuck around with her behind your back. She showed up one day while I was eating lunch in Mobile at Morris Greene's place. She came to the office to talk about you. She would call and leave messages. I had no idea what was going on. I still don't."

The back of Phillip's chair was against the cool cement wall. He leaned his head back to feel it. His tie was already loosened. He realized he couldn't make himself turn to look his brother in the eye, and he knew his words would seem hollow if he didn't. Phillip turned and the brothers looked at each other. Michael said, "I believe you."

Michael meant what he said. He had already seen the witness statement of Sophie Butler about the kiss in the kitchen, and the statements of Phillip's secretary and the people at Morris Greene's restaurant. Michael still carried Suzanne's letter in his shirt pocket. For endless hours over these months he thought about every detail, every turn of fact. The only thing left was to hear it from his brother's mouth.

Phillip asked, "Why would she do that, Michael? Why would she pull me into it?"

Phillip had his own ideas. He wanted to hear Michael's.

"You know why, Phillip. She didn't want you to be able to bail me out of this. She wanted to make sure you couldn't represent me in the courtroom. She wanted you to have to watch, and suffer, from the outside, with no chance to fix this problem like you fix everything else."

Phillip sat up straight in his chair. The words were too true to ignore. The way Michael spoke the words made them seem real, already sorted out, analyzed.

"What the hell happened in there, Michael? What happened in that house?"

"I guess that's the true beauty of this, isn't it? I don't know what happened. I'll never really know. And it seems there isn't another human being in this world who does know. I know I didn't beat her up like she told Betty Riis. I know I didn't put the shovel and the rags in the car, no matter how drunk I was. I know I didn't increase her life insurance to kill her. I know I didn't put that bank statement under the couch, or put a bullet in that gun, or rape my wife. I don't think I ripped her panties, or yanked out her hair. If I did it, I don't remember any of it. But it's all so perfect, sometimes I can't be sure I didn't do it. Sometimes it seems like the only possibility that exists is that I shot my wife in the face in our bed on the night of our anniversary party."

"You couldn't have done it."

Michael said, "Then what happened? She's dead."

"Goddamn it, Michael. Don't you see? Don't you see that evil woman spent the last eight months framing you for her suicide so you can rot in jail?

What kind of a human being is willing to sacrifice her own life to teach somebody a lesson? It's fucked up. The whole thing is just fucked up."

There was a full minute of quiet. Then Phillip said, "If you could ask her one question, just one, about what happened, to clear this up for you, for us both, what would you ask her? What would you need to know?"

Michael thought a moment, "I would ask her if she's in a place where she doesn't have to be afraid anymore."

The men were silent again. Phillip's face was drawn up tight from his question. Michael's eyes were calm with his answer. Something changed between them. Both men felt it. A slow, definite change, beyond description, defined within.

Phillip leaned his face up to the metal screen and spoke, "Do you remember what Grandpa used to call you when you were a little boy?"

Michael didn't answer.

"He used to call you 'the fisherman.' While the rest of us ran around in circles trying to prove ourselves, he used to say that your one true virtue was patience. You could sit and listen to Grandma's stories even when she told 'em for the hundredth time. You used to sit out on that pier and fish all day even if you never got a bite.

"I never told you this before, but I always wished I could do that. I always wished I could sit out there next to you, and not say a word, and not care if I caught a fish. I had to win. I always had to win, catch the biggest fish, run the fastest, hit the ball the farthest."

Michael looked into his brother's tired eyes. He said, "Phillip, maybe I was never in a hurry because I had nowhere to go. Maybe this is where I need to be right now. And I like to believe maybe Suzanne knew that. But there's one thing I've figured out. I'm still here. Suzanne wasn't strong enough to survive, but I'm still here."

Phillip left the jail with a different feeling. It would take him many years to understand completely. "The fisherman" went back to his cell and pulled out the letter from Suzanne. He would wait.

## 9

Tim Tuberville sat in his office around a big table with his three investigators. This day was set aside for the men to sit down and organize the Michael Brace case. The trial was still two months away, but Investigator Tim Tuberville liked to be prepared, and there were several things about the case that bothered him.

He spoke, "Gentlemen, we've gotten back the lab results on the DNA testing. First of all, we've got a match on the semen. It belongs to Michael Brace. Second, the blood on the night table also belongs to Michael. The blood on the rags found in the car trunk is from Suzanne."

Earl Grimes said, "Couldn't be cleaner."

Tim Tuberville continued, "The tox report is back on Suzanne. She had no drugs in her system and only a small amount of alcohol."

Ernie Watson laughed and said, "I don't believe we've ever had a case with so much evidence. We could probably convict the bastard twice if we need to."

Tim Tuberville said quietly, "Remember the rule, gentlemen. If it looks too good to be true, watch your ass."

Eric Anderson was the quiet one. He rarely spoke, but when he did, the other men usually listened. He shuffled through his notes and said, "There are a few things I don't understand. I don't understand the one bullet in the gun. If this was a planned murder, you'd never put just one bullet in the gun and take the chance it didn't do the job. And how the hell did the rags with Suzanne's blood get in the trunk of the car?"

Instinctively the men looked at Tuberville for answers. He said, "The rape kit showed no signs of trauma. I don't think he raped her the first time. At least not by physical force. He's got no scratch marks. The neighbors heard no yelling, and there was very little semen left inside her. Most of the semen was in her panties like they'd had sex earlier, and she'd been up walking around. But I could be wrong. Maybe he held the gun on her and forced her to have sex."

Eric Anderson noticed that Tuberville hadn't answered his question. Tim continued, "The hair in the bed belongs to Suzanne. Somebody pulled it out. Dr. Andrews says she had bruises when he examined her for the insurance policy. The therapist saw signs of abuse. Suzanne told the therapist she was afraid of Michael, he tried to rape her before and that's when she bit him. But gentlemen, I must agree with Eric, there are things about this case I don't understand. Explain the tissue to me.  It had very light traces of gunshot residue like it was used to hold the gun, but Michael's prints are all over the damn thing."

Earl Grimes said, "Tubbie, he was drunk. He probably used the tissue to hold the gun after he'd already touched the gun. Or maybe he touched the gun after the shot. Either way, with the evidence in this case, the jury's not gonna get hung up on tiny details."

Tuberville responded, "Maybe not, but I'd like to know anyway."

Earl Grimes was eager to give his version. "Let me tell you how it happened. Michael Brace is a rich boy. Grew up rich and inherited Grandpa's money before he learned to work for a living. But Grandpa's money was almost gone. No more laying around drinking whiskey by the bay. No more writing books that never get finished. He suspects his wife is screwing around. Maybe he knows it's the brother, maybe he doesn't. Either way, she's screwing around. He can kill two birds with one stone. Get rid of the wife, and collect insurance money so he doesn't have to work like the rest of us.

"So he buys a gun, doubles her insurance, and waits for the right time. Unfortunately for him, he fucks up and gets drunk at the big anniversary party. They get in a fight over it. Maybe he found out about the kiss in the kitchen. Either way, now he's mad. When everybody goes home, he decides he's gonna get a little piece. She gives it up the first time, hoping he'll just fall asleep. But afterwards, somebody says something to start a hell of a fight. He pulls out her hair, rips her panties, and ends up busting his head on the night table. The rush of adrenaline is more than he can stand. He gets the gun. It's not loaded, so he only takes the time to put in one bullet. His grand plan is shot to hell, but there's no turning back.

"He holds the gun on her in the bed. Probably calls her every name in the book. Probably confronts her with the adultery. Maybe she admits it. He gets down in the bed so he can see her, and so she can see the gun. He probably tried to put the tissue around the gun to keep from having gunshot residue on his hand. He shoots her in the face. The face he hates.

"His original plan was probably to take her out and bury the body in the woods somewhere. He starts to pick her up using the rags to cover his hands and realizes it's a bigger mess than he thought. So he puts the rags in the trunk with the shovel before old man Forester wakes up across the street. When he goes back inside to wrap her in the sheet, the light comes on across the street. It's too late. The police car pulls up. There's nowhere to go. It's over.

"He has no idea the letter to Phillip is under the bed. He forgot about the bank statement, but of course it wouldn't have mattered if he could have gotten her body out of the house. He didn't know Suzanne told Betty Riis about the beatings. He didn't try to hide the purchase of the shovel or rags because he would've gotten rid of the rags, and the gun, if the plan had gone right.

"That's it. A perfect murder gone wrong. Rich boy fucks up."

The other men listened. Tim Tuberville knew Earl's version was the only version the facts allowed. Something still didn't make sense. It was just too easy. Michael wasn't a stupid man. Even if he had been planning this murder, he had to know increasing the life insurance policy and buying a gun so soon before the murder would make him the only suspect. Why would he buy a gun so openly? Why wouldn't he get a gun on the street, untraceable? But then again, Tim Tuberville knew that people who kill people are almost never rational. Their motives are almost always tangled with jealousy and bitterness, greed and guilt. And maybe Michael would use the obvious to his advantage, to create doubt.

Tim Tuberville began to put the papers back in his makeshift file. He couldn't stop thinking about his first file that disappeared. It bothered him. He'd never had anything like that happen to him before in a case as important as this one. Since that day he continued to picture the faces of the people in the hallway. He remembered Jerry coming down the hall just before Albert Danley called him to the cameras. It stuck in his mind. He remembered Jerry standing across the street from the Brace house that early morning in February. The idea stayed in pieces, unlike the story told by Earl Grimes, which fit together like a puzzle on a coffee table.

## 10

By the middle of July it was the hottest summer in the history of Baldwin County, Alabama. Many of the prisoners would skip the daily opportunity to go sit outside in the yard or shoot baskets, but Michael made himself go outside every day. He needed proof the world still existed. If he looked up to the sky, there were moments he could imagine the fences and walls weren't there.

The conversations with Laura Simmons were wonderful. They each still stepped lightly around those imaginary lines. There was no talk about what they would do if Michael got out of jail, or what might happen in the trial.

On this particular Wednesday Laura asked, "Are you scared?"

Michael wished she hadn't asked the question, but he knew eventually they would need to go in this direction.

"I was scared before, but not anymore."

Michael continued, "I was scared before this all happened. And I was scared when I first got here. But I'm not scared anymore."

He ended the sentence in a way that allowed Laura to know this part of the conversation was over.

"Have you kissed a lot of girls?" she asked.

Michael smiled. "No. But it's not because I didn't want to. After a while it seemed the temptation of the kiss, or the expectation, was better than the kiss itself."

"Do you really believe that?"

"No. I just didn't have the guts to steal the kiss. And the next best thing is to believe the kiss wasn't worth stealing."

They had stepped over one of those lines, and it felt good. Laura smiled.

"Give me your hand," she said.

Michael slid his right hand through the space under the metal screen. Laura turned his palm up. This was the hand so many people believed had held the gun, pulled the trigger, and sent a bullet through the head of a woman in her bed.

Laura leaned her face down and gently kissed the palm of Michael Brace. She let her lips linger on his skin, and he slowly closed his fingers around her face.

Laura lifted her head. She was not afraid for him. She was not embarrassed. She said, "You didn't have to steal that one."

Michael felt his body react as he watched Laura leave. The jail guard led Michael directly outside to the yard where Virgil stood against the wall.

It was baseball season. Virgil lived for baseball. It was the one constant in his scattered life. Through marriages, jobs, in and out of jail, there was always baseball.

"Where you been, boy? Talkin' to that woman? The Braves won last night. I got a peek at the newspaper on the guard stand. They won five to four. Scored in the bottom of the ninth again."

"Virgil, did you ever play baseball?" Michael asked.

"I played it, boy. I played it, and I watched it. It's God's game. My daddy took me to my first game when I was six years old."

Michael said, "I like football myself." He said it just to aggravate the old man.

Virgil spit. "Football! Football is for idiots. It's a shit game. Do you think football could ever compare to baseball? Do you think football could ever make people feel the things baseball makes them feel?"

Virgil pulled a folded piece of paper from his pocket. Michael instinctively felt his own pocket for Suzanne's letter. Virgil unfolded the paper. It was a page from a book.

"Listen to this," Virgil said, "Listen to this and tell me a writer could write such a thing about football."

Virgil wasn't the best reader, but he had read the page so many times the words flowed like a man who had written them himself.

His entire life he had played baseball and watched baseball, but he had never really seen the game. He hadn't seen the history, consistency, and elegance. A game that has remained essentially the same for over one hundred years, through the generations. A bat made of wood, and a ball that has looked the same, smelled the same, and tasted the same since his father's grandfather stood in the dirt on the empty lot down the street on the pitcher's mound with a steely eye turned toward the batter at the plate. A common thread woven through uncommon ground, past poverty, war, technology, tragedy, race, and ignorance. One of the few threads left from an American tapestry which has held our little worlds together as we travel from the womb to the grave.

As the days passed, it began to seem more like a religion than a game. A certain point in the middle of tomorrow. A time, an event, something to hope for. Something to count on. Something black or white and always there. Always standing with wide-open arms.

Michael asked to see the page. He read the two short paragraphs again. He wondered if anything he would ever write would end up folded in some man's pocket, timeless and important to one person.

"What is this from?" Michael asked.

"I don't know," Virgil said, "And who cares?"

"What are you doing in jail, Virgil? Why aren't you at a baseball game right now eating a hot dog?"

"I already told you," Virgil said, "I got three DUIs in about six months. I'm serving a goddamned year."

Michael asked, "How did you get three DUIs in such a short time?"

Virgil smiled, "Well, I got the first two pretty quick. I decided I either needed to stop drinking and driving, or I needed to come up with a gimmick. So I came up with a gimmick."

"A gimmick?" Michael asked.

"Yeah, I bought a used 'driver's education' car. It still had the 'Driver's

Education Vehicle' sticker on the door. I figured as long as I got drunk early, I could drive home by three thirty in the afternoon. What kind of a cop pulls over a driver's education car? Those kids are just learnin' to drive. Of course they're gonna be all over the road."

"What happened?" Michael laughed.

"What the hell you think happened? I got pulled over. As soon as I came to a stop, I jumped over to the passenger side and put my feet on those other pedals. The son-of-a-bitch arrested me. And here I sit."

Michael couldn't help but think how Virgil could've used his imagination to be somewhere else besides jail. Across the street, through the fence, Michael saw Jerry standing with a green plastic trash bag in his hand. The two men looked directly at one another. Michael heard Virgil's voice, but he wasn't listening. He just kept staring at the strange man, and the strange man just kept staring back.

The guard said, "Time to go, boys." Michael turned away and walked inside behind Virgil. The air-conditioning felt nice. He got back to his cell and found an envelope on his bed. It was a letter from Jimmy Butler.

*Dear Mister Michael Brace,*

*My momma telled me you had to go away. But I knowed where you went to. Uncle Ray say you was in jail and momma say I can't write you a letter but my daddy say it would be OK as long as I don't write nothing about Miss Suzanne. My Uncle Ray been in jail and he say the food ain't too good.*

*I growed one inch. My new shoes are fast. If you get out of that jail can we play football in your yard again? Tomorrow is Saturday. I wish things could be the way they used to be.*

*Your friend,*

*Jackie Robinson*

*(really Jimmy Butler)*

Michael folded up the letter and put it inside his shirt pocket alongside the letter from Suzanne.

## 11

D avid Bailey decided to have a meeting with Michael and his family. They arranged to use a larger room so everyone could sit around a big table. Eddie Creel sat at the far end from David. On one side of the table were Mr. and Mrs. Brace. On the other side sat Michael and Phillip. The trial was only a month away. Michael had agreed beforehand to talk freely with everyone present.

David spoke, "Michael, the trial is four weeks away, and we've got to talk about our defense. I've got three directions we can go. First, we can take the position that someone else came into the house and killed Suzanne. This defense has some very obvious problems. The second option is to take the position that Suzanne killed herself, but framed a murder. I think you know this defense also has problems. If we choose the first option or the second option, it's all or nothing. If the jury doesn't believe us, you'll probably be looking at a capital conviction with a real possibility of the death penalty.

"The third option is to argue you shot Suzanne by accident, or even during a fight while you were intoxicated. This is the more realistic approach. Unfortunately, all we can really hope to accomplish with this defense is a conviction for straight murder. It would eliminate the possibility of the death penalty. On a straight murder conviction you could be sentenced to life in prison. You would technically be eligible for parole in ten years. Ten years is a long time, but at least there'd be something to look forward to.

"Maybe I'm wrong, but I can't see going with self-defense. They'll beat us over the head with the bruises, the hair, the ripped panties. It's time for us to make some difficult decisions."

The room was quiet. Mrs. Brace did everything she could to keep from crying. She fidgeted and looked at Eddie Creel. Eddie's face was the only face that didn't seem to pull the tears from her eyes.

Michael didn't speak.

David Bailey leaned forward and said, "Yesterday, I got a call from Rebecca Mann. She was fishing around about the possibility of your entering a guilty plea to a capital charge in exchange for a recommendation of life in prison without the possibility of parole. She didn't make the offer, and I'm not sure she will, but I had the feeling she wanted to know whether we would take it if it was on the table."

Mrs. Brace rested her eyes on her son Phillip. He looked so tired. She expected him to stand up any minute and take control of this crazy conversation. She expected him to say, "Hold on a minute. This is ridiculous. Michael, go home. I'll handle this. Mom, Dad, don't worry."

But he never did. He sat there, looking small. She guessed he'd lost twenty pounds since February. Phillip was unshaven, and his shirt didn't seem to fit. Ellen Brace turned her attention to her husband. Edward Brace looked as he always looked. She resented Edward's coldness but relied upon it more and more each day.

Michael spoke, "You're my lawyer, David. You decide what to do in the courtroom. I won't plead guilty, and I won't testify that I shot my wife."

David took the opportunity to address the issue of Michael's testimony.

"I don't think we should make the decision of whether you should testify until the time comes. Frankly, I'm afraid your testimony could end up being the final nail in their case. You don't know what the hell happened. You can't even say for sure you didn't shoot the woman. They're gonna pound you with inconsistencies, fingerprints, the gun, the insurance, everything."

David Bailey turned to Phillip and said, "What do you think, Phillip?"

Phillip said, "I want to testify."

"Why?"

"If I can convince the jury Suzanne's letter is a lie, then maybe they can believe all of this is a lie. If I can convince them we never had an affair, never met at the ferry landing, then they've got to consider why she would write a letter like that in the first place. It isn't much, but at least it's a small opportunity to attack the credibility of a person who isn't here to attack straight ahead."

David respected Phillip. He waited a few seconds and said, "I don't have to tell you, Phillip, you'll have to deal with the testimony of Sophie Butler, and your secretary, and the people at Morris Greene's restaurant. I'm not sure if Danley is gonna push the angle of the letter, but if you testify, he'll have no choice except to make this a side issue."

Phillip responded calmly, "Maybe what we need is a few side issues. Let them spend time trying to prove this affair instead of proving their case."

Edward Brace felt he should ask a question. He didn't want his silence to be seen as a weakness, but every question he formed in his mind seemed ridiculous. He refused to ask himself whether he thought his son was guilty. He was afraid of the answer.

David Bailey thumbed through his notes. The witness subpoenas had been sent. He'd been through the file a hundred times. There was no evidence left to gather. It didn't matter anymore whether or not he believed Michael Brace killed his wife. The only thing that mattered anymore was what the jury would believe.

Michael Brace looked around the table. It was a heavy room with no windows. It had the cold metallic touch of a jailhouse, but it was his place, the place he lived.

Michael spoke, "Listen, I know it sounds strange, but no matter what happens, everything will be all right. I can spend the rest of my life in jail if I need to. I created this situation. I didn't kill Suzanne, but I just sat there and let it happen. It's almost the same thing. It's better to understand, and lose your freedom, than to have all the freedom God can give and not know the difference."

Michael smiled at his mother. She smiled back.

## 12

V irgil said, "Mike, you awake?

"Yeah, Virgil."

"What day is this?"

"Sunday."

"Tomorrow's your trial. How you feel?"

"I feel good, Virgil."

Virgil asked, "You feel like you're gonna win?"

"I didn't say that. I just said I feel good."

Michael tried not to spend his time thinking about the legal angles. He tried to think about the months leading up to the anniversary party. He tried to remember the details of his conversations with Suzanne. Had she given him another hint, or left a clue, some way out, some explanation?

Tim Tuberville couldn't sleep. He was ready to testify. He reminded himself that any doubts he might have had were gone. He was an honest man. It was hard to lie to himself. There were still small doubts, but all in all, Investigator Tim Tuberville believed that Michael Brace killed his wife. Maybe it was an accident. Maybe not. Either way, Michael Brace pulled the trigger of the gun that sent a bullet through the skull of a beautiful woman. Through her face. He could live with the outcome.

He still wondered about the missing file. Tim was an organized man.

His notes were good. The file had never turned up. He wasn't afraid the loss of the original file could hurt the case. He just couldn't figure it out. Whose eyes were reading his words? It didn't matter, he told himself.

Laura Simmons saved a weeklong vacation. She planned to be at the trial every day. Her expectations were small and brilliant. There were so many things she didn't understand, but she understood perfectly how she felt when she was with Michael. Maybe all her other feelings could be explained away, but she could rely on the one feeling, the one reality, of how she felt when she kissed his hand.

She was no martyr. The line is thin between sacrifice and selfishness. Her wish was not complicated.

Phillip sat alone on the porch at Michael's house. An empty whiskey glass was on the floor by the chair. Phillip held his face in his hands and cried. When it started, he purposely let go. He cried for his mother and father, for Michael, for Suzanne, for himself, and lastly for the pure shame of God's plan. Surely death would hold solace, he thought. Certainly the pain must bring strength.

"Bring it," he whispered. But he knew only time could bring anything. He was ready. The real pain was right around the corner. Phillip still believed in himself, somewhere.

Suzanne's sister, Elizabeth, packed her bags. She would stay in a motel in Alabama during the trial. She asked herself why she was even going. She had never met Michael Brace. She hadn't seen her sister in years. Blood was her obligation, but it was a sincere obligation. She remembered the night she woke to the sound of breaking glass. She remembered her sister taking her by the hand and leading her to the back door. They ran in the dark from the house where her father screamed. They ran toward the field of Mr. Cates. They were running, little girls in nightgowns, and suddenly Suzanne's hand was yanked from her hand. Suzanne was on the ground next to the barbed-wire fence. Elizabeth could still remember the dark spots on Suzanne's nightgown.

They told her the trial would last at least a week. Elizabeth packed her only five dresses. She was poor, and lonely, and haunted by memories she couldn't afford to understand. Somewhere inside herself she hoped this trial would tell her the things Suzanne never could.

Albert Danley worried even though the case was stronger than any capital murder case he could remember. He could count on Rebecca. She was a true advocate. She believed in her cases without reservation, like a pit bull dropped in the arena. There was no need to worry, he told himself. Michael Brace was guilty. Twelve people would see the truth.

There was talk that he should recuse himself because of Phillip's involvement and allow a district attorney from another county to prosecute the case. Albert Danley wouldn't do it. His election was in November. The publicity from this case alone would ride him through the election. Besides that, Michael Brace was guilty. There was no reason for him to question his motives. Justice is a beautiful motive, he thought. He couldn't sleep.

Jimmy Butler had heard the talk about Mr. Brace. He had a dream. He dreamed Miss Suzanne was alive. He dreamed he was in the grocery store with his momma, and they saw her with her grocery cart full of milk, and cereal, and cans of vegetables. Jimmy wanted to write Mr. Brace another letter, but his momma said no. He wanted to tell Mr. Brace about the dream. About Miss Suzanne in the grocery store.

Jimmy heard his momma tell his daddy she had gotten a subpoena to go to court. She was afraid. She didn't want to go. "Surely they can do this without me," she said. She remembered the kiss in the kitchen like she was a blind woman, and it was the only sight she had ever seen.

Ellen Brace sat in the dining room with a cup of tea. Her husband was asleep. Her baby son, Michael, was in jail. Ellen Brace's life was turned upside down. The damage was done. Nobody makes it through life without misery, she thought. How could she have expected to reach the end without sadness?

Her boys were still boys in her mind. They shot BB guns and forgot to wash their hands. If Ellen Brace closed her eyes, she could smell the smell of little boys.

Jerry pulled the file from behind the couch. It wasn't the first time, but it was almost the last. The file had been hidden in a plastic bag in the woods across the street for weeks before he brought it into the house. On Monday morning, the day of the trial, it would be burned.

## 13

On the morning of Monday, August 18, Michael was taken into a changing room at the jail and given the clothes his mother had picked out with the advice of David Bailey. Michael was led by two guards from the jail across the street to the courthouse at 6:30 A.M. He was taken early to ensure none of the potential jurors would see he was incarcerated. It seemed a ridiculous formality to Michael since the guards would be positioned around the courtroom during the entire trial.

Jury selection began at 8:30 A.M. Five panels of fifteen potential jurors would constitute the jury pool. David Bailey explained to Michael the two sides are able to strike jurors they don't like for any reason other than race, religion, sex, age, or other protected classifications. They don't select jurors they want; instead, they eliminate jurors they don't want until there are only fourteen left. Two people would serve as alternate jurors in the event someone was unable to make it through the trial. The two alternates would be released before the jury began its deliberations. All twelve jurors must agree on the same verdict or there would be a mistrial, and then Michael would probably sit in jail until the case was tried again months later.

David Bailey, Eddie Creel, Michael Brace, and a young paralegal sat at the defense table facing the seventy-five citizens from Baldwin County. Albert Danley, Rebecca Mann, and Tim Tuberville sat at the table for the prosecution. The lawyers were allowed to ask general and specific questions of the potential jurors. They asked about capital punishment, and the burden of proof, and the presumption of innocence. They asked whether the people had served on juries before, and whether they had been selected the foreman of those juries. They asked personal questions, and sometimes people were allowed to approach the judge's bench to give their answers in private. Every word, every single word, was recorded by the court reporter in the trial transcript.

Michael kept notes. David Bailey explained theories about wanting young jurors, or women, or misfits. Michael just looked at the faces. He liked the people he liked. He liked the people that weren't afraid to look at him after the judge announced the murder charges.

Many questions were asked about publicity. People had to try to remember what they had heard on television or read in the newspapers about the Brace case. David Bailey filed motions and made lengthy arguments about many legal issues. He explained to Michael that it was very important to "build a record" for the appeals process in the event the jury found him guilty.

Rebecca Mann argued each of these legal issues for the prosecution. It all seemed like a strange dance to Michael. It seemed that everyone knew David Bailey would lose each of these arguments, but the judge sat patiently and listened anyway. Occasionally, David would strike some legal nerve and Rebecca Mann's voice and demeanor would instantly change. The judge would cock his head to the side and listen intently. These arguments were all conducted outside the presence of the jurors.

Judge Lofton asked Rebecca Mann to read the prosecution's witness list out loud to determine if any of the potential jurors had a relationship with a witness. Rebecca Mann stood and said, "These are the people who may be called as witnesses in the prosecution's case:

Dr. Betty Riis, she's a psychiatrist in Fairhope,
Dr. Martin Andrews, he's a family practioner in Fairhope
Byron Potter, who owns the pawnshop in Fairhope,
Nick Crawford, a life insurance agent
Paul Cooper, who lives next door to the Brace house,
Morris Greene, who owns a restaurant in Mobile,

Kathy Gleason, the secretary of Phillip Brace,

Dr. Garrett, who performed the autopsy,

Joy Creighton, a handwriting expert,

Dr. Matthew Crake, toxicologist,

Lois Jensen from Midsouth Bank,

Hugh Borden, who owns the hardware store in Fairhope,

Rita Welch and

Edna Townsend, who attended church with Suzanne Brace,

Natalie Forester and

Ed Forester, who live across the street from the Brace house,

Sophie Butler, she helped Suzanne clean the house and worked the Brace's anniversary party

Fairhope police officer Marty Draper,

Dr. Janice Preston, DNA expert,

Lou Horne, fingerprint expert,

Investigator Ernie Watson,

Investigator Earl Grimes,

Investigator Eric Anderson, and

Chief Investigator Tim Tuberville."

The jurors were asked if they knew any of the witnesses. They were asked if they knew the lawyers, or Michael, or Michael's family. Jurors were excused for various reasons and finally, after two days, the process of actually striking a jury began.

Fourteen people were left sitting in the box; nine women and five men. The stonefaced engineer in the back row and the young college girl up front were alternates, but wouldn't know it until the trial was over. Michael couldn't tell if David Bailey was pleased or disappointed with the people selected.

## 14

Phillip left the courthouse alone. He found himself walking down the sidewalk behind Suzanne's sister, Elizabeth. Phillip followed her to the parking lot.

She stopped at the old green Toyota next to Phillip's black BMW. The cars were side by side. Phillip thought what a coincidence it was, the only sister of the victim, and the only brother of the defendant, with all the places to park around the courthouse, to end up side by side on the afternoon before the beginning of the actual trial.

Elizabeth slid her key into the door. She saw Phillip and pretended she hadn't. It was hard to hate the man. She didn't know what to think of him. She just wanted to go back to her motel room.

Elizabeth got in her car and watched Phillip out of the corner of her eye through the passenger window standing at the door of his own car to her right. Elizabeth turned the key. Nothing. She turned it again and heard the sound a car makes when the battery is nearly dead.

"Oh, God," she said.

The car was old. It had more than two hundred thousand miles. She bought it from a lady at work. Phillip Brace heard the sound as he climbed into his car. He waited for her to try again, and then he heard the same sound. The battery was dead. They both knew it. Phillip could pretend he didn't know and drive away, or he could help this woman, the sister of

Suzanne Brace, who found herself in a strange town, under strange circumstances, with a dead battery.

Elizabeth removed the key from the ignition, put it back in, and tried once more. This time there was no sound at all. She checked to see if she had left her lights on. And then there was a tap on the window next to her ear.

It startled Elizabeth. She looked up to see Phillip Brace, still in his suit, standing above her. Elizabeth tried the key again and heard the sound.

Through the window Phillip said, "You need some help? I think it's dead."

Elizabeth rolled down the window two inches.

"I think it's dead," Phillip repeated, lowering his voice.

Elizabeth tried it one more time with the hope the car might miraculously roar to life. There was no sound at all.

"We haven't really met," Phillip said. "I'm Phillip Brace. I've seen you in the courtroom. What motel are you staying in?"

Elizabeth tried to remember the name. "The Westwood Inn," she said.

"It's on the way to my house. I'll give you a ride. I know a man in town who can get your car runnin'. I'll give you his number." Phillip didn't want to scare the lady.

Elizabeth thought about the amount it would cost. She didn't have the money to spend on fixing her car right now. It was the last thing she needed. Elizabeth decided to get out of her car, making sure to bring her purse. She wasn't afraid of the man. He wore a suit and drove a nice car. Elizabeth had seen his parents in the courtroom and thought people with parents like those don't do bad things. Then she thought of Michael Brace.

Elizabeth got into the BMW with Phillip. Over the past few days he had noticed how different she was from her sister; a little overweight, homely, quiet. Elizabeth touched the leather seat with her hand.

"I'm sorry about Suzanne," Phillip said softly.

Elizabeth didn't reply. She just looked at Phillip. She had been told by the prosecutors about her sister's letter and their belief Phillip Brace and Suzanne were having an affair.

"Were you and Suzanne close?" Phillip asked as he drove from the parking lot.

Elizabeth turned her head to look out the window.

"She left me and Mom when she was seventeen. I was twelve. She never came back."

Phillip was curious.

"Why'd she leave?"

"Daddy died. She left after he died." Elizabeth watched the town go by. There was no reason not to answer the questions. She didn't think in terms of advantages and leverage. She just talked.

"Did she tell you why?"

In a low voice she said, "She told me I didn't need her anymore."

Elizabeth looked back at Phillip.

"Why are you asking all these questions?" she said.

Phillip was only three blocks from the Westwood Inn. It was the cheapest motel in town and was situated next to a fast-food restaurant. Phillip wanted more from Elizabeth. She seemed lost, almost slow, a whisper of a person.

Phillip said, "I don't know. I could never really figure out Suzanne. I thought maybe you could tell me."

It was quiet. Phillip had never turned on the radio. Up ahead he could see the lights of the motel.

"What was she afraid of?" Phillip asked.

Elizabeth looked from the lights out the window to her hands resting on the purse in her lap. They were strong hands, the hands of a woman who worked.

"She was afraid of us. She was afraid of Daddy, and Mom, and me. Afraid she would be like us, and there was nothing to do to stop it. You don't know what that is. I saw your mom and daddy in the courtroom."

Phillip pulled into the parking lot in front of the motel.

"It's number fourteen," Elizabeth said.

Phillip stopped the car in front of room number fourteen. He wrote the name of his mechanic on the back of his business card and handed it to Elizabeth.

"Thank you for the ride," she said, but she didn't reach for the door handle. She held the card and looked at the name written on the back.

Phillip wanted to ask another question. "Why did you come here?"

Elizabeth put the card in her purse and thought about the question.

"I don't know," she finally said. "I guess I wanted to know my sister. Maybe it's too late. Maybe not."

Elizabeth got out of the car, and Phillip watched her unlock the door to her room and go inside. He could see the light through the curtains. There was so much more to know. What did she mean, "Afraid she would be like us?"

Phillip drove home and parked in front of his big house. It was quiet inside. Phillip sat at the kitchen table in his suit and drank a glass of bourbon. He turned over in his head what Elizabeth had to say, and the contrast between his life and hers, and the reflection of Michael and Elizabeth and himself and Suzanne, like moonlight on water.

Phillip tried to remember what it was like before, when life made sense, when he fit into his family perfectly, between his mother and father, just above Michael.

His mind circled back to a day in high school. Baseball practice. He was all-county shortstop his senior season. Michael tried out for the team. Phillip sat in the coach's office.

"Do you think Michael will make the last cut?" Phillip asked.

The coach fumbled with his clipboard. There were eight kids left, and really only two spots.

"What do you think?" the coach asked.

Phillip leaned up in his chair. "I think having Michael on the team will make us better."

That's all he had to say. Michael made the cut. People said he didn't deserve it. He didn't earn it. They said he only made the team because of Phillip. But Phillip watched his brother on the green baseball field alone before practice every day. He watched him in the batting cage and knew it was right.

In a practice game before the start of the season, Michael was in left field. Phillip came up to bat with a man on third. The pitcher was Gordon Thomas. He was slow, and Phillip knew he could get around on the pitch and send the ball out to deep left. There was only one out, and a long fly ball would score the run from third. If he didn't hit it to deep left field, everyone would know he'd purposefully hit away from Michael.

The pitch came and Phillip took a full swing. His hands felt the concussion of bat on ball and he knew it was solid. He watched Michael turn to his right and sprint back toward the outfield wall. Phillip knew the ball had a chance to get over the wall, but Michael was fast, and Phillip also knew his brother had a chance to come up with the catch.

It was a clear blue day. The white baseball flew through the blue. Michael stretched out his glove. The ball landed in the webbing and Michael crashed into the outfield wall at full speed.

Phillip felt an instant joy at the sight of his brother making a fantastic catch. But the joy was gone in an instant. He heard his brother cry out. He saw the ball roll from the glove and trickle into the summer grass.

Phillip sat in his big house alone and took the last sip from his glass.

## 15

On Wednesday morning, August 20, the trial began. The courtroom was nearly full. Michael recognized many of the faces. There were newspaper reporters with little notepads and television people who were dressed neatly and had pretty faces.

The witnesses were not allowed to sit in the courtroom until after they had testified. Michael's mother and father sat behind the defense table along with Michael's aunt and uncle from Atlanta. Phillip was a potential witness, but the prosecution agreed to allow him to stay with the family in the courtroom.

Mark Simpson and Hardy made their appearance. They sat in the back and nodded when Michael looked their way. Several ladies from the church sat on the side of the prosecution along with Suzanne's sister and people from the District Attorney's Office. Laura Simmons sat alone. It was quiet.

The bailiff stepped into the courtroom from a side door and said, "All rise."

Every person in the room stood. Circuit Judge Cornett Lofton strode to the bench in his black robe. His limp was obvious, and added to the moment. It was almost sacred, the color of the occasion, the respect for the justice system. Cornett Lofton sat down and said, "Be seated."

The judge instructed the jury as to how the trial would unfold. With a strong and certain voice he said, "Ladies and gentlemen, this trial will begin with my reading of the indictment against the defendant, Michael Brace. The indictment is not evidence against Mr. Brace, it is simply the charging instrument. Next you will hear opening statements, first from the prosecution, and next from the defense. These statements are not evidence. They are simply designed to give you an idea of what each side expects the evidence may be.

"Your job, as the jury in this case, is to decide the factual issues, the guilt or innocence of the defendant. Your decision should be based on the evidence that comes to you in the form of testimony from the witness stand and physical evidence that will be introduced throughout this trial. I have no opinion of Michael Brace. I will make decisions on legal issues, and you should not interpret my decisions as an indication of my opinion of Mr. Brace's guilt or innocence.

"Following the presentation of evidence in this case, each side will have the opportunity to give closing arguments to the jury. After these closing arguments you will go to the jury room, along with the physical evidence, and deliberate.

"I expect there will be occasions throughout the trial when I will ask the bailiff to escort you into the jury room so legal arguments can be made. As you know, this jury will be sequestered. Each night the bailiff will drive you to the motel, and each morning you will be driven back to the courthouse. Please do not discuss the case among yourselves or with anyone else. Do not read newspapers or watch news shows. Your televisions will not have local channels and newspapers will not be available."

The judge read the three-count indictment against Michael Brace.

Albert Danley stood to give his opening argument. He was like a preacher. He started calmly, mapping out the details of what he expected the evidence to show about the purchase of the gun, the increase in life insurance, and the bruises on Suzanne. He marched into the anniversary party, leaving out the kiss in the kitchen, and delivering details of Michael's purchase of the shovel and rags, the excessive use of alcohol, and the argument at the party.

His voice began to rise as he spoke of Michael's inheritance being squandered, and his refusal to work for a living like the rest of us. Albert Danley's face began to change, and his hands balled into fists as he spoke loudly of Michael Brace snatching the hair from his wife's head, ripping her panties, and having his way with her probably at gunpoint with the smell of whiskey on his breath.

And he leaned down, looking the jurors in their eyes, shaking with vengeance, and told them how he believed Michael Brace got down the same way, looking his wife in her eyes, and shot her in her face. Two ladies in the front row of the jury box started to cry. A carpenter in the back corner shook his head from side to side. David Bailey tried not to sink back in his chair. It was his turn.

David Bailey stood. He knew how incredibly important it was for him to show no fear, no lack of confidence. Without the first believer, the mountain never moves.

David Bailey said, "Things aren't always the way they seem. Maybe some of you would like to just go back to that room right now, without hearing any evidence at all, and vote to convict Michael Brace for a crime he didn't commit. Is that what you want? Or would you like to get a chance to look behind the picture painted by Mr. Danley and see what really happened that night?"

David continued, but Michael stopped listening. He looked at his wedding band. It wasn't shiny anymore after fifteen years. There were nicks and scrapes and little marks. He began to wonder where every imperfection on that gold band had occurred. He began to wonder if there was at least one visible mark for each year he was married to Suzanne. And then he wondered what they had done with her ring. The autopsy report said she was wearing no jewelry.

## 16

Eddie Creel sat between Michael and David Bailey. At the end of the opening statements Judge Lofton took a fifteen-minute recess. Michael leaned over to Eddie and said, "Eddie, did they ever find a wedding band in the house, Suzanne's wedding band? It matched this one." He pointed at his finger.

Eddie Creel pushed his chair away from the table and looked through his box of files. He was very aware two jurors had remained in their seats during the break. He found the file marked "search checklist."

Eddie's index finger searched the list. When he reached the jewelry items, his finger slowed and he whispered, "Various earrings, bracelets, gold chains, broach, emerald ring, diamond ring."

He continued through the list. When Eddie was finished Michael searched the list himself. There was no mention of a gold wedding band. Michael located the autopsy report and found the part that said, "The subject is wearing no jewelry items."

Jerry stepped from the August heat into the cool courthouse. It was newly built and relocated to Fairhope for convenience. He took his usual route up the steps and down the long hall. This time he walked past the Coke machines without checking the change slot. He walked past the pay telephone without looking for a lost quarter. Jerry was dressed as usual except for a pair of out-of-place church shoes. He went directly to the last courtroom at the end of the hall, opened the door, and sat down alone in the back of the big courtroom. Other people filtered in and sat down. The crowd was smaller now since the opening statements were completed.

Phillip Brace pulled open the door. The first person he saw was Jerry. It took a moment to register. No one sat next to the man with the dirty fingernails and messy hair.

Phillip whispered to the bailiff, "Does anyone know what he's doing in here?"

The bailiff didn't like lawyers. He said, "I don't know. It's a public trial. Unless the judge tells me to remove him, I reckon he stays."

Jerry stared straight ahead. He did not allow his eyes to lock with the eyes of another, any other. Laura Simmons slid past Jerry down the back row and sat down alone.

Judge Cornett Lofton entered and everyone stood.

"Be seated," he said. "Is the State of Alabama prepared to proceed with evidence?"

Albert Danley stood again and said, "Yes, Your Honor, the State would call Investigator Tim Tuberville to the stand." Albert Danley had decided to begin and end his case with the calm Tim Tuberville and his matter-of-fact testimony.

There would be no real surprises. David Bailey thought of a trial like a boxing match. Try not to get knocked out early. Try to plant a seed of doubt in each witness, in each piece of evidence, because sometimes the tiniest doubt to one man can be used as the excuse for the next man looking to overanalyze, looking for a reason to disbelieve.

Tim Tuberville laid out the scene of the crime, the characters' names, and showed the videotape of the inside of the house of Suzanne and Michael Brace on the morning of February 4. Some jurors turned their faces from the videotape of Suzanne's body and the photographs. A diagram was drawn showing the location of the body, and the gun, and the furniture. An aerial photograph taken from overhead was introduced to show the location of the house in relation to the home of the Foresters and the home of Paul Cooper. Michael's car could be seen in the driveway next to the azalea bushes as it was found on the morning the police arrived.

Rebecca Mann had arranged for the witnesses to testify in a certain order. The order was based upon chronology and emotion. Jurors listen better early in the morning before they get tired or bored.

After a lunch break Paul Cooper testified to hearing the shot at approximately 5:00 A.M. and calling 911 at approximately 5:06 A.M. Officer Marty Draper testified to arriving at the house and finding the front door unlocked.

"I called inside. I identified myself. There was a sound. I drew my weapon. My partner was behind me. I looked around the corner of the open bedroom door. That's when I saw Mrs. Brace on the bed, and the blood, and Michael Brace laying in the bed in the fetal position with just his pants on."

The judge had already ruled prior to trial that the officer's entering the home was reasonable under the circumstances. David Bailey made his objections timely and approached the bench to do it outside of the ears of the jurors. He would do this throughout the trial so as not to appear to the jury to be objecting to every little detail.

Investigator Earl Grimes took the stand next. He described taking the gun into evidence, and the bill from Dr. Andrews, the insurance policy, and the bank statement under the couch. He explained and described the lifting of fingerprints from the house and car. Nothing was said about the manuscript of Michael's novel. It didn't fit in the puzzle so it was left to the side.

Earl Grimes spoke about finding the shovel and rags in the trunk of the car, the receipt, the box of bullets in the closet, the clump of hair and piece of tissue in the bed, and the brain matter splattered across the white wall. His descriptions were the descriptions of a man who has taken items into evidence countless times, with rubber gloves, and plastic bags, and the air of detachment.

At nearly six o'clock in the evening Judge Lofton adjourned court.

Michael sat with Phillip in the holding cell.

"It doesn't look good, does it Phillip?"

Phillip rubbed his forehead with the back of his hand.

"No, Michael, it doesn't."

Michael asked, "How bad is it, really?"

Phillip raised his eyes to meet the eyes of his brother.

"Bad. As bad as I've ever seen. They've got everything except a confession. They've got motive, physical evidence, and a goddamned smoking gun.

They've got it all. We've got almost nothing. We don't even have a believable story to tell."

Michael looked across the room at the cold steel toilet in the corner. It stood alone, no dividing wall, no separation from the rest of the little room, the polished metal was out of place between the painted cement block walls and stone floor.

Phillip couldn't think of anything else to say. He couldn't see any solutions. He wanted to change places with his brother, but it was out of his hands. There was a quiet desperation. Phillip stared down at the gray painted floor. Michael reached his hand across and touched Phillip's shoulder.

## 17

By Thursday morning the number of spectators had dwindled. Phillip turned around slowly to see Jerry sitting once again in the back row. His hair seemed to be brushed, and he wore a button-down shirt. The old eye glasses with the elastic strap were gone. Other people had noticed Jerry also. Although he was seen at the courthouse regularly, no one could recall him sitting in a trial. But he was quiet and seemed to be interested in a peculiar way.

Byron Potter, the pawnshop owner, took the stand early.

"Michael just picked the gun out of the glass case. He didn't ask a whole lot of questions. He came in the shop alone to pick out the gun and came in the shop alone when he came back to take the gun home. He also bought a box of bullets."

Nick Crawford was an antsy witness. His collar was too tight.

"I had a conversation with Mrs. Brace. She said Mr. Brace wanted to talk to me about increasing their..."

"Objection," David Bailey said, "Hearsay."

"Sustained," Judge Lofton said.

"So I went to the house to see Michael Brace. He smelled like alcohol. He said he wanted to increase the life insurance policies. I left the paperwork for his wife and we doubled each policy. Actually, we only doubled her policy because Mr. Brace never bothered to go get his physical examination."

"Who was the beneficiary on the life insurance policy of Suzanne Brace?"

"Michael Brace, her husband."

David Bailey attacked when he could. The witnesses came like sharp jabs and body blows, one after the other. At times it was overwhelming.

Dr. Andrews provided details about his physical examination of Suzanne several months before the shooting. David Bailey objected about the relevance, and time span, but the doctor was allowed to describe the bruises and Suzanne's reluctance to answer questions. The point was made. Nobody asked the doctor about how uncomfortable Suzanne Brace made him feel. Nobody asked about how she revealed herself to him at the edge of the white gown.

Dr. Garrett introduced the autopsy report. He gave gruesome medical details about the cause of death and the bullet exiting the skull. Eddie Creel made efforts to make sure the photographs of Suzanne's face did not pass in front of Michael Brace. Michael was very quiet. He watched the jurors and the expressions from the judge. Everything was swirling around him, but he remained still.

The prosecutor elicited testimony from Dr. Garrett concerning the missing hair, the ripped panties, the semen stains, and the bruises found. Michael leaned over across Eddie Creel and whispered to David, "Ask him if she had any jewelry."

David Bailey gave Michael a look. It was the look of a man who must focus on every question and every answer in a courtroom day after day.

Michael said, "Ask it, please."

David Bailey asked the doctor many questions. In the middle of his cross-examination, in an attempt to hide the question, David asked, "Did Mrs. Brace have on any jewelry when you received her body?"

The doctor thumbed through his notes.

"No, I don't believe she did. No."

Lois Jensen from Midsouth Bank took the witness stand. She introduced bank records that showed Michael's inheritance dwindling through the years to $1,100. She introduced the check Michael had written for the shovel and rags at the hardware store. She introduced the check Suzanne Brace had written for the church trip scheduled on February 17.

Hugh Borden, the owner of the hardware store, spoke slowly about the morning Michael had come into the store asking for a shovel and rags. He recollected the check written by Michael and his unpleasant attitude. He also remembered a bite mark on Michael's face that was clearly visible, and he remembered watching Michael look at his face in the rearview mirror while sitting in his car.

Pieces of the case began to come together for the jury. During breaks Michael would try to see Laura Simmons' face. She wouldn't be allowed to sit closer. During one particular break David Bailey and Phillip went into a separate room.

"David, they haven't called any of the witnesses about the letter, or the kiss, or the lunch. I think they're gonna leave it alone and see if we'll bring it up," Phillip said.

"I think you're right. We talked about this before. They don't want to tarnish Suzanne's image. They don't want the jury to think she was some whore who screwed around with her husband's brother and drove Michael to do what he did. It undermines their capital murder arguments. It makes this case look more like heat of passion. I'm not sure yet where to go with it. If you testify, and we bring in the letter, they'll just call Kathy, and Sophie Butler, and Morris Greene as rebuttal witnesses to show you're willing to lie to help your brother. Let's wait and see what they do, Phillip."

Phillip swallowed hard. He was dressed as sharply and neatly as ever before, but he couldn't eat. Sitting in the courtroom while someone else ran the show made him sick to his stomach. He had confidence in David Bailey, but deep inside he had always had more confidence in himself than anyone else. He just wasn't sure anymore.

Edna Townsend from the church was called as the next witness. She was too eager to testify. She recounted the argument at the party between Suzanne and Michael. She exaggerated, but Mrs. Forester corroborated most of what she said.

Mrs. Forester also added the fact that her husband set the clock to go off each morning at 5:00 A.M. She usually woke up and made breakfast. She didn't hear any shots on the morning of February 4 and she didn't see anyone stirring around at the Braces' house until the police arrived.

Michael's parents were exhausted by the end of the second day of testimony, and Ellen Brace's eyes were glazed by the time Judge Lofton recessed at the end of the day. She couldn't hear any  more. She couldn't hear any more about her son killing his wife. She slowly disappeared at the side of her husband. Edward Brace wanted to disbelieve. He wanted not to blame himself for whatever was wrong with his youngest son. Edward Brace sat with his back straight and took it as it would come, one witness at a time.

Suzanne's sister learned very little. She would listen closely, but somehow she couldn't stop thinking about the fact she was already wearing her fourth dress with only one more to go. What if the trial went into a sixth day, or a seventh? Everyone would notice, she thought. Phillip Brace would notice.

## 18

By Friday morning Albert Danley's case was moving along without a
hitch. David Bailey would tell himself he had known how difficult it
would be, but it didn't make it any easier. He felt Michael's life was in
his hands. At night he would rub his eyes and try not to think beyond the
trial.

To David, Phillip had become a wild card. He was clean-shaven, and
held himself upright, but those who knew him knew the difference. David
could smell the alcohol on Phillip's breath after lunch. He was like a man
waiting at a bus station for no one. Phillip's eyes were unclear, but he
intended to testify. It was the only way he knew to help his brother.

Rita Welch from the church started off the morning. She talked too
much but managed to eventually say that Suzanne had signed up for the
church trip to Atlanta scheduled February 17. The purpose of the testimony
was to head off any possible argument from David Bailey that Suzanne committed suicide.

"She wrote me a check one week before her anniversary party. She was
so excited about the trip to Atlanta. I remember she wrote on the bottom of
the check: 'church trip—Feb. 17—can't wait.'"

Dr. Janice Preston was the DNA expert. David Bailey had filed several
pretrial motions to exclude the evidence, but eventually they were all denied.
The blood on the night table matched the blood of Michael Brace. The

semen in the panties matched the DNA of Michael Brace. The semen inside of Suzanne matched the DNA of Michael Brace. The blood on the rags belonged to Suzanne Brace. Several jurors jotted notes on their notepads. Jerry sat perfectly still in the back of the courtroom. He moved his hand down slowly to feel the outside of his pants pocket.

Lou Horne, the fingerprint expert, took the witness stand. He explained the ridges and swirls of a person's fingerprint. It was almost seductive. The prints on the gun belonged only to Michael Brace. The prints on the cellophane window of the bank statement belonged to Michael Brace. There were numerous other prints throughout the house and on the car that belonged to Michael, or Suzanne, or were unidentified.

David Bailey spent a long time stressing the importance of unidentified prints throughout the house, but there was no way to overcome the prints on the gun.

Dr. Matthew Crake was the toxicologist. His testimony centered on the alcohol in Michael's system at the time the blood sample was taken at the hospital. The chain of evidence was linked together through various brief witnesses throughout the trial, as it was for all the evidence. Michael's blood alcohol level at 7:32 A.M. on February 4 was .14 percent. The jury seemed to take notice.

Dr. Betty Riis was called to testify. She was strategically placed as the next-to-last witness. She was as close as the prosecution would come to a grieving family member. Before the first question was asked, Betty Riis began to cry. Her remorse and regret invaded her chest in a peculiar and splendid display. Her glasses remained on her head, and she wore the same dress she wore to Suzanne's funeral.

"I should have done something. She was so afraid."

David Bailey said, "If you were so concerned, why didn't you call the police? Why did you just go to her party?"

"She was strong, Mr. Bailey. She was stronger than you or I will ever be. She believed she could change Michael. But you can't change a man like that. What else do you need? She was scared to death of him. I saw the burn on her hand. She told me about why she had to bite him on the face. I could see the bite mark at the party. The doctor told you about the bruises, and he finally killed her. He finally just killed her."

David Bailey tried to object. He tried to interrupt her sentences, but Betty Riis refused to be interrupted. She cried, and wiped the tears away with her fingers. She looked directly at Michael Brace and said, "There's a special place in hell for you."

Judge Lofton said strongly, "That'll be enough, Dr. Riis."

Laura Simmons didn't hate a single witness. Mr. and Mrs. Brace held hands. It was the first time in twenty years. Edna Townsend prayed. David Bailey imagined himself bloody and beaten. Judge Lofton began to agonize over his impending life or death decision. Many of the jurors had reached a comfort in their duty. Albert Danley and Rebecca Mann would not rest. Michael was calm, and Jerry sat in the back of the room. He took a deep breath.

The last witness for the State was Investigator Tim Tuberville. His final purpose was to wrap the case in a neat ball.

"I've been in law enforcement for twenty-five years."

Albert Danley asked, "Have you worked a lot of suicide cases?"

"Yes, sir, I have."

"Tim, have you ever had a single suicide by a woman where she shot herself in the face?"

"No, sir, I haven't."

"Do you think Suzanne Brace killed herself?"

"No, sir, I don't."

"Why not?"

"In my experience women almost never commit suicide with guns. They use pills or something else. And I just have never seen someone, anyone, shoot themselves in the eye. Maybe a shotgun in the mouth, but not in the eyes. And she made plans for the future, like going on a church trip. It just doesn't make sense under these circumstances that she killed herself. I don't see it."

Albert Danley paused. Slowly he asked, "The defense seems to suggest Suzanne Brace killed herself. In your entire investigation, from all the evidence you gathered about this woman, and this case, did you find anything, anything at all, that would support a motive for this woman to blow her brains out and frame her husband for murder?"

The jurors waited for an answer.

"No, sir. Nothing. Nothing at all."

Albert Danley paused to let the answer hang in the room. He asked, "Did anyone else stand to financially benefit from her death, maybe her sister, or another relative?"

"No, sir. Only Michael Brace."

"Did she leave a suicide note?"

"No, sir."

"Did she owe people a lot of money?"

"No, sir."

"Did the autopsy reveal some horrible disease she had?"

"No, sir."

"Was she on any medication? Did she have a history of mental illness?"

"No, sir. Not that we know of. She seems to have been perfectly healthy. She had friends, she was active in her church, she seemed normal."

Investigator Tuberville introduced the "search checklist" into evidence as State's Exhibit #87. The list included the inventory of items seized at the home of Michael and Suzanne Brace.

On Friday afternoon, August 22, Albert Danley rose from his chair and announced that the State of Alabama would rest. Motions were made and denied after the jury was removed from the courtroom.

Judge Cornett Lofton spoke, "Folks, you know I don't like keeping a jury sequestered longer than I need to. These people have families and jobs to get back to. In California I suppose the case would last six or eight weeks, but this isn't California. Tomorrow's Saturday and we'll be here tomorrow. Mr. Bailey, I assume you'll be prepared to proceed?"

"Yes, sir."

"Court is adjourned until tomorrow morning at 8:30."

## 19

On Friday evening Eddie Creel carried the box of files from the courthouse over to the jail for a meeting with David Bailey, Michael, and Phillip. David had decided there was nothing to lose by allowing Phillip to testify. Maybe the jury would think Albert Danley had something to hide by not telling them about the letter.

David explained, "Michael, I think we'll start off the morning with Phillip testifying. Maybe we can shake things up a bit. The only way we can put up character witnesses is if you take the witness stand yourself."

Michael asked, "Have you decided whether or not I'll testify?"

David rubbed his eyes. He noticed he was hungry.

"Right now I'd have to say I'm leaning toward you testifying. I just don't think we'll have a chance if this jury doesn't hear from you, but I'm not convinced either that your testimony factually will help us. I'd like to put on a stream of character witnesses and people from the community. Like I said, the only way I can get them up on the stand is following your testimony."

The night brought no relief from the heat. Phillip lay awake in bed. He imagined every possible question and every possible answer tomorrow might bring, and his mind scurried around corners and underneath imaginary trip lines. He was unsure of the words, but never once the entire night did he backtrack from his commitment.

And then it was Saturday morning, August 23. The jurors were in their places at 8:30 A.M. Phillip sat in the unfamiliar chair of the witness. The courtroom was packed again. The reporters knew today could be the day when the defendant might take the stand. Headlines and catchphrases formed in their heads.

David Bailey carefully walked Phillip through the direct examination. Much time was spent providing information about the history of the Brace family and Michael's marriage to Suzanne. David Bailey needed the greatest effect possible from his suggestion the prosecution had a motive to hide this letter from the eyes of the jury. Strategically, David had to concede the possibility the jury would decide Michael killed his wife. But if they decided he didn't do it during a rape, or he didn't do it for the insurance money, Michael's life could be spared.

David asked, "Mr. Brace, have you been made aware that a certain letter was found under the mattress of Suzanne's bed?"

"Yes, I have. I've seen the letter."

"Let me show you what's been marked as Defendant's Exhibit #1 and ask you if this is the letter you were shown?"

Phillip read the letter completely in silence and said, "Yes, it is."

"Before the death of Suzanne Brace, did you ever receive this letter, or any other letter like it from Suzanne?"

"Absolutely not."

"This letter is addressed to 'Phillip' and signed by 'Suzanne,' is it not?"

"Yes, it is."

David Bailey spoke to Judge Lofton, "Your Honor, I have made copies for each of the jurors. With your permission I will publish them to the jury."

While David Bailey handed out the letters to the jurors, Phillip Brace saw Jerry come into the back of the courtroom and sit down. He was dressed neatly.

"Mr. Brace, could you read the letter out loud please?" David asked.

*Dear Phillip,*

*Seeing you tonight was like touching the sun. I think of you every minute of every day. Just the few moments we can spend together are the reason I can get out of bed in the morning. A phone call, lunch, the afternoons in your car down by the old ferry landing.*

*Sometimes Michael will look at me like he knows. I am afraid what might happen if he does. I'm not sure I can make it through our anniversary party tomorrow with you across the room. When you tell me you love me, it makes me feel like everything will be OK.*

*I will love you forever.*

*Suzanne*

Although the effect was dramatic, the jurors had no idea where this was going.

"Phillip, did you ever have an affair with Suzanne?"

Phillip's eyes caught the eyes of Elizabeth.

"No. I swear to God. Never. I wouldn't do that to Michael, or my family. She was a different woman. I never really understood her. I still don't. But I know, without question, this letter is a lie. We never went to the old ferry landing. We had lunch one time in the last five years that I can remember, and she just showed up in Mobile at the restaurant."

David asked, "Do you have any idea why she would write this letter?"

Phillip said, "No. I think it's evidence of her mental problems, her delusions."

Albert Danley couldn't wait to rise from his chair for cross-examination. He did not like the idea of humiliating Phillip Brace, but he held the weapons to do it with precision and even subtlety if necessary.

Phillip tried to focus. These many months and the sleepless nights left him dull and far below his normal level of control. He was well aware of his weaknesses.

Albert Danley asked, "Mr. Brace, did you kill Suzanne?"

"No, Mr. Danley, I did not."

"Who did?"

"I don't know, but I don't believe Michael did."

Albert Danley shook his head from side to side slowly as he thought of the next question.

"You've told this jury, Mr. Brace, that you didn't have an affair with Suzanne, is that correct?"

"That is correct. I did not," Phillip repeated.

"Perhaps you can explain to the jury why you were seen kissing her on the mouth in the kitchen alone at the anniversary party that night. Can you explain that?"

"I don't know why she kissed me, Mr. Danley. I went to the kitchen to wash my hands. When I turned around, she was there. She kissed me before I knew what was happening."

"Really?" Albert Danley mocked.

"Really," Phillip said.

"She was a beautiful woman, wasn't she, Mr. Brace?"

Phillip paused and then said, "I suppose she was, Albert."

Albert Danley said, "And you didn't kiss her back?"

It was the moment Phillip knew would come, but for the first time it occurred to Phillip that maybe Suzanne intended it to come. Maybe the letter was written for a reason beyond just paralyzing Phillip. Beyond just making him helpless in the defense of his brother. There was no time to digest the idea.

Phillip spoke slowly, "No. I didn't. And I wouldn't have. I haven't been with a woman in over ten years. Not one woman. Not one time."

The courtroom was quiet. Only the people who knew Phillip Brace knew the sacrifice. For many, the futility of the sacrifice made it spiritual. The circle began and ended with Phillip, but its purpose could not be lost in the selfishness.

Albert Danley tried not to show his surprise. He could not walk away without asking.

"Mr. Brace, are you a homosexual?"

Phillip felt a strength. They looked eye to eye.

"Albert, I don't know. I've chosen to be alone rather than ask myself."

Phillip took a breath and looked past Albert Danley at his brother. Michael felt he was the only person in the courtroom. He remembered as a kid when he had watched Phillip in the pouring rain shooting basketball in the driveway. Michael felt the same bewilderment. The same respect for the unbending dedication and commitment Phillip could achieve.

David Bailey looked immediately at the jurors. He hoped that maybe, just maybe, Phillip's secret would make them wonder why Suzanne would take the time to write a letter that wasn't true and place it perfectly under the mattress beneath her body to be found. But hidden in David's mind he knew his perspective was lost. He knew that compared to the days of testimony, and the mountain of evidence against Michael, this was a side issue that could easily be explained away or even ignored.

## 20

Albert Danley ended his cross-examination. Judge Cornett Lofton sensed it was time for a recess. He did not wish to make Phillip Brace walk across the crowded courtroom in silence from the witness stand to his seat in front of his family and the spectators with their waiting eyes.

"Ladies and gentlemen, we're going to take a midmorning recess. Be back in the courtroom please in fifteen minutes."

Phillip waited. The jurors went to the coffee room. Most of the reporters and spectators stood and walked out into the hallway. It took every drop of energy for Phillip to rise, step down, and walk slowly toward the back of the courtroom. He walked past Michael. He walked past his parents. Phillip sat down alone and let his head rest in his hands. He didn't notice that Jerry was just a few feet away.

In the quiet, Phillip wished the fifteen minutes would last forever. He thought about his father, and how the words he had spoken would stand between them, forever, like an invisible wall.

Jerry spoke softly, "Mr. Brace. I would like to testify now."

Phillip heard Jerry and turned his head in his hands in the direction of the sound. He said nothing.

"I would like to testify now, Mr. Brace. Could you let Mr. Bailey know?"

Phillip had never heard the man speak. He was more aware of the strangeness of the situation than of the actual words spoken.

Phillip said, "I'm not so sure that's a good idea. This is a rather serious trial. I don't think you can help."

Jerry whispered, "Do you want them to execute your brother for a murder he didn't commit?"

Phillip waited a few seconds. He saw something in the strange man's face.

"What do you know about this, Jerry?"

"I know who killed Suzanne Brace."

Phillip let his eyes search the courtroom. The conversation didn't seem real. He wondered for a brief moment if it was. Then he asked, "Who?"

Jerry said simply, "I did."

The two men were just a few feet apart. Phillip thought to himself, even if this man was crazy, even if it turned out to be nothing, it had to be explored.

Phillip asked, "How do I know it's true?"

Jerry whispered, "You don't. I'll tell the story from the witness stand. Then you'll know it's true. Don't just sit back here feeling sorry for yourself. Go tell Mr. Bailey, please."

Phillip stood and walked quickly to the defense table. He leaned over and spoke clearly in the ear of David Bailey. David's head turned to see the man sitting in the back of the courtroom. David walked alone to where Jerry sat. Jerry stood and introduced himself, "Mr. Bailey. My name is Jerry Bannon. I would like to testify now, before you go any further."

David shook the man's hand. He said, "Mr. Bannon, I can't just call you to testify without knowing what you're gonna say. This is a capital murder trial."

Jerry Bannon smiled and said, "Yes, Mr. Bailey, this is a capital murder trial. It's a capital murder trial in which your client is going to be convicted for something he didn't do. I killed Suzanne Brace, but I'm not going to tell you about it until I get on the witness stand. You've got nothing to lose. We both know it. Your choice is simple. Get me on the witness stand, or sit by and watch Michael Brace get sentenced to death."

The legal wheels in David Bailey's mind spun quickly. He couldn't turn his back on a man who wanted to confess to a murder in the middle of another man's trial. Besides, Jerry Bannon was right, there was nothing to lose.

David Bailey went immediately to the judge's chambers with Albert Danley and Rebecca Mann. He asked the court reporter to join them to transcribe the conversation. Jerry Bannon had never been listed as a witness. His competence was a question. The man refused to give any details before testifying. The argument in the judge's chambers was heated.

Albert Danley shouted, "Judge, they can't come waltzing in here in the middle of a trial with a witness they've never identified. They're talking about the guy who's been roaming around town the last twenty years picking up cans. He's liable to confess to the Kennedy assassination if we ask him to."

David Bailey responded, "Judge, until ten minutes ago we had no idea this man was involved. During the recess he confessed to Phillip Brace. He says he killed her. He seems perfectly lucid. It's the jury's place to decide if the man is telling the truth. If he's not allowed to testify, this case will be sent back here so fast by the appeals court our heads will spin. Why should we do this all over again a year from now? Jerry Bannon is here to testify right now."

Judge Lofton sent his bailiff into the courtroom to inform everyone there would be a delay. The arguments lasted for more than an hour. Jerry sat in the back row with his hands together in his lap. He had once considered the possibility of testifying only to what he had seen that morning. But what had he really seen? After he read and reread the file of Tim Tuberville, Jerry knew it could never be enough. It would never be enough for some old bum to say he saw Suzanne in the dark put something in the trunk of the car. He imagined the questions.

"It was dark. You don't really know if it was a man or a woman, do you? Don't you have eyesight problems? And if it was Suzanne, how do you know what she was doing outside? How do you know she wasn't trying to get away? Or maybe she discovered the shovel and rags and that's why Michael killed her? Or maybe you just want to be a witness in a big trial and get in the newspaper? You don't have anything to lose, do you? You'll just go back tomorrow picking up cans."

It would've been for nothing, Jerry thought. Halfway was no way at all. As it was, there were only two people, two people, who truly believed

Michael Brace had not killed his wife. And only one of them, Jerry, could do anything about it.

The jury was asked to stay in the coffee room. The arguments of the lawyers ended by Judge Lofton asking to be left alone in his library. Albert Danley and Rebecca Mann told Tim Tuberville the news. They sent Investigator Tuberville to the back of the courtroom to talk with Jerry.

"How you doing, Jerry?"

"I'm OK," Jerry looked older than his fifty-one years.

"They say you want to confess to killing Suzanne Brace."

"Yes." Jerry looked down at his feet as he spoke.

"How'd you do it?"

"I shot her, Mr. Tuberville. It was an accident. I heard them fighting in the house. The door was unlocked. She was like a princess. She didn't deserve to be treated like he treated her. I was gonna kill that son-of-a-bitch. I'm sorry. I'm not gonna tell you any more until I testify."

Jerry Bannon's words trailed off.

Tim Tuberville said, "I don't believe you, Jerry."

Jerry turned and looked Tim Tuberville in the eye. He said, "You will."

Judge Lofton entered the courtroom. The newspaper reporters sensed a shift, a change in the course of the case. The jury was left outside.

Cornett Lofton spoke, "Mr. Bailey has presented this court with a dilemma. He has a witness who has apparently stepped forward in the middle of the trial who wishes to testify. It is my understanding this new witness will confess to the murder of Suzanne Brace. It is also my understanding the witness will not give details of his testimony to the defense or to the prosecution. He wishes to give details only from the witness stand. Here is my dilemma. If this court refuses to allow the witness to testify, this case will surely be overturned on appeal. This is a capital murder case. The court of appeals will apply the utmost scrutiny to the discretion of the trial court to ensure that the defendant is not denied a fair trial.

"I am not inclined to let the man testify initially in front of the jury. I am ordering Mr. Bannon to testify outside the presence of the jury so both the defense and prosecution will know the gist of his testimony before it is presented to the jury. Also, it will give the court the opportunity to make a determination of the competence of this witness. The court will ask the witness questions."

Strong objections were made by Albert Danley and Rebecca Mann. The objections were overruled and Jerry Bannon was called to the witness stand by Judge Cornett Lofton.

"Do you swear to tell the truth, the whole truth, and nothing but the truth, so help you God?"

"I do."

Jerry Bannon sat down. The courtroom was full. Judge Lofton turned his chair in the direction of the witness stand and began asking questions.

"Tell us your name for the record."

"Gerald Anthony Bannon."

"How old are you, Mr. Bannon?"

"Fifty-one."

"Is it true you wish to testify you killed Suzanne Brace?"

"Yes, sir."

"Why did you wait until now to come forward?"

"I never believed they could convict Michael Brace. I know now that if I don't tell the truth, an innocent man will probably get convicted, and maybe executed. I couldn't just sit back there and watch."

"Mr. Bannon, have you ever been treated for a mental illness?"

"No, sir."

"Have you ever been committed to a psychiatric hospital?"

"No, sir."

"Have you even been declared incompetent?"

"No, sir."

"Have you ever been convicted of a crime?"

"No, sir."

Judge Lofton asked many more questions directed to the issue of competence or a possible motive for a false confession. Jerry Bannon gave all the correct answers.

"Do you have a lawyer, Mr. Bannon?"

"No, sir."

"Mr. Bannon, the Fifth Amendment to the United States Constitution gives you the right to remain silent and not provide testimony that may be used against you. Do you understand you have the right not to testify? And you have the right to consult an attorney?"

"Yes, sir, I understand."

"Would you like to speak with an attorney?"

"No, I would not."

"Do you understand that you will be subjected to cross-examination? You may very well be prosecuted for the murder of Suzanne Brace."

"I understand completely."

"Tell me what happened, Mr. Bannon."

Jerry eased himself up against the back of the chair. His eyes were calm.

"I pick up cans. I sometimes get up early in the morning and go down to the water across from the Braces' house. I've seen Suzanne Brace for lots of years. On this morning, at about 4:30 or so, I heard Michael yelling in the house. He was saying hateful things. Things a man should never say to a woman. When it got quiet, I waited a while and then went to the front door. I don't know why. The door was unlocked, and I went inside. There was a light on in the bedroom. Suzanne was asleep in the bed. She looked asleep. Michael Brace was asleep on the couch. I just wanted to kill him. I wanted her to be away from him.

"There was a gun on the floor in the bedroom. I picked it up with a piece of toilet tissue I got from the bathroom. It was a little silver gun. She looked so pretty and scared. I just wanted to touch her. I just wanted to touch her skin. I leaned down with the gun in my left hand resting on the bed. She woke up and grabbed my hand. The gun went off. It was an awful sound. There was blood everywhere. Everywhere. I just ran. I dropped the gun and ran out the door."

Every person in the room listened to every single word. There was not a sound. Judge Lofton asked, "How did her panties get ripped?"

"I don't know, Judge. When I got inside it looked like there had been a terrible fight. I saw hair in the bed, and her panties were torn. I don't know what happened before I came into the house. I would've killed that son-of-a-bitch. I would have shot him while he slept on the couch. I'm sorry. She didn't deserve to die. It just went off. It was an accident."

Judge Lofton thought a moment and said, "Mr. Bannon, although you've waived your Fifth Amendment privilege and testified, you can still invoke this privilege and refuse to testify in front of the jury. I have no reason to believe that you aren't competent to waive your privilege. What do you want to do?"

"I would like to testify please."

Albert Danley stood. "Your Honor, we would like the opportunity to question the witness."

Judge Lofton responded, "Mr. Danley, you can ask the witness any questions you'd like in front of the jury. If you need additional time to prepare, I'll recess court until this afternoon. That will give you a few hours."

"Your Honor, we'd like to question the witness further outside the presence of the jury. We would like additional information."

Cornett Lofton responded less politely, "I know what you'd like, but I'm satisfied Mr. Bannon is sufficiently competent to testify, unless you can convince me otherwise. I realize he's been in the courtroom for the trial, but his statement is sufficiently consistent with the evidence in this case to allow the jury to have the opportunity to hear what he has to say. You can cross-examine him until the sun goes down in front of the jury."

Rebecca Mann said, "Judge, can we at least get his date of birth and social security number to run a criminal history and background check?"

"Yes," Cornett Lofton said, "Mr. Bannon, please write down your date of birth and social security number. Do not leave the courthouse without my permission. Court will be adjourned until 3:30."

## 21

A lbert Danley sent his investigators in different directions. Eric Anderson pulled into the driveway of Jerry Bannon's little house. The house sat on a tiny lot, covered in vines and overgrown bushes. Eric got out of the car and walked around the back of the house. He cupped his hand and peeked through a window. There was one room. Eric could see stacks of newspapers and books. He could see a couch and an old television set with a crooked antenna. Trash bags full of aluminum cans were piled against one wall.

Ernie Watson learned that the deed to the house was solely in the name of Gerald Anthony Bannon. The property taxes were paid in full each year. There was no mortgage. The man had no debts, no credit cards, no checking accounts or savings accounts.

Earl Grimes ran a criminal history with Jerry's social security number, full name, and date of birth. He had never had an Alabama driver's license and had never been issued a single traffic citation. Gerald Anthony Bannon was not registered to vote. He had never applied for a marriage license in Baldwin County, Alabama. Earl Grimes could find nothing to indicate the man had ever been arrested or committed to a mental institution.

The jury was led into the courtroom and took their seats. The hallway was full of television crews and made-up pretty women with microphones. At the appropriate time David Bailey rose from his chair and said, "The defense calls Jerry Bannon to the witness stand."

All eyes followed Jerry as he walked from the back of the room to the witness stand, placed his left hand on the Bible, and lifted his right hand into the air.

Judge Lofton spoke the same words as before, "Do you swear to tell the truth, the whole truth, and nothing but the truth, so help you God?"

"I do," Jerry whispered.

David Bailey said, "Please tell us your name and age."

"My name is Gerald Anthony Bannon, Jerry, and I'm fifty-one years old."

"Where do you live, Mr. Bannon?"

"I live in Fairhope. I've lived here the past twenty-three years."

"What do you do for a living, sir?"

"I pick up cans, and trash, and sometimes do a few odd jobs."

David Bailey chose to tread lightly. He decided to guide Jerry Bannon through his testimony as gently as possible and force Albert Danley in cross-examination to step into uncharted territory.

"Where were you, Mr. Bannon, on the morning of February 4 of this year?"

"I was on the park bench by the bay across the street from the Braces' house at about 4:30 in the morning. I go down there sometimes early. It's usually quiet."

"What happened on this particular morning?"

"I heard someone yelling from the Brace's house. It was a man's voice. He was cussing and screaming."

David asked, "What did you do?"

"I've seen Michael Brace and Suzanne Brace around town and at their house for lots of years. When I would see how he treated her, it made me angry. She was like a little girl. He treated her wrong. He had no right to yell at her."

"What did you do?"

"I waited until the yelling stopped. It got quiet. I waited twenty minutes or so and walked across the street to the house. At first I didn't know what I was going to do. The door was unlocked, and I went inside."

"What did you do when you got inside the house?"

"There was a light on in one of the rooms. I saw Michael asleep on the couch. He was wearing only his pants. I went into the room with the light. It was the bedroom. Suzanne was asleep on the far side of the bed facing toward me. Her eyes were closed."

"What did you do next, Mr. Bannon?"

"On the floor of the bedroom I saw a little silver pistol. It looked like there had been a terrible fight. There was a clump of black hair in the bed, and Suzanne's panties were torn. She looked sad. I remember getting angry. I remember wishing she could just be away from that son-of-a-bitch forever."

Jerry Bannon looked directly at Michael and said to him, "You didn't deserve to be in the same room with her."

David Bailey moved his body between Jerry Bannon and Michael Brace to break the contact. He said, "Mr. Bannon, after you saw all those things, what did you do?"

Jerry looked back at David Bailey and said, "I decided to kill him. I decided to go into the bathroom and get a piece of toilet tissue to pick up the gun. I was going to kill him on the couch, for her, so he could never do anything to her again."

"Did you get the tissue?"

"Yes."

"What did you do next?"

Jerry looked slowly across the faces of the jurors. He said, "I picked up the gun. Her face was so peaceful. I just wanted to touch her. I wanted to cover her up with the sheet. I leaned across the bed. The gun was in my left hand. I used it to keep my balance when I leaned across to pull up the sheet with my right hand."

Jerry stopped.

"Mr. Bannon, what happened next?"

"She woke up, Mr. Bailey. In a split second her eyes opened, and she saw the gun. Her hands were just a few inches from it. She grabbed my hand. Her face changed."

David Bailey was hesitant to push the man, but they stood at the edge of the cliff, and everyone in the courtroom stood with them.

"Did the gun go off, Mr. Bannon?"

Jerry closed his eyes. He left them closed as he spoke.

"Yes. It went off. It was loud, like a firecracker. I jumped back. There was blood. It was all over. Her face was blown apart. I can still see it. I see it every day."

Michael closed his eyes. At first he tried not to see, but then he let the image form again in his mind. Suzanne's hands rested quietly together on the bed sheets. Her face was no longer her face. It was no longer a face at all.

David Bailey purposefully remained silent to let the picture linger in the minds of the jurors.

"What happened next, Mr. Bannon?"

Jerry opened his eyes and said, "I dropped the gun on the side of the bed and it bounced onto the floor. I ran. I ran out the door. There was no one around. Mr. Forester's light wasn't on yet. I ran past the park bench and down the shore of the bay. It was wrong. I shouldn't have run. There's nowhere to go."

"Was Suzanne Brace alive when you went into that house?"

"Yes, sir."

"Did you see any blood, or evidence that she'd been shot when you saw her asleep on the bed?"

"No."

David Bailey was satisfied. The courtroom had become as thin and sharp as the edge of a razorblade. The most important question is the one never asked, he thought.

David said, "We pass the witness, Your Honor."

Albert Danley stood. He had faced many situations in his career as a trial attorney. He had never faced a situation quite like this. His instincts told him to attack, and he trusted his instincts in a courtroom.

"Mr. Bannon, where did you come from?"

"Washington state, Spokane."

"Why did you choose our little corner of the world?"

Jerry said, "It was as good a place as any."

"Did you collect aluminum cans in Spokane, Washington?"

"No, sir, I was an engineer."

Albert Danley repeated, "An engineer? Why would a man leave a job as an engineer and move halfway across the country to live in a shack and pick up cans, Mr. Bannon? Why?"

Jerry Bannon looked down at his hands. "I can't explain it."

Albert Danley repeated, "You can't explain it?"

"No."

"Did you have a house in Spokane, Washington?"

"Yes, sir."

"Did you have a wife?"

"Yes, sir."

"Did you have any children?"

"Yes, I had two little boys."

Albert Danley asked, "Why would a twenty-eight-year-old man leave his wife, and his baby boys, his house, and his job, to walk around our little town barefoot, smoking cigarettes, picking up cans, for twenty-three years?"

Jerry Bannon rubbed the skin on his hands. For the first time, Suzanne's sister, Elizabeth, leaned forward in her chair to listen. She wanted to know the answer.

"Every day, Mr. Danley, every single day, for twenty-three years, I've asked myself that question. I can't explain it. I think about them every day."

Albert Danley asked, "Do you have any idea what can happen to you for confessing to the murder of Suzanne Brace?"

Jerry said, "Yes, sir, I do."

"Mr. Bannon, you can spend the rest of your life in prison, or the State of Alabama can put you to death for this crime. Do you understand that?"

Jerry felt himself take a breath. He said, "Mr. Danley, I've barely spoken to anyone in twenty-three years. I got on a bus one day, it was a Wednesday, and never saw my beautiful wife, or my beautiful boys again. Every morning, I choose to pick up your trash. There's nothing you can do to me that I haven't already done to myself, nothing."

The man's anguish could be felt like a stone. Albert Danley was without the steady direction of experience. He had reached the uncharted waters that haunt a lawyer.

Albert Danley said, "I don't believe, Mr. Bannon, that you killed Suzanne Brace. You know why?"

"No, sir, I don't."

"You'd never been in that house before. I have a hard time believing you'd go wandering down the hall looking for tissue paper while two people slept. Two people who had only been asleep, at the longest, according to your testimony, twenty minutes. Describe the bathroom, Mr. Bannon."

"It was dark, Mr. Danley. I didn't look at anything except the roll of toilet paper."

Albert Danley felt a crack.

"Well, Mr. Bannon, on which side of the bathroom was the toilet situated?"

Jerry's eyes shifted to Tim Tuberville. Their minds met in the middle. Their minds met on the diagram in the notes of Tim Tuberville's file. They both could see the diagram, on yellow paper, the lines drawn in red ink, the bathroom down the hall. Jerry Bannon took a guess.

"I believe the toilet was on the left side when I entered the door."

For a long pause, Albert Danley's face did not reveal the accuracy of the guess. Finally he said, "Something isn't right, Mr. Bannon. Something just isn't right. Another thing that bothers me is the fact we never found your fingerprints anywhere. Why is that, Mr. Bannon?"

"I didn't touch anything except the bed. I held the gun with the tissue. I used my shirttail to turn the front doorknob. If you test the tissue you'll probably find some gunshot residue."

The palms of Jerry's hands began to sweat. He concentrated on his breathing, in and out, slowly. It was a new concentration, new and old at the same time.

Albert Danley stepped closer to Jerry. He crossed his arms and said, "I think the biggest problem you've got with your story, Mr. Bannon, is the shovel and rags we found in the trunk of the car. The rags had the blood of Suzanne Brace on them. How did you manage to put those in the trunk, Jerry?"

Jerry could hear himself breathe. He felt everyone in the room could hear it. Cornett Lofton shifted in his chair.

Jerry looked down and said, "I don't know how they got there, Mr. Danley. Maybe she cut herself working in the yard."

Albert Danley's voice rose mightily, "You are a liar, Jerry Bannon. You didn't kill that woman any more than the man in the moon. What is this to you, your moment in the sun, your fifteen minutes of fame? Who put you up to this?"

The booming voice echoed off the walls of the courtroom and came to rest in a pool of silence.

Jerry Bannon raised his head and whispered, "I bet you didn't find her wedding band?"

No one moved except Michael. He slowly pulled the folded letter of Suzanne from his shirt pocket and opened it to read. Both of his hands were clearly visible on the edges of the white paper.

Albert Danley's mind sped in five separate directions. He knew a lawyer should never ask a question to which he doesn't know the answer. He knew it was the cardinal sin, but before his mind reached reason, Albert Danley asked, "What wedding band?"

Jerry Bannon leaned back in his chair and reached his hand inside the same pants pocket he had checked the day before. He pulled out a gold wedding band and held it up in his dirty fingers between himself and Albert Danley.

"This wedding band, Mr. Danley. Suzanne's wedding band. Just like the one Michael is wearing."

Every face, every pair of eyes, from the judge, across the jury, to the back of the room, turned to see Michael's left hand on the edge of the white paper he held on the top of the table. Like a man alone in the eye of a hurricane, Michael read the letter to himself.

Albert Danley said, "Anyone can buy a gold wedding band, Mr. Bannon, at any pawnshop or ten-cent jewelry store in the county."

As Michael neared the final lines of the letter, Jerry held the ring close to his face and said, "Not like this one. Inside there's an inscription. It says, 'Suzanne, I will love you forever, Michael.'"

As the words left Jerry's mouth, Michael read the final line of the letter written by his wife. "I will love you forever." Michael held the words for as long as they would last. The winds of the storm around him howled and raged in the quiet courtroom. It was a moment of fierce contrast.

Jerry continued, "I took the ring, Mr. Danley. That's the reason she woke up. I was pulling it from her finger. I wanted to take the ring so I could prove to her later that I was the one who set her free. I was the one who shot Michael on the couch."

To himself, Jerry remembered watching Suzanne in the dark on that early morning as she strode across the yard to the car in the driveway. He could see her again in the light from the trunk placing the shovel and rags in their proper places. And he could see again the woman pull something from her left hand and toss it in the azalea bushes.

He remembered waiting for three days, until everyone was gone, getting down on his hands and knees and feeling under the leaves. He remembered wondering what it was he would find. What would a woman toss in the bushes such a short time before a bullet would explode in her face?

Albert Danley walked to the prosecutor's table and leaned down to speak to Tim Tuberville.

"Tim, check the exhibit that listed everything from the house. See if her wedding band is on there. Rebecca, look at the autopsy report and see what it says about jewelry."

Albert Danley turned to face the judge and said, "Your Honor, we'd like to reserve the right to continue cross-examination of this witness and ask the court for a brief recess."

Judge Cornett Lofton said, "Ladies and gentlemen, this court will be in recess for fifteen minutes."

Albert Danley turned back to his table.

Rebecca Mann said, "The autopsy report says she was wearing no jewelry."

Tim Tuberville said, "The wedding band isn't listed in the items found in the house."

Albert Danley said, "Tim, go out to the witness room and ask Edna Townsend, Mrs. Forester, and Sophie Butler if they remember Suzanne wearing the wedding band the night of the anniversary party. Rebecca, let's talk a minute."

The courtroom cleared. Tim Tuberville pushed his way past the reporters as they asked questions. Jerry Bannon remained on the witness stand. Michael folded the letter and placed it back in his top shirt pocket. He turned to see Phillip sitting behind him with his eyes closed.

Albert Danley whispered to Rebecca, "If any of these ladies remember her wearing that wedding band, this case is over. I think we should end it now and explain to those people outside that justice will be done. We can have Tim arrest Bannon in the courtroom and lead him past the cameras. People will understand. The man didn't come forward until this morning. The evidence against Michael was overwhelming. But a confession is a confession. Jerry Bannon dug his own grave when he pulled that ring from his pocket."

In a few minutes Tim Tuberville stepped back into the courtroom. He sat down at the table with Albert and Rebecca.

"Albert, Sophie Butler remembers the ring. She says she saw Suzanne take it off to help wash dishes and then put it back on. The other two women aren't sure, but both of them say Suzanne wore her wedding band all the time. Edna Townsend had even seen the inscription."

Albert Danley's mind shifted quickly.

"Tim, I'm going to dismiss the charges against Michael in front of the jury and ask you to arrest Jerry Bannon here in the courtroom. Get Grimes and the other guys in here so you can put him in handcuffs and take him over to the jail. It's the only thing to do."

The courtroom slowly filled. Every seat was taken, and people were standing against the back wall. The congregation rose as Judge Cornett Lofton limped slowly to the bench and sat down.

"Be seated please. Mr. Danley, you may continue."

Albert Danley stood like justice rising. With a clear and steady voice he said, "Your Honor, the State of Alabama moves to dismiss the charges against Michael Brace. Gerald Anthony Bannon will be arrested for the murder of Suzanne Brace. Mr. Tuberville, if you would."

There were no cheers. In silence, Tim Tuberville and his investigators approached the man sitting alone on the witness stand. The wedding band was removed from his hand. He was arrested without words, led across the courtroom to the door in handcuffs, and walked slowly past the crowd of cameras and reporters. Jerry Bannon never raised his head.

## 22

Michael hugged his mother in the courtroom after Jerry Bannon was led away, and the jury was dismissed. Ellen Brace smiled with tears in her eyes. Michael motioned for Laura Simmons to come up front. She was safe to touch. They hugged, and Michael hugged his brother, Phillip. Phillip felt like bones in Michael's arms. They held on until Phillip let go.

The guards walked with Michael across the street to the jailhouse to complete the paperwork. Michael stepped out of the freedom of the August heat through the door into the air-conditioned confinement. He was taken to his cell to collect his things. Virgil had already heard the news.

"I'll be damned, boy. If I had a lawyer like yours, I'd be layin' on the beach drinking cold beer."

Virgil shook Michael's hand.

Virgil said, "I knew you didn't belong here."

The two men talked while Michael gathered his papers and personal items. Michael was led to the booking room. He was asked to sit in a chair facing a woman in uniform.

Jerry Bannon was led from the holding cell into the room with Michael. He was asked to sit down in a chair across from another lady only ten feet from Michael. There they sat, Michael being booked out, handed his walking papers, and Jerry Bannon being booked in, prepared to have his photograph taken.

Once there had been two men, only two, who really believed Michael Brace didn't kill Suzanne Brace. Now there were two men, the same two, who knew Jerry Bannon didn't kill Suzanne Brace. There were many things Michael Brace did not know, but he knew for sure he didn't wake up on the couch that early morning. He knew for sure he hadn't yelled at his wife. And he knew for sure Jerry Bannon didn't find the gun on the floor.

The question remained. Why? It was the only real question that mattered. But Michael knew he might never understand the answer. He watched the side of the man's face. He watched Jerry Bannon sign the papers, and he watched him be taken away to the photograph room. Michael hoped he was right in his belief that Jerry Bannon had his reasons. The reasons were real, and personal, and came from a place far away. Far from anyplace Michael had ever been, or might ever go.

Michael Brace felt the burn to write. He thought, the souls of men are touched by different hands. They were meant to be strange to one another. It is this strangeness that can sometimes bring us together, at certain times, in certain places, for a certain purpose. He asked the deputy for a pen, and on the back of a piece of paper, he wrote the words.

## 23

Jimmy Butler sat quietly in the front seat of his mother's car as they drove to the home of Michael's parents. There was going to be a party, a celebration, and Sophie Butler was asked to help as if nothing had ever happened. Jimmy couldn't wait to see Mr. Brace. Soon it would be football weather again.

Michael sat in the backseat of his father's car. Ellen Brace had made phone calls while Michael was being booked out of jail to invite friends and family to the house to celebrate. During the slow drive there were periods of silence. Ellen Brace was so happy to learn her son hadn't killed his wife. Now she could think about finger sandwiches and punch bowls. Her world had come back together in only a few minutes, and now she couldn't think of a thing to say to her boy. She would never talk about any of it again. It was as if Suzanne never existed, but Edward Brace couldn't forget. He couldn't forget any of it, and the words he had heard would change him forever.

When they pulled into the driveway, Michael recognized Mark Simpson's big red Chevrolet. He was sure the old hamburger was still shoved under the seat. He hoped Hardy and Rake were inside.

Jimmy Butler peeked around the edge of the curtain in the living room. He watched Michael Brace get out of the car. There were hugs, and smiles, and more cars. Jimmy walked through the dining room into the kitchen to find his mother.

"Momma, how come when Uncle Ray got out of jail, nobody had a party for him?" Jimmy asked.

Sophie Butler was uncomfortable. Even though she had never testified, everyone knew what she had seen in the kitchen that night. Phillip Brace was only a room away. She didn't answer her son's question.

The house began to fill. Michael stood next to Phillip. There was a preseason football game on the television. They both pretended to watch. In the background ice clinked in glasses.

Phillip stirred his whiskey with his finger. He said, "Have you figured out yet this party isn't for you?"

Michael looked around the room.

"Sure are a lot of folks here."

Phillip said, "They're here to forget. During the last six months, every person in this room believed at one time or another you killed Suzanne. Even me. Most of them believed you beat the shit out of her, and raped her, and planned to get the insurance money. Look around, every person."

Michael put his hands in his pockets and said, "Except for one."

"Who? Name one," Phillip said.

"Me, Phillip. But I don't blame any of them, you or Mom or Dad, any of them. How could they know me well enough to know I couldn't do it? All we learn about people is usually what they let us learn, and all they can let us learn is what they understand."

Phillip looked at his brother and said, "If Jerry hadn't come forward, that jury would have convicted you of capital murder. Lofton would've sentenced you to death."

Michael stayed next to his brother. In this room full of family and friends he felt like he shouldn't leave him alone. People would spot Michael from across the room and practically bounce to him for hugs and kisses and reassurance. Phillip was right, Michael thought, these people were far too happy. They needed a separation from their guilt, a relief from the possibility that anyone they knew could kill. No one actually knew Jerry, and no one seemed to remember Suzanne. They were shadows.

Jimmy Butler watched from the kitchen door. The brothers stood side by side, and Jimmy wished he had a brother. The rich people complained about the heat and drank gin and tonics. Jimmy's mother cut another lime and put the pieces in a crystal bowl. She sent Jimmy out to the bar with the limes so she wouldn't have to walk past Phillip Brace.

Jimmy took the bowl in both hands. He walked around the dinner table carefully and past the brothers. He set the bowl down next to Mark Simpson, who poured himself a new drink. When Jimmy turned around, Michael Brace was looking him in the eye. He motioned for Jimmy to come over by the television.

Michael knelt down and opened his arms. The boy gave him a hug.

Michael said, "Man, you've grown at least a foot. Let me see those shoes."

Jimmy stuck his right shoe out. They weren't brand-new anymore, but they were still fast. "Did you get my letter?" he asked.

"I did," Michael said. "I got it. It was the best letter. I'm sorry I didn't write you back."

Michael smiled, and Jimmy Butler smiled back.

"Is your momma OK?" Michael asked.

Jimmy said, "She's OK, I guess. She worries a lot."

"That's what mommas do sometimes," Michael said. "They worry."

Michael was down on one knee so they were eye to eye.

Jimmy said, "Mr. Brace, I wish we could go to your house again."

Michael hadn't thought about going to the house. After a moment he said, "There's nothing there, Jimmy. No one's home."

Michael imagined the walls and windows. He imagined the doors and ceiling fans. It was dark outside. From across the big living room he could hear the voices of David Bailey and Eddie Creel. He could hear laughter from Hardy and Mark Simpson.

"Maybe we can throw the ball later under the streetlight. I can see how fast those shoes really move."

Jimmy Butler went back to help his mother. Michael asked his brother for the car keys and slipped out the back door. He was almost to Phillip's car when he saw the red pickup truck parked across the street. Laura Simmons sat on the driver's side. Michael walked to her open window. She'd been in the truck thirty minutes, afraid to go inside, afraid her place in Michael's life only existed in the little visitation room of the jail, or inside her own mind.

They looked at each other. She couldn't tell from his face.

Michael leaned inside the truck and kissed Laura Simmons gently. Not too long. Not too dramatic. Just a kiss. Like they'd done it a million times before, in the morning on the way to work, or in the evening.

Michael said, "Go inside. I'll be back in a little while. I've just got a few things I need to do."

He left her feeling the way she'd always felt around Michael Brace. Alive.

It had been six months since Michael had driven a car. He turned up the radio in the BMW and rolled down the windows. Michael's mind was alive. He had to know. He had to sit down across from the man and ask the question.

The jail seemed different. Now he was a visitor. Michael asked to speak with a certain deputy who was a longtime friend of Eddie Creel and Phillip.

"Tony, I'd like to see Jerry Bannon. I know you don't owe me any favors, and it's not visitation hours, but it's important."

Tony looked hard at Michael Brace.

"I'll see what I can do, Michael."

Michael sat down in the jail lobby and waited. He needed the time to put his thoughts and questions together. There were butterflies in his belly like the ones he felt in those Little League football games before the first kickoff. Tony came back into the room and motioned for Michael to follow.

"The man says he'll see ya. I can only give you thirty minutes."

Michael Brace sat in the same room where he had sat each Wednesday with Laura Simmons. This time he sat in the chair on the other side of the metal screen. It seemed less cold with the unlocked door behind his back. He waited for Jerry Bannon.

Michael remembered as a boy how slowly time had seemed to pass when he stared at the clock. On one particular Friday he had brought home a bad report card from school. He knew his father would be home at five thirty. Michael remembered running from the bus, through the front door, and straight to the kitchen clock. He stared at the red second hand as it would climb and fall back around again and again. He wanted those two hours to seem like two days. If he concentrated hard enough, maybe the second hand would slow to a crawl and eventually actually stop.

The door on the other side of the screen opened and Jerry Bannon came into the room. He sat down in the chair and the men were face to face.

Neither spoke.

The orange jail jumpsuit on Jerry Bannon had short sleeves. Michael could see his arms were brown from the years of walking around town in the sun. Jerry was not uncomfortable with the silence. He had expected Michael to come.

Michael spoke.

"I don't know exactly why you did this, Mr. Bannon, but I know you didn't do this for me, so I won't thank you."

Jerry listened. He watched the man's mouth move.

Michael continued.

"I need to understand, Mr. Bannon. I need to know why you would confess to a murder you didn't commit."

Jerry Bannon asked softly, "Why?"

"I can help you, Jerry. I can write this. People will listen. Words are powerful. We can prove you didn't kill Suzanne. I can write about this. A book, or maybe newspaper articles."

Michael's face was close to the screen. His hands were up and down with the enthusiasm of the idea. He felt for the pen in his pocket to make sure it was still there.

Jerry Bannon said, "I remember when you had that story published. I kept the magazine for a long time. It was good. You're good."

There was silence. Somewhere, the red second hand on a clock started on the seven, rose evenly upward, reached the peak of the twelve, and began the journey down the hill.

"Michael, I sat in that courtroom to learn whether or not the truth would be enough to keep you from being convicted. It wouldn't have been. For the first time since I walked away from my family, I found myself in a situation where I was the only one who could make things right. The only one."

Jerry paused and continued. "I thought about this a long time. You're right, it doesn't have anything to do with you. It has to do with me. It has to do with not wasting this opportunity. It wasn't courage, it was desperation. There's nothing I will ever be able to do or say to fix what I did when I walked away from my family twenty-three years ago. For a few years it seemed OK, but it was never OK. I left out of fear. There was something the matter with me. I was sure that one day, any day, those little boys, and my wife, would see I could never be the father and husband they deserved. I could never be the person they needed me to be. It was like I couldn't breathe.

"At dinner, the night before I left, I remember looking at them across the table. I remember my hands shaking under the table. The next morning I woke up, got dressed for work as usual, left the house, walked past the door to my office, and straight to the bus station around the corner.

"I can never get those years back, my boys, their first baseball games, my wife, holding hands by the lake in the summer. But every now and then, sometimes only once in a lifetime, a person gets a chance to make something very wrong, right. You can't do it for other people. You can only do it for yourself."

Michael wanted to write it down. He wanted to remember every word, and the way they rolled from the mouth of this calm man on the other side of the metal screen. This man he would never understand.

"Write it, Michael. Write whatever you want. But do it for yourself. Don't do it for me. Leave me alone. Let me have this. They won't kill me. They won't execute me for an accidental shooting. It doesn't matter anyway. I've made my peace with the devil. He'll keep his distance now."

The room grew silent again.

Jerry Bannon stood from his chair and turned toward the locked door.

Michael spoke softly, "At least tell me this: Where did you get Suzanne's ring? I need to know."

Jerry stood in front of the door, his hand on the knob. The lie was prepared. He turned to Michael and said, "I was on the bench that morning, across the street, where I said I was. Suzanne came outside in her robe and sat down on the front steps by the door. I could hear her crying. Not loud. Soft. The way a child cries when they're alone.

"She pulled something from the pocket of her robe. I couldn't tell what it was at first. She held it to her face. It caught the light as it dropped to the step and bounced into the grass.

"I watched her get down on her knees and run her fingers through the grass trying to find it. She cried the whole time. She finally went back inside. I walked across the street and found the ring. The light from the streetlight caught it perfectly. I just walked over and picked it up."

Michael listened.

"I don't know why I took it, Michael. When I got back across the street and sat down, I saw Suzanne come outside with a flashlight. She looked and looked. She wiped her eyes with the sleeve of the robe. I wish I could give it back to you."

Jerry knocked on the door to get the guard's attention. Michael found himself imagining Suzanne, in the night, sliding her hand slowly across the grass waiting for the touch of gold or the shimmer of reflection. He could see it like he had been there, sitting on the step behind her, listening to the sounds.

The door in front of Jerry Bannon clicked and opened.

"Go home, Michael," he said.

24

Michael took the long way to his old house across the street from the bay. He drove slowly and pulled Phillip's car into the driveway next to the azalea bushes. It started to rain as he rolled up the windows. Michael sat in the car listening to the drops on the windshield. The house was dark. A sadness rested around him.

Michael got out of the car and headed up the walkway. He half expected Suzanne to open the door. The spare key was still hidden under the loose brick. The door opened like a place in his mind. It was warm, and quiet. The quiet itself was a presence.

Michael walked to the porch with his hands in his pockets. Some of the furniture remained. He stood at the window and looked across the water at the gathering cloud full of rain. It seemed strange that clear raindrops could cause a cloud to be so dark and angry. Thunder rolled slowly in the distance.

Michael turned to see the path he would take from the porch to the bedroom door. There was no one else. He walked and stood to see the half-empty bedroom. The bed was gone. On the floor, under Suzanne's side, the dark stain on the hardwood floor could be anything, Michael thought. It could be water, or a glass of whiskey spilled, or paint.

Michael walked to the spot. He bent down on one knee and touched the stain with his two fingers. There was nothing to feel except alone. Alone is what we decide for ourselves. It has nothing to do with anyone else.

Michael laid his body down. The only sound was God's raindrops on the tin roof, steady and indifferent. He closed his eyes and remembered with every detail the night they had taken off all their clothes and driven around town in that old Volkswagen. All he could see was Suzanne. She laughed like a little girl. She was funny, and smart, and had a way. Her spirit played in the house.

Michael pulled the ring from his finger. He held it up to his eyes and struggled in the darkness to read the inscription. To himself he said, "Michael, I will love you forever, Suzanne."

He set the ring down on the floor and left through the front door in the rain.

## ACKNOWLEDGMENTS

Without certain people, this book would not exist for one reason or the other. They include David Poindexter, Pat Walsh, Kate Nitze, Sonny Brewer, Hoss Mack, Kevin Shannon, Kip Howard, Michael Strecker, Charlotte Robertson, Sally Hollon, Smokey Davis, Kyle Jennings, Rodney Criswell, Paige Bensen, Michael Dasinger, Sharon Hoiles, Melissa and James Bass, Ellen and Bob Gentle, Bill and Linda Cone, Gabriel Black, Dad and Virginia, Mom and Skip, Robert Bell, Matthew Guma, Allison, Dusty, Mary Grace, Lilly, Tasha, Melanie, and Dorothy.

A special thanks goes to my secretary, Melissa, for your endless patience. Thank you.